Crisis

CRISIS

Ken McClure

SIMON & SCHUSTER

LONDON·SYDNEY·NEW YORK·TOKYO·SINGAPORE·TORONTO

First published in Great Britain by
Simon & Schuster Ltd in 1993
A Paramount Communications Company

Copyright © Ken Begg, 1993

Simon & Schuster Ltd
West Garden Place
Kendal Street
London W2 2AQ

Simon & Schuster of Australia Pty Ltd
Sydney

A CIP catalogue record for this book is
available from the British Library
ISBN 0-671-71794-4

Typeset in Palatino 10.5/12.5pt by
Hewer Text Composition Services, Edinburgh
Printed and bound in Great Britain by
Butler and Tanner Ltd, London and Frome

'And we are here as on a darkling plain,
Swept with confused alarms of struggle and flight,
Where ignorant armies clash by night.'

'Dover Beach', Matthew Arnold (1822–1888)

PROLOGUE

The Island of Barasay, The Western Isles of Scotland. 19 January, 1992.

Lawrence Gill's lungs demanded more and more oxygen until, unable to comply, he was forced to his knees on the wet shingle. He knelt there, weakly supporting himself, until the deficit had been reduced. As soon as his laboured breathing subsided he struggled painfully to his feet and continued trying to run on a surface that seemed hell-bent on denying him grip. The wind howled in from the Atlantic and whipped up the rain until it felt like icy rivets being driven into his face. It seemed that nature was attempting to render him as featureless as the barren beach that so begrudged him every inch of progress.

Gill's hands were bleeding by the time he had clawed his way to the top of the cliff and started out for the old stone cottage where he planned to seek refuge. It had lain abandoned for more than two years, ever since Shona's father had given up the unequal struggle against the elements and returned to the mainland. Gill was hoping that there would be enough there to sustain him in the way of shelter until the hunt had tapered off. The rucksack on his back held enough tinned food and supplies to see him through two weeks if necessary.

Through the rain Gill could see the outline of the cottage on the corner of the headland. It still had a roof and that was something of a bonus considering its location. He had once

1

asked Shona what had possessed her father to build a cottage on such an exposed site. Shona had said that he had felt closer to God there than anywhere else.

It was true that, when the sea was calm and the sky clear, you could see for thirty miles from the top of the cliff and watch the sun sink into the western horizon like a huge ball of orange fire; but the sea was almost never calm, and the sky was seldom clear. More often than not westerly gales whipped up the Atlantic into a frenzy and sent huge breakers crashing against the rocks below sending fingers of spray high into the air to clutch at the cottage as if to tear it from its perch.

Gill moved into the lee of the back wall and rested for a moment with his shoulder against the rough stone. The rain had sought out the vulnerable points in his clothing and he could feel the water trickle down his back as he once more gasped for breath. There was a back door to the cottage. He moved along to try it rather than expose himself to the wind again by going round the front. The handle was rusty and stiff but it did turn and Gill put his shoulder against the door to overcome the reluctance of the hinges.

The room he was in had been the kitchen but broken windows had allowed access to the elements and the sea birds and it was in a mess. With a heavy heart Gill wondered if the other rooms had fared any better. He opened the door leading to what had been the living-room and stopped suddenly in the doorway. Two men were standing there. They were clad in oilskins and they looked at Gill as if they had been expecting him. Neither said anything; the guns in their hands were supposed to say all that needed to be said.

Gill felt a strange, sad sense of resignation come over him. It seemed ironic but it was almost a feeling of relief. He had been on the run for four days and that's all it had taken to turn his life completely upside down and make him the running victim in a living nightmare. Four days to undo everything he had worked for, career, marriage, prospects, the imagined solid

2

foundations for success and future happiness, had been swept away with an ease that now seemed obscene. It all seemed so unfair.

One of the men ransacked his belongings while the other held a gun on him. When the man kneeling on the floor looked up and shook his head the man pointing the gun said, 'Where are they?'

'You're too late,' said Gill. 'They're already in the post.'

The two men looked at each other without saying anything. The man with the gun motioned that Gill should back out the door.

Gill was no longer mindful of the wind and the rain; his head was full of images of the things he would never see again. God! he wasn't ready to die! He was suddenly overwhelmed by panic. He veered off to the right and ran into the wind, hoping that his captors would have difficulty aiming with the driving rain in their faces.

In his mind's eye, Gill imagined a path leading down from the far end of the cliff to the shore where he would run along the sand with the wind behind him and get into the boat to make good his escape. But when he got to the edge he saw that there was nothing but a sheer drop. He sank to the ground and lay full length looking over the edge at the rocks far below. He felt all hope drain from him; he was left with a desperately empty void inside. He relaxed his grip on the tufts of grass and turned slowly over on to his back to wait for his pursuers.

One of the men signalled that he should get to his feet and he did, leaning back against the wind to keep his balance. The two men put away their guns and each took an arm. For a moment Gill wondered why when there was no place for him to run to, then he understood. Almost before he could cry out the men lifted him bodily off his feet and swung him back over the edge of the cliff. For a moment his arms flailed against the dark sky then he plunged headlong to his death on the jagged rocks below, his last scream of protest carried off by the wind.

*   *   *

3

The Medical Research Council, Park Crescent, London

'I apologise for the inconvenience caused by the calling of this meeting at such short notice gentlemen, but I have been asked by the Prime Minister to brief him and the cabinet on our findings with regard to our survey on brain disease in this country.' The secretary of the MRC, Sir John Flowers, paused and looked over his glasses at the men sitting round the table.

'The studies are nowhere near complete, you know that,' said a middle-aged man with the trace of a Scots accent.

Flowers shook his head and said, 'Won't do Hector. We as scientists know we have to evaluate properly all the data but the government see it as sitting on the fence. They would like assurance that there are no major problems brewing in this area.

'What they really want us to tell them is that human beings can't get brain disease from sick animals!' said another man whose ample girth was barely restrained by a waistcoat of maroon silk material which almost matched the colour of his nose.

Flowers gave a slight nod.

'Why the sudden rush?' asked Hector Munro, Director of the MRC Neurobiology Unit in Edinburgh.

'Ever since *Mad cow disease* hit the headlines a year or so ago, the opposition have been waiting for the right moment to cause embarrassment to the government. The sale of British meat and meat products to the continent has still not recovered from the bad publicity generated at the time. In fact, they fell again sharply last month and the agricultural lobby is up in arms. They are going to demand to know what the government is doing about the problem. They want positive assurances that British meat products are safe. We for our part have been monitoring the incidence of brain disease in the country and following the experimental work of the Agricultural Research Council,' exclaimed Flowers.

'There *has* been a rise in figures,' said a thin man with the pointed features of a bird and the appropriate name of John Lark.

'But it's of doubtful statistical significance,' said Flowers.

'We can't give them a definite assurance yet because the experiments take such a long time but we could tell them that, at the moment, there is no evidence to link diseased animals with human brain disorder,' suggested Munro.

'I'm afraid we can't even do that,' said Flowers, and the murmuring round the table died away.

'Something wrong?' said Lark as if the words were reluctant to come.

Flowers looked around the table at each man in turn. 'Very wrong,' he said quietly. 'I have just received a report which amounts to something of a nightmare,' he said.

'Go on,' said Munro.

'It comes from the north of Scotland, a place called Achnagelloch.'

Munro shrugged and shook his head. The name failed to register with any of the others.

'It records an outbreak of degenerative brain disease.'

'How many people are we talking about?' asked Munro.

'Three deaths.'

The answer came as an anticlimax. 'That's hardly an outbreak, John,' said Lark.

'Unfortunately, there's more to it,' said Flowers. 'The three concerned were relatively young men. All three worked on a sheep farm which has recently been subject to an outbreak of the sheep brain disease, *Scrapie*.'

'Oh, I see,' said Munro slowly.

'Could be coincidence,' said Lark, but without much conviction.

'It gets worse,' said Flowers. 'The preliminary pathology report suggests that the men died from a brain disease identical to *Scrapie*.'

'But there's a species barrier between sheep and humans!'

'That's what we've always maintained, gentlemen,' said Flowers quietly.

Munro rubbed his forehead in a subconscious effort to avoid the implications. 'We thought a species barrier applied to cows too and look what happened,' he said.

'Has the link been established for sure?' asked Lark.

Flowers nodded. 'The ARC labs have shown that cows got BSE from eating sheep meat infected with *Scrapie*.'

'So why didn't they get it before?' asked Lark. '*Scrapie* has been round for long enough in sheep.'

'The renderers changed their method of treating sheep carcasses. The old way killed the infective agent off. The new way didn't. As simple as that.'

'So there wasn't a species barrier at all?'

'No.'

'Ye gods,' said Lark. 'But surely *Scrapie* couldn't cross to humans?'

Flowers held up a sheaf of papers in his hand and said, 'This case suggests otherwise.'

'I have always maintained that *Scrapie* in sheep should have been made notifiable all along, just like BSE,' said Munro.

'Well, it's too late to bolt that particular stable door,' said Flowers. 'Our problem is that not only can we not allay the government's fears about an increasing incidence of brain disease but we have to inform them of the existence of a potential disaster in the making.'

'I take it lambs can be affected with the disease too?' asked Lark.

'Yes,' said Munro, 'and to answer your next question, roasting would not kill the agent. It's one of the toughest viruses on earth. It can withstand the temperature achieved in a hospital steam sterilizer.'

'Then I hope to God that the report is mistaken,' said Lark.

'Who is reporting for the Scottish region?' asked Munro.

'George Stoddart.'

'Edinburgh University?'

Flowers nodded.

'Have you spoken to him?' asked Lark.

'Yes,' said Flowers.

'And?'

'Stoddart says that his man is adamant that the men died of *Scrapie* but there will be the usual difficulty in assigning the cause.'

6

'I'm not sure I understand,' said Lark. 'What difficulty?'

Flowers looked to Munro and said, 'You're the expert in this field. Perhaps you would explain.'

'Of course,' said Munro, clearing his throat. 'We know very little about the infecting agent which causes *Scrapie* in sheep, or BSE in cattle for that matter. The only reliable way of demonstrating the infection is by injection of infected material from one animal into another. In this way we can show that the agent is transmissible and has a similar pathology.'

'What sort of infected material?' asked Lark.

'The standard test is for macerated brain obtained at autopsy to be injected into mice to see if they develop degenerative brain disease.'

'Has such a disease ever been seen in man?' asked Lark.

'Yes,' replied Munro. 'In man it's called Creutzfeld Jakob Disease. It's a brain disease of the old. It's a relatively rare condition and thankfully it has a very long incubation period.'

'What was the incubation period in this case?' asked Munro.

All eyes turned towards Flowers. 'Stoddart says that his man reports that the patients developed the disease almost overnight and were dead within three weeks. The brain pathology was identical to *Scrapie* or Creutzfeld Jakob Disease. They're practically indistinguishable in terms of histopathology.'

'Damnation,' said Lark. 'Three is not a big number. I still feel we may be jumping to conclusions.'

'I'd like to agree,' said Flowers, 'but three men working on a farm with infected sheep die of a brain disease indistinguishable from *Scrapie*? We have to take this seriously.'

This comment was digested for a moment in silence then Lark said, 'It's still very hard to believe that a sheep disease that's been around for years without causing the slightest trouble in man has suddenly managed to jump the species barrier and start killing people.

'Surely there would have to have been some additional factor involved; a change to the infecting agent; a mutation of some sort; an alteration, either spontaneous or induced.'

'Let's hope, if that's the case, that the mutation was induced by some local factor and that this is an isolated incident,' said Flowers.

'Then it's of the utmost importance to establish just what caused the mutation,' said Munro.

'Agreed.'

'Are there any clues?' asked Lark.

'There is one prime suspect,' said Flowers.

'What's that?' asked Munro.

'The area around the farm in question includes the Invermaddoch nuclear power station.'

'Radiation,' said Lark.

'What better inducer of mutation?'

'I need hardly tell you what a delicate position this business puts us in,' said Munro. 'If we suddenly announce that a highland region is reporting that people living in the vicinity of a nuclear power station are developing an infectious brain disease which resembles sheep *Scrapie* in every way, we can expect a storm of panic and protest. Apart from public outcry, we will face the combined pressure of the agricultural lobby insisting that there is no link between infected animals and human brain disease, and the nuclear lobby maintaining that atomic energy is safe and clean.'

'So what *do* we do?' asked Munro. 'And what do we tell Her Majesty's Government?'

'I think we have to treat the Scottish thing as a separate, isolated problem for the moment,' said Lark. 'In broad, general terms there is still no evidence that animal brain disease can be transmitted to man. I think we should admit that there has been an increase in reported cases of brain disease in the population but it is too early to assign a cause or say whether it is significant or not. Let the government's statisticians present the figures in whatever way they want.'

'But the government must be made aware of the potential problem in Scotland just in case it leaks out in the press,' said Munro.

'The area doesn't get much attention from the press so we should be able to investigate quietly on our own for a while,' said Flowers.

'No disrespect to Stoddart and his people but I think we should see the pathology evidence taken from the three men who died,' said Lark.

'I've asked for it,' said Flowers.

'Did Stoddart say who the investigator on the ground was?' asked Munro.

'Yes he did,' replied Flowers, referring to his notes. 'A pathologist named Dr Lawrence Gill.'

ONE

Dr Ian Bannerman sorted his notes before him on the lectern and waited for the hubbub to die down. He thought his audience of medical students looked depressingly familiar but quickly reminded himself that this was a cynical thought. Sometimes the borders between cynicism and realism were a bit fuzzy.

Despite a solid middle-class background with its attendant adherence to Christian ethics and values he had always failed to be convinced that human beings were 'individuals in their own right'. People, as he saw it, fell into certain discreet 'types'. There was a type of person who became a vicar, a soldier, a policeman and so on. From lecturing to medical students for the last five years at St Luke's Hospital he had come to recognise that there was a definite type of person who became a medical student.

Medicine was seen by society as a profession for winners and because of this medical schools could demand the very highest academic entry standards. This meant that the cleverest pupils on paper were encouraged to 'try for medicine' as if entering a competition to prove their worth. Egged on by parents and teachers alike, such people would often find themselves railroaded into something they had not given much thought to.

Equipped with a brand new stethoscope from proud parents and a dissecting set from Aunt Mabel they would turn up at St Luke's, ready to start passing more exams because that was what they were good at. 'Doesn't anyone ask the buggers if they care about sick people?' Bannerman had asked at the last faculty meeting. The remark had been met with good humoured tolerance. This did not please Bannerman, it only confirmed his thesis on people 'types'. He reluctantly acknowledged that he was seen as the rough-diamond type; the kind of man who spoke his mind but was accepted because he was good at his job, and when it came to pathology there was none better.

Bannerman looked at the sea of faces, trying to spot a few who might become 'real' doctors. It was practically impossible but he always tried. It was easier to spot the ones who wouldn't, the loud-mouths who would bluster their way through the course, the quiet note-takers who would copy everything down and rely on hours of study and a retentive memory to see them through exam time. There would be some who would fail, of course, and not necessarily because they were bad students. Although the course was tough and academically demanding the entry standards ensured that not many idiots reached the starting line. The 'failures' were often students who discovered that they were square pegs in round holes; they were simply doing the wrong subject.

Bannerman always took time to reassure such students that it was better to have found out at an early stage than to have been faced with the truth when someone's life was resting in their hands. He always had much bigger problems with the students who passed the exams yet clearly were not cut out to be physicians. The frustrating thing was that there was little he could do about it. He would do his best to instil a genuine concern and regard for the sick in them but he suspected that many would go through their entire careers without ever seeing patients as anything more than 'cases', temporary intellectual puzzles to be solved along the path of their careers.

Despite not being able to spot the 'real' doctors in his audience Bannerman knew that they would be there and saw it as his duty to deliver the best possible lectures he could for their sake.

'Today we shall continue with our study of diseases of the central nervous system,' he announced. 'A subject I know will be close to your hearts because your essays on the subject of my

11

last lecture suggest that many of you are suffering from one or other of them . . .'

There was general laughter because although Bannerman had an acid tongue he was popular with the student body. He was a good lecturer, always on top of his subject and had never been known to prevaricate when asked a question to which he did not know the answer. Instead, he would say so immediately and tell the student to look it up and let him know. This saved a lot of time and the students appreciated it. Too much course time could be wasted by lecturers waffling to cover up deficiencies in their knowledge. The words, 'I don't know' were too seldom uttered in the realms of academia.

'Creutzfeld Jakob Disease and Kuru are the two conditions we will consider today. Both result in nervous degeneration, loss of coordination of the limbs and mental deterioration. Both are invariably fatal.' Bannerman switched on the slide projector and clicked in the first slide with a hand held controller. 'On the left is a brain section from a patient who died of CJ disease. The section on the right is from a normal brain. Note the spongioform appearance of the diseased brain and the typical SAF fibrils.'

Bannerman changed the slide and altered the focus slightly with his thumb. 'This is a photograph of a patient who contracted CJ disease after corneal graft treatment. Note the vacant expression in the eyes and the lack of facial muscle tone.'

A voice from the darkness said, 'Are you suggesting that the patient got the disease from the graft?'

'Almost certainly,' said Bannerman.

'Then this is an infectious condition?'

'Yes, but not conventionally so.'

There was a murmur of amusement as the student body began to believe that they had caught Bannerman about to prevaricate at last.

'Yes or no?' demanded the cocky student voice.

'Officially the diseases are said to be caused by unconventional *slow* viruses,' said Bannerman.

'How 'unconventional?'

'The truth is that no virus has ever been isolated from an infected brain but in all other respects the material behaves as if an infectious agent is present.'

'Then the disease can be transmitted?'

'Yes.'

'Are there any other diseases like these?'

'Several, in animals.'

'Such as?' asked the student, determined to catch Bannerman out if he could.

'*Scrapie* in sheep; Bovine spongioform encephalopathy in cattle.'

'*Mad cow disease*?' asked the student.

'Yes, also transmissible encephalopathy in mink.'

'But surely a bit of research would determine the cause of these conditions?' said the student.

For a moment Bannerman was taken aback at the arrogance of the proposition then he said, 'Mister . . . ?'

'Marsh,' replied the student.

'Mr Marsh, there is a small but significant graveyard containing the careers of several top flight researchers who insisted they had discovered the cause of these diseases. Perhaps you would care to do "a bit of research" and give me your written submission on where you think they went wrong? Shall we say by next Wednesday?'

'Yes sir,' mumbled the student, all trace of youthful arrogance gone.

'Is there a species barrier?' asked a female student voice.

'Good question Miss . . . ?' said Bannerman.

'Lindsay.'

'Good question Miss Lindsay. Everyone thought there was a barrier until *Mad cow disease* caught us on the hop. Recent research suggests that the cattle got it from eating foodstuffs containing *Scrapie*-infected sheep brains.'

'Then it's not inconceivable that man could contract brain disease from eating infected animals?'

'It's not inconceivable, but there's no evidence to support such a view.'

'At the moment,' added the student.

'At the moment,' conceded Bannerman.

'It could be that Creutzfeld Jakob Disease in man is actually derived from eating infected meat?'

'I repeat, there's no evidence to support such a view.'

'But you would advocate a vegetarian lifestyle anyway,' said a student at the back.

There was general laughter and Bannerman joined in. 'I have no intention of becoming vegetarian,' he said.

'At the moment,' added Miss Lindsay and there was more laughter.

'What about Alzheimer's. Is it related to *slow* virus disease?

'There are distinct diferences in pathology.'

'Is it known what causes Alzheimer's?'

'There is a genetic form of the disease but no clear proof about the more common type apart from the suggestion of some chemical involvement.'

'Aluminium?'

'There is some published evidence about the involvement of aluminium,' agreed Bannerman.

'Would it be true to say that research on dementia is woefully inadequate, Doctor?' asked a confident voice.

Bannerman looked at the student who held his gaze from beneath a mop of red hair which clashed with the colours of his medical school scarf. There was almost an air of insolence about him but Bannerman had seen it too often before to be upset by it. It was simply the holier-than-thou righteousness of the young. 'Yes I think it would,' he said evenly.

'Why?' demanded the red-haired young man.

'Every society has a limited amount it can spend on research,' said Bannerman. 'Dementia is primarily a disease of the old. There are enough diseases of the young to occupy our resources. It's as simple as that.'

'Personally I think it's disgraceful,' said the student.

Bannerman could feel that the sympathy of the class was not with him. 'Perhaps you should be reading social sciences, not medicine,' he said.

'Or politics,' suggested another student voice to a murmur of laughter.

'Medicine is a practical business,' said Bannerman. 'You work with the resources you have and make decisions accordingly. If you are faced with two patients in kidney failure and you have only one kidney machine it's no good shouting about how disgraceful it is. You have to decide which one lives and which one doesn't.'

Bannerman gave the class a moment to think about what he had said before saying, 'Perhaps the class would care to compare the pathology of the more common forms of dementia and we can discuss it next time.'

Bannerman returned to his office in the hospital and lit a cigarette. His secretary, Olive Meldrum, appeared a few moments later with strong, black coffee without being asked.

'How did it go?'

'Not bad,' replied Bannerman. 'Not bad at all. They're quite a bright lot. Any messages?'

'Stella phoned. She's operating this afternoon but she still expects you for dinner at eight and would you bring the wine?'

'Did she . . .'

'She said chicken,' said Olive, anticipating the question.

'Anyone else?'

'Dr Vernon asked that you call him if you have a spare moment. That was all.'

'Thanks Olive, get me Vernon would you?'

Olive closed the door behind her and a few moments later the buzzer on Bannerman's phone announced his call.

'Hello George, what can I do for you?'

After a few pleasantries Vernon got down to business. 'I've had a forty-seven-year-old man in for treatment on his arm. He burned it badly in an accident with a kettle of boiling water.'

'Not exactly my area of expertise,' said Bannerman.

'It's not the burn I'm concerned about,' said Vernon. 'I think he may have other problems.'

'What makes you think that?'

'I've noticed that in several conversations I've had with him he appears to have forgotten what I said to him only a few moments before. The first time I thought nothing of it but it's happened more than once. Brain disease is your thing; I wondered if you might take a look at him?'

'Of course,' said Bannerman, looking at his watch. 'How about now?'

'Absolutely,' answered Vernon, saying that he was obliged. He would meet Bannerman at ward seventeen in five minutes.

Bannerman rinsed his mouth with the antiseptic wash he kept by the basin in his office; he didn't want the patients to smell the cigarette smoke on his breath. He put on a fresh white coat and started out for the ward. The pathology lab was in the hospital's basement so his journey took him up two flights of stairs and along a corridor which was busy with lunch trolleys and nurses in transit between their wards and the dining-hall. Vernon met him at the entrance to ward seventeen; they entered together.

'I rang Sister to say we were coming,' said Vernon.

As if on cue, a stout woman dressed in navy blue with a white frilly cap on her grey hair emerged from a door to their left and smiled at them. 'Mr Green is all ready for you,' she said. 'Nurse will screen him off.'

Vernon and Bannerman were accompanied down the ward by a student nurse who pulled green, cotton screens round the patient's bed, corralling the three of them inside. The ward had a meal-time smell, a mixture of food and antiseptic.

'Mr Green, this is Doctor Bannerman. He would like to ask you a few questions.'

The patient, a well-built man with a tanned face and good teeth smiled and said, 'What can I tell you Doctor? My arm is coming along well thanks to Doctor Vernon here and they tell me I'll be getting home soon.'

'I'm glad to hear it,' said Bannerman. 'What happened exactly?'

The patient smiled and said, 'You chaps are like the police. You keep asking the same questions over and over again.'

'I hope that's not from personal experience,' smiled Bannerman.

'Indeed it is,' replied Green.

Bannerman was taken aback and Green noticed. 'I'm a policeman Doctor, a sergeant in CID.'

'Oh I see,' said Bannerman with a smile. 'I didn't know. So what happened?'

'Happened?' asked Green.

Bannerman noted that Green appeared to have forgotten the original question and exchanged a quick glance with Vernon who nodded. 'Your accident,' said Bannerman.

'It was just carelessness really. I grabbed at a kettle thinking it was empty. I was going to fill it to make some tea and it turned out to be full of boiling water. It went all over my arm.'

'Nasty,' said Bannerman with a grimace. 'Who else was in the house at the time?'

'Nobody,' replied Green.

Bannerman looked at Green wondering whether or not he would realize anything from his own reply but he didn't appear to. 'What happened then?' he asked.

'I tried to get my shirt off to hold my arm under the cold tap for a bit but the pain was something else. I could see the damage was pretty extensive so I called the ambulance and waited.'

'Did the ambulance take long to come?'

'Eight minutes,' replied Green. 'I watched them all pass on the clock.'

'Do you know how long it took to get to the hospital?' asked Bannerman.

'Ten minutes,' replied Green. 'It would have been quicker but there was a big snarl-up of traffic in Graham Road where they are laying new gas pipes. We got held up there for a couple of minutes despite the siren and flashing lights.'

'What day is it today?' asked Bannerman.

Green smiled as if he hadn't heard properly but Bannerman's expression assured him that he had. 'Why it's . . . it's . . .'

'Tuesday,' said Bannerman, 'Tuesday the 23rd of January.'

'Of course,' smiled Green. 'I couldn't think for a moment there. That's the trouble with being in hospital, the days just come and go and they all seem the same.'

Bannerman nodded sympathetically and said, 'I want you to start counting backwards from three hundred taking away seven at a time.'

Green shrugged his shoulders and began. 'Three hundred, two hundred and ninety-three, two hundred and eighty-six, two hundred and seventy-nine, two hundred and eighty-six, two hundred and eighty-six . . .'

'That's fine,' said Bannerman.

'How did I do?' asked Green with a smile.

'Just fine,' said Bannerman. He looked to Vernon and nodded.

Vernon thanked Green for his cooperation and he and Bannerman left to walk back up the ward to the ward duty-room while a nurse pulled back the screens on Green's bed.

'What do you think?' asked Vernon.

'I think you were right to be suspicious,' said Bannerman. 'He's showing all the signs of early Alzheimer's.'

'I feared as much,' said Vernon.

'His long term memory is fine but short-term is practically lost. I suspect that was the cause of his accident. I think he put the kettle on to boil then forgot that he'd done it. He went to do it again and poured the scalding water over his arm. He said there was no one else in the house. It must have been him who boiled the kettle in the first place.'

'He's only in his forties,' said Vernon shaking his head.

'He can only get worse,' said Bannerman softly. 'To all intents and purposes his useful life is over.'

'He has a wife and two teenage sons, one of them is a black kid they adopted when he was three. Sometimes I wonder if there's a God at all.'

'I came to my own conclusion on that one some time ago,' said Bannerman without elaborating. He said goodbye to Vernon and returned to the Pathology Department.

*   *   *

Olive Meldrum had gone to lunch; the outer office was empty. Bannerman made himself some more coffee and took it through to sit down at his desk and light up a cigarette. There would be no lunch for him today he decided. The bathroom scales this morning accused him of being twelve and a half stone and he had not been able to offer any defence. The band of thickening flesh round his middle, a legacy of over-indulgence at Christmas, was conclusive and could not be denied. Something had to be done.

Bannerman looked at the date on his desk diary and remembered that in eight days time it would be his thirty-eighth birthday. Thirty-eight and still unmarried! he could hear his mother declare. He had been up to see his parents at Christmas and had suffered the annual accusations along these lines. Luckily he had a sister Kate who had provided, with the aid of her husband, two grandsons to take the pressure off a little. 'When are you and Stella going to get together properly?' his mother had wanted to know.

Bannerman had countered by declaring, as he had so often in the past, that he and Stella were just old friends. It was true but then Stella was the only woman he ever mentioned at home. Some five years before there had been a romantic element to their friendship but it had not come to anything and had been abandoned in the cause of their continuing friendship. Occasional liaisons with members of the nursing staff were usually short-lived and seldom mentioned at home for fear of maternal probings worthy of the Spanish Inquisition.

Bannerman took a deep lungful of smoke and rested his head on the back of his chair to wonder why he had never married. He liked women and they seemed to like him well enough. But there had always come a point in relationships when he had backed off, unable to make a final commitment. He closed his eyes for a few seconds reflecting on the irony of never being able to make clear decisions about his own life when he made so many about other people's with no apparent trouble at all.

If he were to be honest with himself he would have to admit that there had been a string of women in his life with whom he had formed affectionate relationships but nothing more. Stella

19

had once pointed out that there was a difference between wanting someone and needing them. A woman liked to feel needed. Was that it, he wondered. Was he so self-contained that he didn't need anyone? An island?

Bannerman stubbed out his cigarette and decided that he had had enough of self-analysis for the moment. He checked his schedule for the afternoon and saw that he had a post-mortem to perform on a patient who had died of a brain tumour. He had also promised to be on call for any emergency analysis that theatre required during a breast operation that was being carried out by John Thorn, a surgeon colleague of Stella's for whom she had particular regard. 'The lump is in an awkward place,' Thorn had said. 'If I get it wrong the patient won't have a second chance.'

The operation was due to begin at three-thirty. It was five minutes to two. Bannerman decided that he would start on the PM and leave a message that he was to be called if any section analysis was required by the theatre team. He clipped his bleeper to his top pocket and started out for the mortuary.

His prompt arrival at two o'clock took the mortuary attendant by surprise. The man was sitting at a small wooden table in his office with a newspaper in front of him. A sandwich with a bite taken out of it lay on some greaseproof paper and a thermos flask with its lid off stood beside it.

'I was a bit late in getting off for my lunch,' explained the man. 'Doctor Leeman took longer than he thought this morning.'

'Just when you're ready,' said Bannerman.

'Who is it you're doing Doctor?' asked the man, getting up from the table and wrapping the paper round his half-eaten sandwich.

'Thomas George Baines from ward eight; he died on Sunday night.'

The attendant checked a wall chart which depicted the refrigerated body vault. The names on it were written in pencil so it could be used indefinitely with the aid of a dirty eraser that lay on the table below. 'Baines, number five,' he said to himself.

Bannerman moved back to allow the attendant to exit from

20

the room and then followed him to the body vault. This was located in a long, white-painted room, one side of which was entirely taken up with a series of tall doors, each secured with a heavy metal clasp. The doors were numbered from one to eight. The attendant opened one and revealed three sliding trays, one on top of the other. He checked a label on the middle one and said, 'Here we are, Thomas Baines.'

The man pulled an adjustable trolley into position and locked it in position before winding up the platform to match the height of the middle cadaver. With a practised tug he slid the body of Thomas Baines out onto it and unlocked the trolley to swing it round in a semi-circle before slamming shut the door of the vault. 'Table one all right?' he asked.

'Fine,' said Bannerman.

The man manoeuvred the body on to the post-mortem table and removed the shroud. He turned on the cold water supply to the slab and water started to gurgle down the gulleys. Bannerman himself turned on the overhead light and switched on the extractor fans.

'Do you want the air freshener on?' asked the attendant.

Bannerman shook his head. 'It's a head job,' he said. Bannerman loathed the smells of pathology as much as the next man but found the scent of the air freshener almost as bad in terms of pervasiveness. It would cling to him. There would be no need to open up the chest cavity of Thomas Baines. The examination would be confined to the head so he would do without the air freshener.

'Want me to open the skull?' asked the attendant.

'I'll do it,' said Bannerman. 'Go finish your sandwiches.'

'Cheers Doc,' said the man.

Bannerman donned a pair of Wellington boots which he selected from the row standing along the back wall and took down one of the green, plastic aprons from a clothes peg above. He fastened the ties behind him and snapped on a pair of surgical gloves which he took from the box marked 'Large'. Using a power tool he trephined around the skull of the corpse on the table, pausing at intervals to rinse away the accumulating bone grit and allowing the smell of burning to subside. When he had cut right round, he lifted off the cap of Thomas Baines' skull as a complete unit and laid it beside the head. Changing to surgical instruments he removed the brain and placed it on a metal tray on an adjoining table.

Bannerman weighed the brain then examined it visually from several angles. 'Doesn't take too much to see what killed you my friend,' he murmured. A large tumour was protruding from the left side of the excised brain. It was a livid red colour against the greyness of the normal brain material. Bannerman removed the tumour and placed it in a glass specimen jar for removal to the lab. He placed the brain back in the skull cavity and told the attendant that he was finished.

'Right you are Doc,' exclaimed the man. 'I'll put his "hat" back on, eh?' He broke into a cackle of broken laughter.

Bannerman did not join in. Gallows humour was not his thing. 'You'll do it respectfully,' he said.

'Of course Doctor,' said the man, realising he had made an error and wiping all trace of amusement from his face.

Bannerman stripped off his gloves and threw them into a plastic bin. Walking over to a large porcelain sink he levered on the taps with his elbows and took pleasure in sluicing the liquid soap and warm water over his hands and forearms. As he dried his hands he watched the attendant fitting the skull cap back on to the body. The man was whistling quietly as he did it, checking the fit on all sides as if he were a plumber changing a tap washer.

Bannerman had to concede that the attendant had achieved a far greater degree of ease with his job than he himself had ever managed. There were still times when he found himself vomiting in the bathroom over certain aspects of his work. It didn't happen nearly as often as it once had but it still happened. It was something he had never confessed to anyone, not to Stella in their closest moments, not even to his own father, also a doctor. He didn't like to think about it too much. The bleeper went off in his pocket and stopped him thinking about it now.

'I'll be right up,' he said in response to the information that theatre had requested an urgent biopsy examination. The door to the PM room shut with a loud echo as he swung it closed behind him and ran along the tiled corridor to the base of the stairs leading up to the lab. The technicians had already processed the tissue by the time he got there and one of them was examining a slide of it under a Zeiss binocular microscope.

'What do you see, Charlie?' asked Bannerman.

'A toughie,' said the technician.

'Bad prep?'

'Could be. Karen's doing another one. It'll be ready in a couple of minutes.'

The man stood up to allow Bannerman to take his place at the microscope. Bannerman altered the distance between the eyepieces to compensate for the fact that his eyes were slightly further apart than the technician's. He adjusted the fine focus then manipulated the stage controls to permit a stepwise examination of the slide without going over the same area twice. 'Shit,' he said under his breath.

'You've found something?' said the technician.

'It looks bad,' said Bannerman, moving the focus control as if there was a perfect level that still eluded him. 'Take a look, just there at eleven o'clock.'

The technician sat down again and said, 'Yes, I see it but it's not as clear as . . .' His voice tapered off as he showed himself unwilling to commit himself to a definite opinion.

A young woman came into the room and interrupted them. She said, 'Theatre say they must know right away.'

'I'll see if the other prep is ready,' said the technician who had been examining the slide. He came back a moment later looking sheepish. 'It's going to be another ten minutes I'm afraid. Something went wrong.'

Bannerman looked at the embarrassed expression on the technician's face but did not pass comment. He turned to the woman and said, 'I'll talk to theatre.' He got up and followed her through to the main lab where he picked up the receiver. 'This is Bannerman. Can you give us ten minutes?'

'Negative,' said the surgeon's voice. 'I have to know now.'

23

Bannerman closed his eyes for a moment and then said, 'It's malignant.'

'Understood,' said the surgeon and the line went dead.

There was a silence in the room which threatened to overwhelm all of them. Bannerman broke it. He said, 'I'll be in my office. Let me know when the other prep is ready.'

Bannerman walked over to the window of his office and lit a cigarette with fingers that trembled slightly. There was little to see, save for a stone wall barely seven feet from the window with rain water running down it from a faulty gutter somewhere above, but then he wasn't really looking at the view. There was too much going on in his head.

A light tapping came to the door and Bannerman said, 'Come in.'

'The prep's ready.'

Bannerman nodded and walked over to the door where the technician held it open for him. As he passed through, the technician said quietly. 'You were right. I had a look. It's malignant.'

Bannerman paused in the doorway for a second and felt the tension melt from him. He took a couple of shallow breaths and said, 'I didn't imagine for a moment that it wasn't, Charlie.'

'Of course not,' said the technician with the barest suggestion of a smile. For a moment they held each other's gaze then the technician said, 'The second prep is as clear as a bell . . . poor woman.'

TWO

Bannerman left the hospital at six-thirty. He noticed that Stella's white Volkswagen Golf was still in the car-park as he edged his own Rover out of its sardine-like space at the end of the line reserved for 'Medical Staff'. He had hoped that the worst of the rush-hour traffic would be over but he still had to wait for nearly a minute at the gate before he could ease out into the slow moving line. He swore as he had to clear the windscreen yet again with his glove as condensate built up because of the rain. 'Living in London is like living down a dark wet hole,' he muttered, turning up the fan and switching on the rear screen demister.

The traffic came to a halt because of some unknown obstruction up ahead; it did nothing to improve his temper. He pushed a cassette of Vivaldi into the car's tape player and tried to concentrate on the music rather than the frustration of city driving. The tapes had been Stella's idea. Fed up with his bad temper at the wheel, she had embarked on a programme of 'sound therapy', insisting that he try out the soothing effect of various musical styles as an aid to relaxation.

So far the biggest success had been a tape of Gregorian chant, recorded by French monks in an alpine monastery. The sonorous tolling of bells and echoing prayer chants had induced a marked improvement in his driving demeanour with their constant allusion to human mortality. The ironic drawback was that Stella found the ecclesiastical aura in the car almost as irritating as his bad temper. She had insisted on him finding something else. It had been Mozart's turn last week, which had

25

only moderate success; now it was Vivaldi's big chance with *The Four Seasons*.

The traffic started to move but again ground to a halt less than fifty yards further on. Bannerman slipped the gear stick into neutral and sighed in frustration. *Winter* wasn't doing too well. It took a further thirty-five minutes to reach the turn off for his apartment block. A few twists and turns through quiet back streets and he was safely through the gates and into the haven of Redholm Court.

As he got out and locked the car he suddenly remembered that he had yet to get some wine to take over to Stella's. He toyed with getting it on his way there but decided that if he did that it would be warm. There was an off-licence a quarter of a mile down the road so he pulled up his collar and hurried along to it. He was back within fifteen minutes.

With the wine safely in the kitchen fridge Bannerman took off his coat and poured himself a large gin from a bottle which stood on a tray beside the window. He closed the curtains and switched on the television to catch what was left of the early evening news on Channel Four.

Bannerman lived on the third floor. It was a pleasant two-bedroomed flat rented at a price which included all services. He had stayed there for the last two years and had no intention of moving unless he had to. It was quiet, warm in winter and pleasant in summer because of the south-facing balcony and roof garden. The building itself was surrounded by private gardens which included several mature beech trees and a series of well-kept flower beds which the gardeners stocked according to the season. There was also a garage for his car although he seldom used it, preferring instead to leave it on the tarmac apron facing the row of lock-ups.

There was little in the way of furniture in the apartment, something which owed nothing to 'minimalist' fashion but much to Bannerman's lack of interest in matters domestic. Most of what there was was designed to hold books although even these pieces were insufficient to cope with his collection and several volumes lived permanently on the floor, something his cleaner was at pains to point out at frequent intervals. She maintained that it interfered with her 'Hoover'.

Unknown to her, this fact gave Bannerman perverse pleasure. Anything that impeded the progress of that monstrous machine was to be applauded. He had an almost irrational loathing of the 'Hoover'. It was a hated enemy, the ultimate symbol of domestic drudgery. On the odd occasion he found himself in the flat when the dreaded noise started up he would be into a track suit and off running round the grounds before the cleaner had finished saying, 'I hope this won't disturb you too much Doctor . . .'

Bannerman finished his drink, kicked off his shoes and padded off to the bathroom to shower. He noticed a message on the hall table and stopped to read it. It was from the cleaner and said that one of his shirts had gone missing in the laundry. She hald 'told them off' about it and, 'by the way' he needed some more shirts anyway. Several were looking 'weary'. Bannerman had to admit that that was fair criticism. He was probably one of the laundry company's best customers.

As a medical student he had discovered that pathologists carried the smell of their profession about with them. Even on social occasions he had noticed the sweet tang of formaldehyde or some other tissue fixative clinging to their clothes. For this reason, when he became a pathologist himself, he decided that this must not be the case with him. To this end, he kept two separate sets of clothes, one for work and the other for social use. They were never allowed to mix. Each day when he came home he would strip off and shower before putting on fresh clothes and placing his working ones in the laundry basket, the *Ali Baba* basket as the cleaner called it. It was a nice allusion; he liked it. It was a 'working' shirt that had gone missing and it was his range of 'working' shirts that were looking decidedly faded. It was only Tuesday. He would put off dealing with the problem until the weekend.

Bannerman lingered longer than usual in the shower, letting the warm water cascade on the back of his neck and slacken off the tension there while he mulled over the events of the day. Uppermost in his mind was the decision he had been called upon to make on the breast biopsy. It had worked out well in the end but it had also given him more than a few bad moments. What worried him most was the fact that he had noticed a distinct tremor in his fingers while he waited for an improved prep to be made. He had had worrying moments before in his career, many, but he could not recall ever having seen his hands shake before.

When he stepped out of the shower he towelled himself down in front of the big mirror at the back of the sink and examined himself critically, something he rarely did. Perhaps the appraisal was inspired by earlier thoughts of his approaching birthday but he hadn't really looked at himself in a long time. He leaned forward to examine his hair, thinning a bit, a state exaggerated by it being wet but undeniable nevertheless. He frizzed it at the front with his fingertips.

His clean-shaven face carried no spare flesh and his chin line was still firm – well, reasonably firm. Perhaps there was just the vaguest suggestion of a double chin there but it disappeared when he pushed his jaw out a little – so he did. His brown eyes, when examined closely with the aid of a finger pulling down the lower lid, seemed clear and bright and his teeth were straight and reasonably white. His upper body was well muscled, though softer than it had been some ten years ago, and the thickening round the middle he would ascribe to Christmas for the time being.

He had a slightly low centre of gravity which kept his height a couple of inches under six feet. His thighs were a bit too thick and muscular when they could have done with being a bit slimmer and longer, a fact which nevertheless had helped him in his rugby playing days. He had played for Glasgow University when he was a medical student there. 'Frankly Bannerman,' he thought, 'you're not going to be in demand as a romantic lead . . . but then,' he reasoned, 'you never were.' He wrapped the towel round his waist and went through to the bedroom to dress.

*   *   *

The entryphone crackled into life and Stella Lansing's voice said, 'Come on up, Ian.' The door relay clicked and released the lock without waiting for him to say anything.

'It's not Ian,' said Bannerman. 'I'm a multiple rapist and I've come to have my way with you.' He climbed the stairs to Stella's apartment, bottle in hand, and found the door ajar. He let himself in and closed it with enough noise to let Stella know he had arrived.

'I'll be with you in a moment,' came her voice from the kitchen. 'I'm behind as usual. Help yourself to a drink.'

Bannerman ignored the suggestion and went straight to the kitchen where he came up behind Stella and kissed her on the cheek. 'Hello.'

Stella half turned and said, 'I think I've ruined the potatoes.'

'Good,' replied Bannerman. 'I'm on a diet.'

'Since when?' asked Stella.

'Since this morning.'

'It's not like you to care about things like that,' said Stella.

Bannerman digested the comment in silence. It deserved some thought.

'Why don't you pour us both a drink,' said Stella, intent on stirring something on the hob.

This time Bannerman did as he was bid. Stella joined him a few moments later, undoing her apron and throwing it casually away as she walked towards him. Bannerman smiled at the gesture. Stella did everything with grace and panache. He was reminded of a story he had once heard about Fred Astaire. It was said that he could walk across stage smoking a cigarette, throw it away, stub it out with his foot and all without breaking stride.

Stella smoothed her brown hair back from the sides of her head and straightened her dress before sitting down. Both gestures were unnecessary. Stella always liked to maintain that she was disorganised and 'in a tizzy' but it was seldom, if ever, true. If she had messed up the potatoes it must have been because God had decreed that they should be messed up.

Stella sat down beside him and smiled. 'How was your day?' she asked. She had a slightly round face which tempered

29

perfectly her slim elegant figure, whereas sharper features would have made her appear forbidding. A pleasantly wide mouth broke into a smile and bestowed on her what Bannerman always thought of as an air of amused detachment. An enemy might have seen it as patronizing.

'Fair to middling,' he said. 'How about you?'

'No problems,' said Stella. 'Routine removal of ovarian cysts. What happened about John Thorn's patient?'

'I'm afraid the section was malignant. What was the problem there, anyway?'

'The patient had multiple breast lumps and John suspected from the X-rays that there was a deeper tumour which they couldn't reach by needle biopsy beforehand. He wanted you on hand to examine it if they came across it during the op. Everyone trusts your opinion.'

Bannerman rubbed his forehead in a nervous gesture, then realized he was doing it and stopped.

'Is something wrong?' asked Stella. She put her hand on his.

'No, nothing,' smiled Bannerman. 'I'm just a bit tired that's all.'

'Poor Ian,' said Stella.

The comment was affectionate but it made Bannerman feel guilty. He felt sure that Stella had more reason to feel tired than he.

'I'll just check the sauce,' said Stella, getting up and disappearing into the kitchen. 'You could open the wine.'

Bannerman opened the wine and removed the cork slowly from the end of the corkscrew. 'Stella?' he said.

'What?' came the reply from the kitchen.

'Why do you think we've remained such good friends?'

'I don't know,' said Stella, coming into the room holding a hot dish with two hands and protecting her fingers with a dish cloth. 'Is it important?'

'Maybe,' said Bannerman.

'Why,' asked Stella, depositing the dish on the table and turning to face Bannerman. 'What's brought this on?'

'I've been thinking,' said Bannerman.

'About what?'

'Life.'

'And?'

'I don't know,' said Bannerman.

'Well, what can I say?' said Stella with a grin.

'Why haven't you got married? Why haven't I? Do you think it's some defect in our characters?'

'Personally speaking I'm quite happy as I am,' said Stella. 'Perhaps we don't need the hassle. We both have demanding careers and busy lives. Maybe that's enough?'

'Yes but . . .'

'But what? Who has been getting at you? Or have you been stricken by a sudden bout of middle-age?'

Bannerman reacted to the word 'middle-age' with a slight wince and Stella noticed. Stella noticed everything. 'So that is what this is all about,' she said knowingly.

'I don't know what you mean,' said Bannerman hastily.

'You're having a mid-life crisis! That's what I mean,' exclaimed Stella. 'You're indulging in an orgy of self-analysis! Do you want to lie along the couch and tell me all your innermost fears?'

'Certainly not,' insisted Bannerman, feeling vulnerable and wishing he had never broached the subject. He should have known that Stella would see through him right away. 'I was simply thinking.'

'Ugh huh,' nodded Stella. 'And putting yourself on a diet while you were doing it . . .'

'Sometimes I hate you,' smiled Bannerman.

'Eat up,' said Stella. 'You can always dance it off at the disco on the way home . . .'

Afterwards, as they sat on the couch with their coffee, Bannerman said, 'I almost bottled it today.'

'What do you mean?'

'Lost my nerve. The tumour section wasn't as clear as I would have liked and theatre insisted on an answer before the new prep was ready.'

'That isn't exactly the easiest of positions to be in,' said Stella.

'I know but it's what they pay me for,' said Bannerman.

'Tell me about it,' said Stella.

Bannerman told her the details of what had happened and Stella looked at him in disbelief. 'You call that losing your nerve?' she exclaimed. 'That was an absolutely nightmarish situation to be in, and you got it dead right.'

'That's the way it worked out but it could have been so different,' said Bannerman. 'The woman could have lost her breast unnecessarily.'

'Nonsense!' exclaimed Stella. 'She had the best histopathologist in the country examining the biopsy.'

'Thanks,' said Bannerman, but his expression showed that he wasn't convinced.

'You really are down aren't you?' said Stella. 'What brought all this on?'

'I'm not sure,' said Bannerman, 'I had a lecture this morning and before it I suddenly found myself thinking what a waste of time it all was.'

'We've all thought that from time to time, especially if you get a bad class,' said Stella.

'But they weren't bad at all as it turned out. We were discussing *slow* virus brain disease and they seemed genuinely interested. I finished up feeling guilty for misjudging them.'

'What you need is a change,' said Stella. 'Take some time off, re-charge your batteries.'

'I can't. I've got too much to do.'

'No one is indispensable Ian, not even you. I'm sure the hospital could survive for a couple of weeks. Leeman could cope with the lab couldn't he?'

'Yes,' agreed Bannerman.

'And you have a first-class chief technician in Charlie Simmons?'

'Yes.'

'So, do it.'

'I have two more lectures to give on brain disease for the course.'

'Ah,' conceded Stella, 'that's more difficult. When do your lectures finish?'

'The last one is a week on Friday.'

'That's not long,' said Stella. 'Finish your lectures and then take time off.'

'I'll consider it,' said Bannerman.

'Do it!' urged Stella.

Bannerman thought for a moment then said, 'Maybe I'll do something I've planned to do for a long time but haven't quite got round to.'

'What's that?'

'Go winter climbing in Scotland.'

'You're serious?' asked Stella.

'Absolutely. I used to do it when I was a student at Glasgow. I promised myself that I would do it again one day.'

Stella looked bemused and said, 'I must confess I was thinking more along the lines of you lying on the beach in the sunshine, chatting up dolly birds, drinking ice-cold beer, but if this is what you really want . . .'

'We'll see,' said Bannerman attempting to close the subject, but Stella made him promise that he would give it some serious thought.

'I promise,' said Bannerman. 'Can I give you a hand with the washing up?'

Stella declined the offer, saying that she would do it in the morning. She wasn't due at the hospital until eleven. 'How about you?'

'I said I'd do the autopsy on the Bryant kid who died at the weekend and I've got a meeting at ten-thirty so I'd better get an early start.'

'I heard about that,' said Stella. 'Very sad, brain cancer wasn't it?'

'Almost certainly,' said Bannerman, 'but I suppose I'll know for sure tomorrow. If it is, the MRC will want a full report for their survey.'

'What survey?'

'They're monitoring the incidence of brain disease in the UK to get an overall picture of the situation.'

'Is this a routine survey or has something prompted it?' asked Stella.

'They're pretending it's routine but it has a lot to do with the

BSE scare we had last year. People suddenly realized that no one has a clear picture of what is going on because brain disease is so difficult to diagnose and classify. The temptation is always to use vague generalities like, "dementia".'

'Somehow I get the impression that things like Alzheimer's disease are on the increase. Is that right?'

'I fear so,' said Bannerman, 'But the survey should give us a clearer picture when it's complete.'

Stella looked at her watch and said, 'It's late and if you've got to get up early . . .'

Bannerman nodded and got to his feet. He thanked Stella for dinner and took hold of both her hands to say, 'Thank you for being my friend.'

'Off with you,' smiled Stella, 'And . . .'

'Yes?'

'Don't stay too long at the disco.'

Bannerman woke at three in the morning with the sweat pouring off him. He had awoken from the nightmare just at the moment when the naked woman had raised the knife above her head to stab him. The act of stretching had caused the jagged surgical wounds on her chest, where her breasts should have been, to split open and weep blood over him.

Bannerman sat bolt upright, breathing heavily and repeating an oath under his breath. After a few moments he swung his legs out from below the duvet and sat on the edge of the bed to light a cigarette. He took a deep lungful of smoke and let it out slowly while he massaged his forehead with his fingertips.

The nightmare had been so vivid that there was no question of lying back down again and risking sleep. The woman with the knife would be waiting for him just below the brim of consciousness. He pulled a dressing-gown round him and went through to the living-room to turn on the television. It didn't seem very interesting – some American film from the sixties by the look of it – but it provided a distraction, and that was the main thing. The soundtrack was therapeutic as he shuffled into the kitchen to turn on the kettle to make tea.

James Stewart and an actress he didn't recognize were about to live happily ever after and there were two more cigarette stubs in the ashtray before Bannerman felt like risking sleep again.

At ten-fifteen in the morning, Bannerman returned to his office from the post-mortem suite with the taped report he had compiled of the autopsy on Paul Bryant, aged nine. 'I'll need an MRC report form Olive,' he said to his secretary on passing. 'He had cancer of the brain.'

'You aren't forgetting the monthly Health Board meeting at ten-thirty are you?' said Olive.

'No,' replied Bannerman without enthusiasm.

Olive Meldrum smiled. She knew how much Bannerman hated routine meetings.

Bannerman sat down behind his desk and picked up the telephone. The events of the previous day and night had been preying on his mind too much. He resolved to do something about it. He pressed a four digit code and waited for a reply.

'Drysdale,' said the voice.

'Dave, it's me, Ian Bannerman. Do you think we could have a talk sometime today?'

'What about a drink at lunch-time?'

'I meant a more professional talk,' said Bannerman.

'Oh I see. Well I think I should warn you that I suspect your "patients" are a bit beyond psychiatric help,' said Drysdale.

Bannerman did his best to respond to the joke but it was laboured and Drysdale sensed it. 'How about two-thirty?' he asked.

'That suits me fine,' said Bannerman. 'Your place or mine?'

'Come up,' replied Drysdale.

For Bannerman to arrange a meeting with a psychiatrist it had been very much a case of the singer not the song because he had little time for psychiatry. On the other hand, he had great respect for David Drysdale whom he had known and liked for five years. Drysdale knew and freely admitted the shortcomings of his speciality. He never hid behind meaningless jargon as Bannerman suspected so many of his psychiatric colleagues of doing. When he heard Drysdale describe electro-convulsive therapy as 'wiring the patients up to the mains to see what would happen' he knew that he had found a psychiatrist he would like. As he got to know him better, he discovered that the man had a genuine and sincere concern for the welfare of the mentally ill. It was his regret that so little could be done to help in so many cases.

Drysdale's office was two floors above the pathology department. The walls were decorated with examples of schizophrenic art and a small print of Edvard Munch's, *The Scream*. Drysdale, a sallow-skinned man with dark hair and heavy-rimmed spectacles, which made him look like an East European student, invited Bannerman to sit. 'What can I do for you Ian?' he asked.

'I think I may need help,' said Bannerman awkwardly.

Drysdale considered making some comment about 'not thinking he would see the day' but thought better of it, seeing the troubled look on Bannerman's face. 'Tell me about it,' he said.

Bannerman told him about his experience with the emergency section. 'My hands were actually shaking,' he said. 'And then I had a nightmare about it last night.'

Drysdale nodded and said, 'Tell me.'

Bannerman related all that he could remember about the dream and then asked, 'Do you mind if I smoke?'

Drysdale made a sign with his hands that indicated resignation but not approval. 'You should give it up,' he said.

Bannerman ignored the comment.

'What else should I know?' asked Drysdale.

'Sometimes I'm sick after doing post-mortems.'

Drysdale nodded. He had started making notes. 'How old are you Ian?'

'I'll be thirty-eight next birthday.'

'How do you feel about that?'

'Rotten.'

'Me too,' said Drysdale. 'I'll be thirty-nine. Any other problems?'

'Insomnia.'

'You waken up at three in the morning and feel wide awake.

You can't get back to sleep for about an hour. This happens every second night on average?'

'How did you know that?'

'Sheer bloody brilliance,' said Drysdale. 'But apart from that, I recognized the symptoms. They're textbook. It's depression not insomnia.'

'So you think I'm clinically depressed,' said Bannerman.

'A little,' replied Drysdale, 'but the main problem is stress.'

'Stella thinks it's a mid-life crisis,' said Bannerman.

'She's right,' said Drysdale, 'But there's another factor involved and I'm not quite sure what it is. I'll have to have a think about it.'

'What do I do about it in the meantime?' asked Bannerman.

'I can suggest pills but you know as well as I do they'll just dull your senses so you won't feel so stressed. That's probably not such a good idea in our line of work. How about booze in the evening?'

'I think I've used up that option,' said Bannerman.

'Me too,' said Drysdale. 'How about a break? A holiday might be just what you need.'

'Stella suggested that. I'm considering going climbing in Scotland.'

'In January!' exclaimed Drysdale. 'You're sicker than I thought!'

'To each his own, Doctor,' said Bannerman with a smile. He got up to go.

'I'm sorry I couldn't be of more help,' said Drysdale, 'but keep in touch. I don't think it's anything serious and Stella's probably right about it being fear of forty but if you should begin to feel worse give me a call, any time, day or night.'

Bannerman thanked Drysdale and promised to buy him a drink in the near future. He returned to the Pathology Department where Olive had left a package on his desk. It was marked 'On Her Majesty's Service' and had come from the Medical Research Council by special delivery. He opened it and found three microscope slides and a covering letter. The letter was from the coordinator of the MRC's Survey on Degenerative Brain Disease, Dr Hugh Milne. It asked if he would mind examining them and reporting his findings as quickly as possible. There was also a message to say that Stella had phoned; it was nothing important but he was to be reminded that he couldn't call her back because she would be in theatre all afternoon.

Bannerman took the slides to his personal microscope and removed the dust cover. He clipped the first to the stage and adjusted the tungsten light before focusing on the stained section of the brain. There had been a marked lack of details with the package and no indication about the source of the material, save for the fact that they were brain sections. There was an air of anticipation about him as he scanned around to find the clearest fields. It didn't take long to find what he was looking for – unequivocal evidence of degenerative disease.

It was so obvious that Bannerman was puzzled to the point of feeling mildly annoyed that he had been asked for his opinion on something so clearcut. He had rarely seen spongioform areas so well marked. This was the kind of slide that could be used for illustrating text books. The second and third slides were almost identical to the first. 'What on earth are they playing at?' he muttered as he removed the last slide and turned off the lamp. He asked Olive to get him the MRC coordinator on the phone.

'Dr Bannerman? Good of you to call,' said Milne after a short wait. 'I take it you received the slides?'

'I've just had a look,' said Bannerman.

'What do you think?'

'I think I've just looked at three perfectly prepared brain sections from the same patient. He or she would be in their mid to late seventies and has just died of Creutzfeld Jakob Disease.'

'You'd be wrong,' said the coordinator.

'What?' exclaimed Bannerman.

'What would you say if I told you that each of the slides came from a different patient, all were under thirty and none had been ill for longer than three weeks?'

'I'd say there had been a mix-up in the slides,' said Bannerman.

'We are assured that there has been no mix-up.'

'I find that incredible,' said Bannerman.

'Suppose I was to add that the three dead patients worked with infected sheep?'

'What?' exclaimed Bannerman. 'You're not suggesting that they died of *Scrapie* by any chance?'

'I wish I wasn't. Can we meet to discuss this further?'

'When?' asked Bannerman.

'I think it had better be as soon as possible,' said the coordinator.

'Why me?' ventured Bannerman.

'Your reputation, Doctor. Your work on degenerative brain disease is second to none and right now we need the best we've got. I'll explain more when I see you. Would tomorrow at eleven be a possibility?'

Bannerman checked his diary before saying that it would.

'Did you see about taking time off?' asked Stella when Bannerman saw her later.

Bannerman brushed the question aside and told her about the call from the MRC. 'I saw the slides Stella! They were classic Creutzfeld Jakob but Milne said they came from three men who had been working with *Scrapie* infected sheep!'

'You mean the men died of *Scrapie* not Creutzfeld Jakob?' exclaimed Stella.

'That's what Milne seemed to be saying.'

'But that can't happen surely? *Scrapie* is a disease of sheep. It can't pass to man. There's a what-do-you-call-it?'

'A species barrier,' said Bannerman. 'Last year cows, this year people . . .'

'What was that?' asked Stella.

'I was just thinking that last year *Scrapie* was shown to have passed from sheep to cows through the food chain . . .'

'You're not seriously suggesting that it could do the same to humans?'

'Up until today I would have said that there was no chance of that at all,' replied Bannerman.

'Then what do you think is going on?'

'My initial reaction is to think that some kind of mistake has

39

been made, some kind of mix-up in the path lab, but the chap I spoke to said not.'

'Maybe I should think twice about having lamb for Sunday dinner?'

'It's a bit early for that,' smiled Bannerman. 'I'll know more when I see the MRC people tomorrow.'

THREE

It was raining heavily when Bannerman's taxi pulled up outside the headquarters of the Medical Research Council in Park Crescent. It turned to hail and battered deafeningly on the roof of the cab as he paid the driver before getting out and making a run for the entrance.

'What a day,' smiled the woman behind the desk. 'Rain, sleet, hail, whatever next?'

Bannerman brushed at his shoulders and said who he was, adding, 'Dr Milne is expecting me.'

'Take a seat Doctor,' replied the woman, indicating with one hand while picking up the telephone with her other. A few minutes later a young man appeared in the hall and said, 'Dr Milne asks if you wouldn't mind waiting in the library until everyone is here?'

'Of course not,' replied Bannerman automatically, but wondering about the word, 'everyone'. He was under the impression that this was to be a meeting between himself and Milne. He followed the young man up to the library where he was invited to sit beside a small table that was bedecked with magazines. He picked up one with two smiling Africans on the front and flicked through the pages without taking in too much. The magazine was comprised of a series of reports on successful projects undertaken to improve health care in the Third World.

There was a young clerk in the room. She was replacing books on the shelves but was aware of Bannerman's presence. She saw

41

the magazine he was looking at and said, 'It's wonderful what they're doing in Africa isn't it?'

Bannerman looked at the innocent smile on her face and smiled back. 'Yes it is,' he replied but inside his head he was thinking what a load of twaddle the magazine was. It was exactly the kind of rubbish the West wanted to read about Africa. Comfortable, optimistic nonsense about success in the field without any reference to the enormous scale of the problems of pestilence and famine. Yet, would it really help if they did understand? he wondered. Would it encourage people to give more if they understood the true scale of the problem? or would it put them off altogether?

'If you would follow me Dr Bannerman?' said the young man who had re-appeared in the doorway putting an end to his philosophising.

Bannerman put down the magazine, smiled goodbye to the female clerk and followed the young man downstairs, where he was shown into a large room with a long table as its main feature. Four men were sitting at one end; one of them got up and came towards him as the young man left.

'Dr Bannerman? I'm Hugh Milne. We spoke on the telephone. We are all obliged to you for coming here at such short notice. May I introduce, Sir John Flowers, Secretary of the MRC, Dr Hector Munro, Director of the Neurobiology Unit in Edinburgh and Mr Cecil Allison from the Prime Minister's office.'

Bannerman nodded to each of the men in turn and took his seat.

Flowers said, 'I understand from Dr Milne that you were kind enough to examine some brain sections we sent you.'

'It didn't take long,' said Bannerman. 'They were very clear. Typical Creutzfeld Jakob Disease.'

'So I understand,' said Flowers. 'Hugh also explained their origin?'

'I understand the sections came from the brains of three young men who died after a short illness and that all three worked with sheep.'

'Quite so,' said Flowers. 'What was your reaction when you heard this?'

'I thought there had to be some kind of mistake, a mix-up with the slides perhaps.'

'We are assured that there was no mix-up,' said Flowers.

'So I was told,' said Bannerman.

'This puts us in a very difficult position,' said Flowers. He turned to the man from the Prime Minister's Office and said, 'Perhaps Mr Allison would like to explain?'

Allison nodded, cleared his throat and said, 'Her Majesty's Government is very anxious to assure our European colleagues that there is absolutely no problem with British meat products. Ideally we would like to be able to say categorically that *slow* virus diseases of animals cannot be transmitted to man through the food chain.'

'I see,' said Bannerman.

'We have reason to believe that Her Majesty's Opposition is about to press us very soon to make a statement to this effect. If we cannot do this with the backing of the Medical Research Council then the effects on the farming community might well be catastrophic.'

'All the evidence has been pointing to an effective species barrier between animals and man and then suddenly, we have this report from Scotland,' said Flowers.

'I can well understand the problem,' said Bannerman.

'Naturally, we are hoping that the report is mistaken in some way,' said Allison.

'But even if it is, and please God it is, I understand that there has been an overall increase in the incidence of degenerative brain disease in the population. Is that not so?' asked Bannerman.

Allison appeared to move uncomfortably in his seat. He said, 'Our statisticians have concluded that that is not necessarily the case. Data in the past has been scant and very difficult to obtain so what represents a true increase percentage-wise is quite hard to define . . .'

Bannerman looked at Flowers but the Secretary diverted his eyes and looked down at the table. 'I see,' he said.

'If this report is accurate however,' said Flowers, 'and an

animal brain disease has been transmitted to man, then that would be quite another matter.'

'Quite,' said Allison.

Flowers looked up at Bannerman and said, 'Might I ask what your feelings are at this stage Doctor?'

'I think that if this report is real, then some extra factor must have come into play,' said Bannerman.

'What sort of extra factor were you thinking of?' asked Allison.

'If the *Scrapie* agent caused the deaths of these men then I believe it must have changed in some way; something caused it to mutate, enabling it to cross the species barrier.

'This is largely the conclusion I and my colleagues have come to. It would be very worrying of course, if the change were due to a spontaneous mutation occurring in the animals because that would mean that this sort of thing could happen at any time and in any place. If however, the mutation was induced by some outside factor then it may be possible to identify such a factor. With luck we should be able to take steps to prevent it happening again.'

'Something tells me that you have identified a factor,' said Bannerman.

'I think we may have,' said Flowers. 'The area where the three dead men farmed the sheep is adjacent to the Invermaddoch power station.'

'The Invermaddoch *nuclear* power station,' added Allison.

'Oh,' said Bannerman, taking a moment to consider the possible implications. Radiation was one of the most common inducers or mutation in living things. 'I suppose you couldn't hope for a better candidate,' he said, 'assuming there has been a leak. Has there?'

'Officially no,' said Allison.

'What does that mean?' said Bannerman.

Allison took off his glasses to clean them, unnecessarily.

'There was a slight problem at the station some six months ago,' he admitted hesitantly.

'Which was covered up,' said Bannerman.

'We were assured that it was very slight and we didn't want

to cause unnecessary alarm,' said Allison.

'But it happened,' said Bannerman.

Flowers moved in to defuse the situation. 'I think it's about time we came to the point,' he said to Bannerman. 'We were rather hoping to enlist your professional help with this affair.'

'I would be happy to help you with the lab work if that's what you mean,' said Bannerman.

'Actually, it isn't,' said Flowers. 'What we would like, would be for you to investigate this whole matter.'

Bannerman was taken aback and left speechless for a few moments.

Flowers said, 'We need a first-rate pathologist to go up to Scotland and report back. We have to know; one, if the men's deaths were really due to *Scrapie*; two, what caused the disease to cross the species barrier; and three, whether or not we can regard this as an isolated incident.'

'And it has to be done discreetly,' added Allison.

'Presumably no mention of *Scrapie* was made on the men's death certificates?' asked Bannerman.

'No. The official cause of death was given as meningitis.'

'What about the sheep in the area?'

'The *Scrapie*-infected sheep were, of course, destroyed but there has been no general alert,' said Allison. 'That would have attracted immediate and unwanted attention.'

'And you wouldn't want to cause unnecessary alarm,' added Bannerman, acidly.

'You must see how delicate the situation is, Doctor,' said Allison.

Reluctantly, Bannerman had to admit that he could. 'But you must have a pathologist working on it already,' he said. 'The man who reported the problem in the first place.'

'That's another thing, I'm afraid,' said Flowers. 'Dr Gill has disappeared.'

'Disappeared?' exclaimed Bannerman.

'He left home nine days ago and hasn't been seen since.'

'Some domestic upheaval, we're told,' said Munro.

Bannerman shook his head in bemusement but didn't know what to say. 'Where is the pathology lab work being done?' he asked.

'Edinburgh, in George Stoddart's department at the medical school,' said Flowers.

'Edinburgh is full of experts on *Scrapie* and *slow* viruses,' said Bannerman, looking to Munro.

'My people are scientists Doctor,' said Munro. 'We would give you all the back-up you required but the investigation calls for a medic.'

'Insistent but discreet,' added Allison. 'I'm sure there's no need to tell you what the press would make of this.'

Bannerman sighed and looked down at the well-polished surface of the table.

'We appreciate that you will need a little time to think this over,' said Flowers, 'but you must know that time is of the essence and we would have to ask for your decision by say, ten o'clock tomorrow?'

'You'll have it,' said Bannerman.

'Perhaps I should add that we would provide the hospital with a locum in your absence,' said Flowers.

Bannerman was about to say that he had intended to take some time off anyway but he thought better of it. His morale had been given an unexpected boost by what had been said about his professional reputation. He did not want to diminish the effects with talk of stress and strain.

'Would you like me to call you a taxi, Doctor?' asked the woman at the front desk as Bannerman prepared to leave. He looked out and saw that it had stopped raining. 'I think I'll walk for a bit,' he replied.

The air was damp and fiercely cold after the heat of the offices; for a moment it made his eyes water. He grimaced and pulled up his collar as he made his way down Park Crescent to cross Marylebone Road and continue down into Regent's Park. The grass stretched before him like a wet, green desert below a leaden sky. What the hell was he to do? he wondered.

An investigation of this importance was hardly a job for someone undergoing any kind of personal crisis but on the other hand the whole thing intrigued him deeply. It would be no picnic but at least, if he took up the investigation, he would be away from the pressures of the hospital and there would be no emergency diagnostic work for a while. He might even be able to do some winter climbing in Scotland after all.

Bannerman was suddenly aware of a woman standing in front of him. She was swathed in loose-fitting clothes which disguised her shape and consequently her age; she carried two bundles wrapped in what appeared to be bed covers. A head scarf was supplemented by a further scarf wrapped round the lower portion of her face. She hooked two fingers over the scarf round her mouth and pulled it down slightly. 'Have you anything for a cup of tea?' she mumbled.

Bannerman took out his wallet and gave her a five pound note.

'Bless you, mister,' said the woman clutching it tightly with gloved fingers which left the tips free.

'You too,' said Bannerman quietly. He turned to watch her shuffle off and began to see executive stress and strain in a new light. Until that moment he had planned to discuss the morning's events with Stella before reaching a decision. Now he decided to accede to the MRC's request.

Olive Meldrum handed Bannerman an envelope on Friday evening. It contained, she said, his first-class ticket on the night sleeper to Scotland. Bannerman thanked her, saying that he would see her soon.

'Good luck,' said Olive. 'Bring me back a haggis or whatever they call it.'

'I promise,' smiled Bannerman. He checked his watch and saw that he should be leaving. He wanted to get back to the flat and finish his packing before Stella arrived. They had arranged to have dinner together at a restaurant they both liked and then she would run him to the station in time for the train. He added a few last-minute notes to the file that he had prepared for Nigel

Leeman who would take over in his absence. They had already had a meeting that morning but several things had occurred to him during the course of the afternoon that he thought Leeman should know about. He closed the file with a paper-clip, wrote Leeman's name on it and left it on Olive's desk. With a last look round, he switched off the light and closed the door.

'Why don't you have another brandy,' said Stella. 'You're not driving.'

'You've talked me into it,' smiled Bannerman, summoning the waiter.

'This has all happened so fast I'm not sure what to say,' said Stella. 'Are you absolutely sure you're doing the right thing in taking this MRC thing on?'

'No,' admitted Bannerman, 'but it's important to find out the truth.'

'Send me a postcard?'

'Of course,' smiled Bannerman.

'And if you have time to pursue this crazy notion of heading off into the Scottish mountains in winter these may help.' Stella reached into her bag. 'I know you don't need lectures about the right equipment and all that, but I got you a little present.' She brought out a small package which she handed to Bannerman.

Bannerman opened it and pulled out a pair of gloves. 'Goretex gloves!' he exclaimed. 'I'll be the best dressed climber on the mountain.'

'In January, you'll be the *only* climber on the mountain,' retorted Stella.

'Thank you, that was a kind thought,' said Bannerman.

'I think we'd better go if we've to get you on that train,' said Stella.

They arrived at the station with ten minutes to spare. Bannerman insisted that they say their goodbyes there and then, knowing that neither of them liked hanging around draughty platforms in order to wave at a moving train. He watched Stella's back until she turned round at the exit, then he waved and walked through the barrier to board the train.

Bannerman woke at six. The train was crossing a particularly intricate piece of track, and the change from regular sound patterns to a series of irregular clacks and jolts had disturbed him. He opened the blind and looked out at a misty, grey morning with dampness clinging to the trees and fences bordering the track. Maybe a holiday in the sun wouldn't have been such a bad idea after all, he thought, but then he stamped on the heresy and got back into his bunk. He propped himself up so that he could catch occasional glimpses of the countryside. If the train was on time they must be soon approaching Berwick and the Scottish border.

As he got out on to the platform at Waverley Station in Edinburgh, Bannerman considered his options. The medical school were expecting him any time after nine so he still had some time to kill. He was hungry, but not hungry enough to eat in the station buffet. He walked up the hill, out of the station and up to Princes Street, where he admired the sight of Edinburgh Castle looming out of the morning mist before opting for breakfast at a large hotel. His third cup of coffee took him up to a time when he could hail a taxi and ask to be taken to the university.

'Nice to meet you,' said the white-haired man who stood up and introduced himself as George Stoddart, when Bannerman was shown into his office.

Stoddart was a small man in his sixties with silver hair and a neatly clipped moustache. He was wearing a dark suit with a Bengal striped shirt and a university tie. The shirt seemed a bit too tight around his middle, thought Bannerman, as he took the outstretched hand and said, 'How do you do Professor.' He wondered if the slight coldness he detected in the man's manner was real or imagined. If it was real it was not entirely unexpected, after all, he was an outsider being foisted on the department by the MRC. There had been no opposition from Munro because his people were scientists not medics, but Stoddart's department was different. It *was* medical and it was not inconceivable that he might be seen as an interfering interloper from the south.

'We've arranged an apartment for you in the old town,' said Stoddart. 'Would you like to be taken there right away or would you rather settle in here first?'

'Here I think,' said Bannerman.

'Very well,' said Stoddart. 'I'll have someone show you to your lab and then we can talk. He picked up the phone and requested that 'Dr Napier' come up.

Bannerman was introduced to a woman in her mid-thirties. She was pleasant looking but her appearance was tempered by what he regarded as middle-class notions of respectability. Her clothes, hairstyle, shoes, all deserved the adjective, 'sensible', and when she spoke she did so with just the genteel accent he expected her to have. The soul of discretion and reliability, he thought; there's a woman like her in every university department. He noticed that she was wearing an engagement ring. That didn't quite fit with his appraisal of her as a 'bride of the university'.

'Morag Napier,' said the woman, holding out her hand with a smile.

'Ian Bannerman.'

Bannerman followed Morag Napier along a corridor and down some stairs to where she opened a half-glazed door and ushered him inside. 'I think you'll find everything you need here,' she said. 'If not, I'm only next door. You only have to ask.'

'Thanks,' said Bannerman, looking about him with a heavy heart. The building was old. It was part of the original medical school at the university and consequently high ceilings and tiling were much in evidence. The cold, grey light coming in from a north facing window did nothing to lighten the atmosphere.

A modern microscope stood on a turn-of-the-century lab bench, and a calendar from a laboratory supply company decorated the wall above it. There was a blackboard on one of the other walls with a duster and a cardboard box containing an assortment of coloured, mainly broken, chalk sticks.

There were some dusty pathological specimen jars arranged along a wooden shelf with labels that were peeling and practically indecipherable with age. Bannerman looked closely and saw that one patient's liver had achieved immortality, courtesty of formaldehyde fixative. Diamonds ain't the only things that are forever my son, he thought.

'I hope everything's all right,' said Morag.

'Everything's fine,' replied Bannerman, with his back to her.

'I'll leave you for a bit, then, when you're ready, I'll take you back to Professor Stoddart,' said Morag.

'No need,' said Bannerman, turning to face her. 'I can remember the way.'

'If you're sure?'

'I'm sure.'

There was an old oak desk beside the blackboard. Bannerman sat down at it and opened the drawers to see if they had been emptied. In the main they had, although half an eraser, two pencils and a broken plastic ruler lingered on. He opened his briefcase and transferred some of his own things to them. He saw this as an act of self-psychology – a conscious effort to persuade himself that this was where he was going to be working for the time being. He was considering how oppressive the room was, when a slight knock came at the door. It was Morag Napier.

'I forgot to give you these,' she said. In her hand she held a series of brown cardboard files. 'These are the notes Lawrence and I made on the brain disease patients.'

'Lawrence?' asked Bannerman.

'Sorry. Dr Gill, the man I work with.'

'I hear he's not around at the moment,' said Bannerman, taking the files and resting them on his knee.

'No, we're very worried about him.'

'No word at all?'

'Nothing.'

'Have the police been informed?'

Morag Napier looked uneasy at the question. 'No,' she replied, looking down at her feet. 'The feeling is that Lawrence's disappearance was for domestic reasons.'

'You mean he's run off with someone?' said Bannerman.

'Something like that,' agreed Morag, coldly.

'Can I ask what makes you think that?' asked Bannerman.

'His wife,' said Morag.

'Oh,' said Bannerman, 'well, I hope he kept good notes,' he said, tapping the files.

'I think you'll find everything you need to know there,' said Morag.

'Did you work with him on the MRC survey?'

'Yes, I did.'

'Then you know all about the three men who died?'

'I went up to Achnagelloch with Lawrence when the report came in. I carried out the preliminary lab work.'

'Are the bodies here in Edinburgh, or still up north?'

'They are in the mortuary downstairs,' said Morag. 'Do you want to examine them?'

'Yes,' said Bannerman.

'Today?'

'Tomorrow.'

Bannerman found his way back to the office of George Stoddart, where Stoddart gave him some general information about the brain disease survey in the area that Lawrence Gill had been responsible for. He added the file to the others that Morag Napier had given him.

Stoddart opened up a map and spread it over his desk. He traced a pencil line round an area in the north west of the country and said, 'This is the area Lawrence was concerned with. The main communities are at Achnagelloch and Stobmor.'

Bannerman saw that the line Stoddart had drawn marked out an area to the west of the Invermaddoch power station. He asked, 'What about east of here?' pointing to it with his finger.

'There are no people living to the east of the station within fifty miles,' replied Stoddart. 'It's barren moorland, not even good enough for sheep.'

'I see,' said Bannerman.

'Do you have access to the public health records for the area?' asked Bannerman.

'If you mean, do I know if the region has a higher than normal incidence of child leukaemia and the like, then yes I do. The figures are higher than for non-nuclear areas, but not high enough to cause alarm or be in any way conclusive in a statistical sense.'

'How about the figures for carcinoma?' asked Bannerman.

'Again, the figures for tumours are statistically higher than the norm but the population for the region is so low that it's very difficult to reach firm conclusions. Here they are.' Stoddart handed Bannerman a clear plastic file.

'Was it ever different?' murmured Bannerman.

'Pardon?'

'Trying to make sense out of statistics,' answered Bannerman. 'It's often a case of the singer not the song, don't you think?'

Stoddart's blank look said that he didn't know what Bannerman was talking about. Bannerman said, 'I think I've managed to collect enough in the way of paper to keep me busy for a bit. I wonder if someone could tell me how to get to my accommodation? I'll settle in there and start going through these files.'

'Of course,' said Stoddart. 'I'll have someone drive you.'

'That's not necessary,' protested Bannerman, but Stoddart insisted, saying that they had a pool of drivers 'sitting on their hands'. 'You won't mind if it's a van will you?'

The driver sent up from the pool to drive Bannerman was a short, round-faced man with ruddy cheeks and a lop-sided grin. His peaked cap was pushed to the back of his head, emphasizing a probable easy-going approach to life. 'Let me take that for you,' he said, stretching out to take Bannerman's bag from him and opening the passenger door of a black, 15 cwt van with darkened glass windows at the back. It was no great challenge to guess what the van was usually employed in transporting. The driver confirmed this by saying, 'It's nice to have a live passenger for a change.'

'Do you know Edinburgh at all?' asked the driver, as they drove towards the castle.

Bannerman said not, adding, 'I was a medical student in Glasgow many years ago.'

'I'd keep quiet about that if I was you,' said the man, with a grin.

As they turned into the High Street, the driver, who by now had introduced himself as Willie MacDonald, said, 'You'll be staying in the Royal Mile. That's the main street in the old town of Edinburgh; it connects the Castle at the top with Holyrood Palace at the foot.'

They turned off into a courtyard on the left and Willie said, 'Here we are, Darnley Court.'

Bannerman got out and looked up at a recently restored tenement building, judging by the cleanness of the stonework. There was a paved courtyard at the front with large flower tubs posted around it. In January they were empty, save for wet earth.

'You are on the top floor,' said Willie. He led the way into the building and went up with Bannerman to open the door and then hand him the keys.

'This is wonderful,' said Bannerman, walking over to the window to look at the view and marvel at how high up they were.

'It's a beautiful city Doctor.'

'Breathtaking.'

'You're looking out over Princes Street Gardens, to the new town down there,' said Willie, 'and beyond that, the Firth of Forth with its islands.'

'What's the big one?' asked Bannerman.

'Inchkeith,' replied Willie. He pointed out several other prominent landmarks far below them and joked that he hoped Bannerman had a head for heights.

Bannerman felt that at least one good thing had happened to him today. He thanked MacDonald and tried to tip him, but the driver declined, assuring him that Professor Stoddart would have his guts 'for one of his practical classes' if he accepted.

After a quick look round the apartment, Bannerman unpacked and took advantage of the coffee that someone had thoughtfully supplied along with a few other basic necessities in the kitchen. He pulled a chair over to the window, and settled down in it with his mug to peruse the files he had been given. He had barely begun when the telephone rang and startled him. It was George Stoddart.

'I forgot to say,' said Stoddart, 'that my wife and I would be delighted if you would join us for dinner this evening?'

'That would be very nice,' replied Bannerman, thinking it would be nothing of the kind. He took down details of the address and agreed to be there for eight. There were few things Bannerman liked less than 'academic' dinners but he accepted it as part and parcel of life, a necessary evil. It did however, put paid to his plans to explore the neighbouring hostelries that evening. He got back to reading through the files.

FOUR

After an hour, Bannerman stopped reading and taking notes to make more coffee. He looked out of the window while the kettle boiled and mulled over what he had learned so far. The medical records for the region had failed to provide him with what he was looking for. Although it was true that there had been an increase in leukaemia and cancer in the area round Achnagelloch and Stobmor, it was not a striking one – even when he examined the raw data instead of the statistics, which he didn't trust.

He had been hoping to find something in the figures to indicate that the radiation leak from the power station had been severe enough to affect the health of the local community. This, in turn, would have indicated that the levels of radiation around the immediate area of the power station would have been high enough to account for a mutation occurring in the *Scrapie* virus. A twelve per cent increase in childhood leukaemia sounded a lot, but it was based on a relatively small number of cases. It might have been due to a radiation leak but, on the other hand, it might not. This conclusion merited an expletive from Bannerman.

He sat down with his coffee and turned his attention to the details of the three deaths. It made alarming reading. The dead men had been employed as farm labourers on Iverladdie Farm, to the north of Achnagelloch. Only one of them, Gordon Buchan, had been married; he had lived with his wife in a tied cottage on the farm. The other two had stayed in lodgings in Achnagelloch. An outbreak of *Scrapie* had been reported in the sheep of Inverladdie and all three had been involved in the disposal of the carcasses.

The men had died within a three week period of working on the slaughter, after suffering headaches, vomiting, and finally, dementia. One of the two bachelors had run amok in the streets of Achnagelloch, smashing windows and screaming obscenities before being constrained and taken to the cottage hospital where he died the following day. Witnesses had described him as being 'out of his skull'.

The married man had been nursed by his wife until he had gone into a coma. His eyes had remained open but he had not been able to communicate or respond to anything she said. Just before she called the doctor for the last time, who in turn called the ambulance, the man had appeared to develop some unbearable itch and had scratched himself all over until he bled.

There were no details of how the third man's illness had progressed. He had been found dead in his room by his landlady. She had, however, noticed that his arms had been scratched and bloody and there had been a wax candle in his mouth, as if he had been trying to eat it.

Bannerman knew that there was not much to be gained by studying the behaviour of deranged patients. Once control of the brain had been lost, the patient would be liable to do anything without necessary rhyme or reason. His or her entire behavioural pattern would be indicated by circumstances and events in his or her immediate surroundings. The reports of scratching, however, were alarming and Bannerman saw the significance in them. The sheep disease had been given the name *Scrapie* because of the infected animals' habit of scraping themselves against fences, as if fighting a constant itch. It sounded like the men had displayed the same symptoms.

The pathology reports from Lawrence Gill and Morag Napier reported extensive spongioform encephalopathy in the brains of all three men, just as Bannerman had seen for himself in the microscope slides the MRC had sent him. He could find no loophole in the report as it stood. Many of the lab tests had yet

57

to be completed but all the circumstantial evidence pointed to the dead men having been infected with *Scrapie* while handling contaminated carcasses on Inverladdie farm.

Gill had included some notes on *Scrapie* research. It had been established that the disease could be transmitted from one animal to another through scarified tissue. Bannerman supposed that this must be how the dead men had been infected. The agent had got into their bodies through cuts and grazes on their hands while they worked on the disposal of the slaughtered sheep. The supposedly mutant *Scrapie* virus had breached a normally impassible barrier and attacked their brain cells.

Bannerman had a nightmarish thought. Perhaps there was no species barrier at all. Maybe the virus could cross to man quite readily under normal circumstances but the incubation time was so long that the disease did not appear until old age. Under these circumstances it might be called senile dementia. The Achnagelloch mutation might be one which speeded up the disease rather than allowing it to cross any barrier. It was a complication he would have to bear in mind.

Although Gill had referred to the possibility of 'mutant' *Scrapie* in the notes he had not offered any thoughts on what might have caused the mutation. No mention was made of radiation or the proximity of a nuclear power station. If it hadn't been radiation, what else could it have been? Bannerman wondered. Chemical or spontaneous mutation were the other two possibilities. Viruses were notorious for changing their structure. The AIDS virus did it all the time. The 'flu' virus did it too. UV radiation? UV light was a powerful mutagen. It was not inconceivable that changes in the ozone layer might allow UV levels to reach mutagenic levels. Chemical mutagenisis? Modern society produced a host of chemicals capable of altering DNA and inducing mutations. The possibilities seemed endless.

There were several practical questions that Bannerman wanted to ask. How soon after the diagnosis of *Scrapie* in the sheep of Inverladdie had the infected animals been slaughtered, and by what means? Had the corpses been buried quickly? Dead sheep lying around the hillside would be prey to vermin and carrion who would spread the virus.

Gill's notes indicated that the local vet, Finlay, had been called in quickly by the farmer. According to Finlay's report, the infected sheep had been slaughtered without delay and the corpses had been buried immediately in lime pits on the farm. Everything seemed satisfactory. Compensation had been paid to the farmer at Inverladdie and the veterinary inspectorate were keeping an eye on other farms in the area for further signs of *Scrapie*.

Bannerman found a problem with the research notes, however, when he tried to find out what experimental measures had been taken to investigate the pathology of the men's deaths. He checked through all the papers again but found nothing. He felt sure that brain samples would have been sent to the Neurobiology Unit for testing in mice. He would check. He got out his diary where he had made a note of Hector Munro's number, and called it. He remembered that Munro had said at the meeting in London that his people would be happy to give any help they could.

'Munro.'

'Dr Munro? This is Ian Bannerman. We met at the MRC in London.'

'Of course, you decided to take the assignment then?'

'This is my first day,' said Bannerman. 'I've been going through the case notes and I find I need some information.'

'Fire away.'

'I presume Gill asked your people to test the brains of the dead men for confirmation of *slow* virus infection and to measure incubation times in mice. Do you have any results yet?'

'I'm afraid you presume wrongly,' replied Munro. 'Gill did not send us anything from the autopsies.'

'But your people are the acknowledged experts on this sort of thing!' said Bannerman. 'The short incubation time is one of the most striking and worrying features about this whole business!'

'I wouldn't disagree with that,' said Munro, 'but nothing has come to us. I supposed that Stoddart's people were carrying out their own investigation.'

Bannerman let out a sigh of frustration. 'Departmental politics,' he complained. 'I'll check on that. In the meantime would you mind if I sent you some brain biopsies for mice inoculation. I understand the men's bodies are in the medical school here in Edinburgh. I'll take the samples myself.'

'We'd be delighted to help in any way,' said Munro. 'The sooner we got this sorted out the better.'

'Thanks. I'll get them to you as quickly as I can.'

Bannerman put down the phone and cursed under his breath. What the hell was Gill playing at? He must have seen the awful implications in the men's deaths, and yet he had failed to send samples to Munro's Unit, and he had picked this very moment to bugger off with some dolly-bird. 'Clown!' he murmured. He called Stoddart to be told by his secretary that he had left for the day. He looked at his watch and muttered, 'Short day George.' He remembered that he would be seeing him later for dinner. He could ask about it then.

The Stoddarts lived in a spacious Georgian Flat in Edinburgh's new town, the elegant area to the north of the castle and Princes Street, favoured by the professional classes. The room was freezing. Bannerman had to exercise great restraint in not rubbing his arms to keep the circulation going. A 'small problem' with the heating, as George Stoddart called it, had been compensated for by placing a single-bar electric fire at the head of the dining-room. In a room which was thirty feet long and something like fourteen feet high, this did not make a lot of difference.

The room was also oppressively quiet. Bannerman was the only guest, since Morag Napier and her fiancé had had to call off at the last moment. Every clink of the cutlery seemed to resound in the long silences that punctuated the meal between infrequent, staccato bursts of polite conversation.

Bannerman gathered, when introduced to Stoddart's wife, that she did not have a medical background. He therefore thought it improper to pursue the subject of brain pathology while eating the haggis which the Stoddarts had thought appropriate to welcome him to Scotland. He had managed to glean, however, that she was a leading light of the university wives' 'Friends of Rumania' circle, and did his best to make conversation about that.

Stoddart seemed totally uninterested in anything his wife had to say and would interrupt, at will, with completely unrelated observations. 'Of course I'm a pituitary man myself,' he suddenly announced in the middle of a discussion about orphanage conditions.

'Really?' said Bannerman, embarrassed on behalf of Stoddart's wife, who looked down at the tablecloth and appeared to be holding her tongue in check.

'I suppose you're familiar with my work?' asked Stoddart.

'Of course,' lied Bannerman, thinking it must have been twenty years since Stoddart had last published anything.

Stoddart saw this as his cue to launch into an after-dinner lecture on his life's work.

Bannerman sought solace in the brandy while nodding at appropriate intervals and sneaking surreptitious glances at his watch. When, eventually, Mrs Stoddart asked to be excused so that she could begin clearing the table, Bannerman took the opportunity to interrupt Stoddart and find out what he wanted to know.

'Professor, I must ask you, what animal tests were set up on the brains of the three men from Achnagelloch?'

Stoddart adopted a serious expression. He thought for a moment, and then said, 'I think you would have to ask Lawrence Gill that.'

'But I can't can I?' said Bannerman.

'I suppose not,' agreed Stoddart. 'Then I suppose Dr Napier would be your best bet.'

'You haven't been taking an interest in this investigation yourself then?' asked Bannerman.

'I'm the collator for the MRC survey figures, of course,' said Stoddart, with comfortable self-importance.

'I see,' said Bannerman, who was seething inside. Jesus

Christ, he thought. He's confronted with something like this and he's collating the figures. If ever there was a candidate for early retirement, he was currently listening to him drone on about the pituitary gland.

The following morning was Saturday, but Bannerman was in the medical school just after eight-thirty. He wasn't sure if Morag Napier would be around but he thought he might be able to get her home phone number from someone. Apart from that, he wanted to carry out an examination of the bodies of the three dead men and to get brain biopsies to send to Munro at the Neurobiology Unit. He found his way to the mortuary and collared the duty attendant. He told him what he wanted.

'I don't know about that,' said the man, shaking his head.

'What do you mean, you don't know about that?' asked Bannerman, irritated but trying to keep his temper.

'I've no note of this,' said the man. 'It's not on my list.'

'Then put it on your list!' exclaimed Bannerman.

The man shook his head with a pitying smile and said, 'It's not as easy as that I'm afraid. There are procedures to be followed.'

Oh Christ, thought Bannerman. A traffic warden in charge of the mortuary is all I need. 'Do you have a phone?' he snapped.

'Not an outside call, I trust,' replied the man.

Bannerman brushed past him and called Stoddart, not caring if he was still in bed. As soon as Stoddart answered, he said curtly, 'This is Bannerman. I'm at the mortuary and I want to examine the cadavers of the men Gill brought down from the north. Will you please tell your man that this is in order.' Without waiting for a reply, he handed the receiver to the attendant and stared down at the desk, taking deep breaths as Stella had advised him to do when losing his temper. He heard the man say, 'Yes sir, certainly sir, right away Professor,' and then put the phone down. 'I was just following the rules, sir,' he said to Bannerman.

So were the guards at Auschwitz, thought Bannerman.

'Any particular order sir?' asked the attendant.

'Doesn't matter,' replied Bannerman, taking off his shoes and putting on Wellingtons. He gowned-up while the attendant brought the first body through the narrow, tiled corridor leading from the vault and slid it on to the table. The light above the table stuttered into being and produced a background hum as Bannerman, fastening the last of the ties on his gown, walked up to the table and peeled back the shroud.

Even if no one had told him beforehand, he could have guessed that the dead man had had an outdoor occupation and that it involved physical effort. Despite the pallor of death there were still signs of a ruddy complexion, and the muscular development of his legs was marked. A jagged, dark line round his skull indicated where the skull cap had been removed when Gill had carried out the previous post-mortem.

'I'll need some specimen containers,' Bannerman said to the attendant, who was keeping his distance.

'What type?'

'Glass, one ounce, Universal.'

The attendant brought four containers to the head of the table while Bannerman removed the top of the skull. He picked up a scalpel and forceps from the instrument tray that had been opened for him and looked inside the skull cavity. He felt stupid. There was nothing there!

Feeling as if he had been given a bad line to say in an amateur production, Bannerman said to the attendant, 'Where is the corpse's brain?'

'If it's not in his head, I don't know, sir,' replied the attendant, with an apparently straight face.

'I take it you were not in attendance when Dr Gill carried out the first autopsy?'

'No sir. I'm just weekends.'

'Are copies of the reports kept down here?'

'No, sir.'

Bannerman hadn't really imagined that they would be. It was a forlorn hope. He was beginning to feel as though he was running in soft sand. 'Put him back. I'll check the other two.'

the story was the same with the other two cadavers. The

brains had been removed and, by the look of them, the cranial cavities had been cleaned out afterwards.

Bannerman washed and went upstairs to see if he could find someone to give him Morag Napier's telephone number. If he couldn't, then it would mean another call to Stoddart. In the event he saw a light on in one of the labs and knocked on the door. He was invited to enter by a foreign sounding voice. He learned that Dr Klaus Lehman was on an exchange visit from the Max Plank Institute in Germany to work on a research project on allergies. Bannerman said he hoped that he would be able to talk to him about his project at some later date, but in the meantime, did he know if there was a staff telephone list? Lehman said that there was and that he had a copy.

The phone rang eight times before Morag Napier answered. 'You caught me in the bath,' she complained.

'I'm sorry, but it's important. I couldn't find any details about the animal tests that you and Dr Gill must have set up on the brains of the three men from Achnagelloch. You must have left the notes out of the file.'

There was a pause before Morag Napier said, 'I gave you everything there was in Lawrence's desk. I wasn't involved with the animal tests.'

'But surely you must know what animal tests he set up?' said Bannerman.

'I'm afraid not.'

Bannerman tapped the heel of his right hand against his forehead in suppressed frustration. 'All right,' he said. 'Where is the animal lab, and will there be someone there today?'

Morag told him where the lab was and added, 'One of the technicians will be in around noon.'

'Good,' said Bannerman. 'Now can you tell me where the brains of the dead men are?'

'I don't understand,' said Morag. 'The bodies are in the mortuary.'

'But their brains aren't,' said Bannerman.

'Lawrence must have removed them.'

'Where would he keep them?'

'There's a fridge-freezer in Lawrence's lab. He sometimes stores specimens in that until they are no longer current.'

'Can I get into it?'

'It will be locked, and so will the lab.'

Bannerman's silence prompted Morag Napier into saying, 'I'd better come in. I know where the keys are. Give me twenty minutes.'

Bannerman went back to his own lab to wait. He tried to read the Sunday paper he had bought on the way in but found he couldn't concentrate. He had flicked through all the pages without really having read anything.

Morag Napier arrived wearing a navy-blue track suit with a university logo on it. Her trainer shoes were pristine white and she had tied her hair back in a bun. Bannerman noticed that she smelt of shampoo. She was carrying a bunch of keys in her hand. 'Lawrence's lab is open,' she said.

Bannerman thanked her for coming in and followed her into Lawrence Gill's lab.

Morag unlocked the large fridge-freezer and stood back for a moment to allow the frosty mist to clear. Bannerman saw that the fridge was well packed with a variety of plastic bags and boxes all containing bits and pieces of the human body. He made a superficial inspection for tell-tale grey material but there was no obvious sign of brains being stored there.

'There's an index,' said Morag. She slid out a hard backed notebook from the space between the freezer and the wall and turned the pages until she reached the list of current contents. 'That's funny,' she said. 'They don't seem to be here.'

Bannerman rolled his eyes. 'I'll have to talk to Gill,' he said. 'Does anyone know where he is?'

'I'm afraid not,' replied Morag.

'What conclusions did you and Gill come to about the deaths?' asked Bannerman.

'That the men had died from a degenerative brain disease and Lawrence thought that there might be some connection with *Scrapie*.'

'The pathological evidence points to the men having died of *Scrapie!*' said Bannerman.

65

'Or Creutzfeld Jakob Disease,' said Morag.

'But the incubation time was too short for that,' said Bannerman.

'Yes.'

'So they must have died of something that looks like Creutzfeld Jakob,' said Bannerman. 'That's what made Gill think of *Scrapie*. It's possible that the agent which killed the men is a mutant form of the sheep disease. That's why the animal tests are of vital importance. If it transpires that *Scrapie* can cross the species barrier into man, for whatever reason, then we may have a major crisis on our hands.'

'You mean if it can do it once, it can do it again?'

'Yes. We have to find out how and why it did that,' said Bannerman. 'The animal tests will tell us.'

'But surely the danger is over,' said Morag. 'The agent would be wiped out when the infected sheep were slaughtered?' said Morag.

'I hope you are right, and that all this was just a chance in a million, but we have to know for sure. We have to know why this happened in the first place. We know very little about the spread of *Scrapie* in the sheep population. It may be that the new virus, if that's what it turns out to be, has already been spread all over the country through bird and animal food chains.'

'What a thought,' murmured Morag.

'Unless Gill set up animal tests, the only source of infected material is the brains of the three men who died, and they are missing. We've got to find them so that the people at the Neurobiology Unit can run tests on them. That's why I must talk to Gill.'

Bannerman saw from the clock on the wall that it was coming up to twelve o'clock. 'How do I get to the animal lab?' he asked.

Morag said, 'I'll take you there.'

Bannerman followed her through a maze of basement corridors until he knew that they were getting near the animal lab from the unmistakable smell of mice. She knocked on a glass-fronted door that was reinforced by wire.

'Who is it?' came a voice from inside.

'Morag Napier.'

The door was unlocked, and Morag and Bannerman walked through into the animal house. The room was a whitewashed, basement room, lit by fluorescent strip lighting. One entire wall was decked with metal shelves upon which stood row after row of mouse boxes, each equipped with an automatic water feeder bottle. Another section of the lab housed rats, guinea pigs and rabbits. There was a preparation table in the middle of the floor and a row of sinks stood beyond. There were two small rooms leading off the main room. Bannerman could seen an animal post-mortem board in one of them with a tray of instruments laying beside it.

The girl who answered the door continued with her feeding schedule, dropping a handful of mouse 'nuts' into each box and checking to see if the inhabitants were still alive.

'We need some information,' said Morag.

'Uh huh,' replied the girl.

'We need to know if Dr Gill asked for any mice tests to be set up when he returned from the north.'

'It will be in the book,' said the girl. 'The red one in the office.'

Morag and Bannerman took this as an invitation to look for themselves. They started scanning back through the pages of the animal records.

'Here we are,' said Morag, underlining an entry with her finger. Bannerman looked over her shoulder.

The entry read, 'Six mice, Dr Lawrence Gill, three samples, two mice per sample. Ref. W 17–22. Cross Ref. MRC 3'.

'MRC 3,' repeated Bannerman. 'These must be the ones.'

'How do we find W 17–22?' Morag asked the technician.

The girl stopped feeding her charges and moved along the row to tap one of the boxes with her palm. 'From here to the left,' she said.

Morag took down the box the girl had touched and looked inside. 'Alive and well,' she said, handing the box to Bannerman and bringing down the next one. 'Same.'

All six mice were alive and apparently healthy.

'Well, it's a relief to know the tests were set up,' said

Bannerman. At least Gill had done something right. He put on protective gloves and picked up one of the mice from its box to let it run over the back of his hand. It seemed perfectly healthy in every way. The mouse tried to get a grip of his gloved thumb with its teeth and Bannerman massaged the black spot in its otherwise white fur until it let go. He dropped the animal gently back into its box and closed the lid. 'I suppose it's a bit soon for any brain disease to have developed, even if it is a new strain. We'll have to keep an eye on these chaps. They may hold the answer to this whole business.'

Morag nodded and said, 'I'll see to it.'

'But I still have to talk to Gill,' said Bannerman. 'Does his wife live in Edinburgh?'

Morag Napier looked at him in surprise. 'Yes but surely you're not going to . . .'

'I need to see her,' said Bannerman. 'If she knows that her husband has run off with someone, she probably knows who with and possibly where to.'

'But she'll be upset!' protested Morag. 'How can you be so heartless?'

'If three young men have died of *Scrapie* we have a great deal more to worry about than the sensibilities of Lawrence Gill and his wife,' said Bannerman.

'I suppose so,' agreed Morag reluctantly. 'I'll get you the address.'

Bannerman invited Morag Napier to have lunch with him, but she declined, saying that she had 'things to do'. It wasn't too big a disappointment; the offer had been made out of politeness. He suspected that Morag did not hold a single opinion that hadn't been vetted by her subconscious for 'suitability'. Instead, he had lunch at a pub in the High Street and watched the world go by for an hour or so before phoning Lawrence Gill's wife.

'Vera Gill.'

'Mrs Gill, my name's Bannerman. I'm a pathologist working for the MRC.'

'What can I do for you, Mr Bannerman?' said a polite voice.

'I'd like to talk to you about your husband.'

'What about him?' The voice had gone cold.

'I'm sorry. I know it seems insensitive in the circumstances, but please, it's very important.'

'I can't think what that could possibly be,' said Vera Gill.

'I'd rather not talk over the telephone. Could we meet?'

Vera Gill hesitated, and Bannerman repeated how important it was.

'Very well. Come round this afternoon.'

Bannerman scribbled down the address and they agreed on a meeting at three-thirty.

Vera Gill lived with her children, two girls, in a pleasant semi-detached house in the Colinton area of the city. The girls, who were wrapped up warmly against a cold east wind, were playing in the garden when Bannerman arrived. As he opened the gate and started to walk up the path the youngest girl asked, 'Have you brought my daddy home?'

Bannerman was struggling for a reply when the older child said, 'She doesn't fully understand yet.'

Bannerman smiled apologetically. The older child could not have been more than ten.

Vera Gill appeared at the door and invited Bannerman inside. As she ushered him past her she said to the older child, 'Keep Wendy amused will you, darling. Mummy has to talk to this man for a little while.'

'She is quite a young lady,' said Bannerman as the door was closed.

'She's very mature for her age,' agreed Vera Gill. 'I don't know what I would have done without her support over the last week or so. Now, what did you want to know?'

'Mrs Gill, it's very important that I find your husband. I need some vital information from him.'

Vera Gill's face clouded over. She said, 'I have heard nothing from my husband since he left here on the 16th of January. Not a word.'

'So you don't know where he is?'

'No.'

Bannerman maintained a silence for a few moments, hoping

69

that it might oblige Vera Gill to reconsider a little. She didn't, so he pressed her a little further. 'Mrs Gill, if your husband has just gone missing surely you would have reported the matter to the police?'

'All right,' snapped Vera Gill. 'He's gone off with another woman. Is that what you wanted? But I don't know where they are.'

'Do you know this other woman?' asked Bannerman, aware of the pain in Vera Gill's eyes but also knowing that she was his only hope of finding Gill.

'No,' replied Vera Gill, but Bannerman could see that she was lying. It wasn't difficult. She wasn't used to doing it. She diverted her eyes and looked guilty, just like a child.

'Mrs Gill . . . I know how much this must have hurt you . . .'

'Oh no you don't!' snapped Vera Gill with a venom that surprised Bannerman. 'You couldn't possibly know anything of the sort!'

It was Bannerman's turn to divert his eyes. 'I'm sorry,' he said quietly. 'Of course I don't.'

Vera Gill took a number of deep breaths in the ensuing silence, which was only broached by a ticking clock on the mantleshelf and the muted sound of the children playing in the garden. 'Her name is Shona MacLean,' she said quietly.

Bannerman wrote it down.

'Some years ago she and Lawrence had an affair, when we lived in the north. He said it was all over but there were occasional letters that arrived with a give-away postmark.'

'Did your husband tell you he was going off with this woman?' asked Bannerman.

'No, but that was Lawerence,' said Vera Gill, with a snort.

Bannerman felt confused. He asked. 'What exactly did he say before he left?'

'Almost nothing. I could see he was in a blue funk over the whole thing but, as I say, that was Lawrence. He hated making unpleasant decisions. He got more and more agitated and angst-ridden and then suddenly he announced that he had to go away for a bit, and that was the last I saw of him.'

'Where does this Shona MacLean live?' asked Bannerman. 'The village of Ralsay on the Island of North Uist.'

On the way back to his apartment Bannerman stopped at a large newsagents and bought some road maps of north-west Scotland and the Western Isles. Without access to the brain tissue of the dead men there was very little in the way of pathological investigation to be done at the medical school. The brains of the infected laboratory mice would provide more diseased material for him to work on, but even if his worst fears surrounding incubation times were realised, that would not be for another couple of weeks. He was beginning to think in terms of a visit to the north to see the Achnagelloch area for himself. If this could be combined with a trip to North Uist to find Lawrence Gill, then so much the better.

FIVE

Bannerman's original plan had been to eat out at one of the restaurants in the Royal Mile that evening, but the visit to Vera Gill had left him with little heart for playing the tourist. Instead he decided to make do with what was in the apartment. There were a couple of packet meals. One of them had a nice picture on the front. If he felt better later he might go out for a drink. Instead, he phoned Stella just after eight.

'How's it going?' she asked.

'Not well,' confessed Bannerman. 'The pathologist who raised the alarm has disappeared and so have the brains of the victims.'

'What?' exclaimed Stella.

'I know it sounds crazy, but their brains were completely removed at autopsy and nobody knows where they are except the missing pathologist, and he's run off somewhere.'

'Sounds like a Whitehall farce,' said Stella.

'If it wasn't so serious,' added Bannerman.

'What's the head of department doing about it?' asked Stella.

'Collating the figures,' said Bannerman drily.

'Pardon?'

'Nothing. He's about as much use as a keep left sign in a one way street.'

'Distinguished, eh?'

'Distinguished,' agreed Bannerman, sharing an old joke between the pair of them that ageing incompetents in the world of academia were never called so; they were invariably termed 'distinguished'.

'So what are you going to do?' asked Stella.

'I've read Gill's lab notes and looked at the microscope slides, as you know; it looks serious, but I have to talk to Gill. I'm thinking of trying to find him myself.'

'Surely that's a job for the police,' protested Stella, 'Besides, where would you start?'

'I've been pointed in the right direction,' said Bannerman. 'Gill ran off for domestic reasons.'

'And with immaculate timing,' added Stella.

'Quite so,' agreed Bannerman. 'I think I might find it hard to be civil to him when I find him.'

'Where's the "right direction"?'

'His wife thinks he's on the Island of North Uist.'

'This could turn out to be a holiday after all,' said Stella.

'I have to go north to see the location of the sheep farm and talk to the local GP and vet. I also want to take a look at the power station, find out where it fits into the scheme of things. My plan at the moment is to take in the island on the way up.'

'A proper little Doctor Johnson,' said Stella.

'I'm beginning to wish I'd never got into this,' said Bannerman.

There was no point in delaying his departure for the north, thought Bannerman, but on the other hand, trying to reach the Western Isles on a Sunday was probably not such a good idea. He probably wouldn't be stoned to death as a heathen intruder, but transport might be a problem. He toyed with the notion of travelling to Inverness by train on Sunday night and getting a connection to the Kyle of Lochalsh on Monday morning, but then he had a better idea. If he were to rent a car he could start his journey on Sunday morning and stop off somewhere on the way to do a bit of hill walking. He could do with some fresh air to rid himself of the claustrophobic feel of the medical school and its brooding walls. He could stay overnight at a small hotel and then head for North Uist on Monday morning.

The idea filled him with enthusiasm; he consulted the local telephone directory for details of weather forecasting services for the areas he would pass through on his way north. Ten minutes later he had decided on tackling the Tarmachan Ridge, north of Loch Tay. He had been assured by the weather people that the region north of Loch Tay was to be cold and clear with blue skies and sunshine. Fine settled weather.

Bannerman called Hertz and, using his credit card, arranged for a Ford Sierra to be made available to him until further notice. He tried calling Morag Napier to let her know his plans but there was no answer. He would call her in the morning before he left.

Bannerman approached Loch Tay from the east and stopped in Lawers village to book himself into the Ben Lawers Hotel for the night. The weather was as good as had been promised, and he enjoyed coaxing the Ford along the narrow road that faithfully traced the north shore of Loch Tay until he swung north to park at the entrance to the old quarry road that crosses the estates of Tarmachan and Morenish. He reflected that it had been fifteen years since he had last come here. As far as he could see, nothing had changed.

The sun was warm on his face as he sat on the edge of the car boot to change his socks and pull on his boots. It was the kind of day that made you want to just put on a sweater and sprint off up into the mountains, but he knew better. In the Scottish hills you had to prepare for the worst. The weather here was among the most fickle in the world, a fact that had been the downfall of so many who had succumbed to the beauty of the mountains from the car park and ventured too far without thinking what would happen if the temperature fell like a stone and the wind screamed down from the north like a demented demon.

Bannerman checked his rucksack for everything he might need and some things he hoped he wouldn't. Bandages, pain killers, torch, survival bag, spare clothing. He set off along the quarry track until the approach to the south ridge of Meall nan Tarmachan became less steep, then he climbed up strongly through the bracken to join it. He then headed north up the ridge, pausing occasionally to catch his breath and look back along the length of Loch Tay sparkling below in the sunshine. Ten years ago he might have climbed directly up on to the ridge at the north-east corner but now he was content to take a more leisurely line.

As he neared the end of the ridge where the ground fell away sharply, before the final steep ascent to the summit of Tarmachan, he paused again and took off his rucksack to sit down and chew a chocolate bar. Far below he could see that another car had parked behind his own, but there was no sign of its driver on the hill. The sun slid behind some clouds that had crept down from the north and Bannerman realized that he was getting cold. He had only been sitting still for a few minutes but the height he had gained in the last hour, and the fact that there was now a north easterly wind to contend with, told him that the temperature was now below freezing.

He got to his feet and put on a Berghaus Goretex shell jacket and a pair of woollen mitts before removing his ice axe from its holster and swinging his pack on to his back and tightening the straps. He would soon be above the snow line and the axe would give him a feeling of security on the slippery slopes. It may not have been a technique for the purists, but sinking the axe into the ground and holding on to it at awkward moments was a psychological comfort and provided at least one hand-hold he could rely on.

The clouds above him were now thickening and their speed was increasing. This gave him a clue as to what to expect when he came out of the lee of the south face and crested the main ridge. As he did so, he had to drop to his knees to maintain balance when the full force of the wind hit him. Pride would not let him move on without first touching the summit cairn, but caution and common sense made him approach the final rise on his hands and knees. He touched the stones and looked briefly over the edge down to Loch Tay, now three thousand feet below. He had a brief impression of movement in the bracken below the crags to his left but concluded that it must have been a trick of the light which kept changing as successsive banks of cloud crossed the sun with varying degrees of thickness.

Bannerman had a decision to make. The wind was much stronger than either he or the weather forecasters had antici-pated, and he knew that the section of the ridge to the west of

Meall Garbh, the next mountain on the ridge, was very narrow and exposed. Should he go on, or turn back and descend in the lee of Tarmachan. After some consideration he put off making the final decision until he had reached the second summit.

As he descended into the small hollow between the summits of Tarmachan and Garbh, to where the ground was interrupted by a series of small lochans and where he could be out of the wind for a few minutes, he made a plan. He would linger for a while in the shelter of the hollow and have something to eat and drink. This would give him time to get his breath back and also give the wind a chance to subside. It was always possible that it would fade away as suddenly as it had arisen.

Bannerman checked his watch and saw that forty minutes had passed. He decided that he should not delay any longer. In January the days were uncomfortably short. He looked at the sky to the north for signs of encouragement but found none. If anything the sky was darkening over Glen Lyon and there was a threatening purple tinge to it. Feeling instead that he had to expect the worst, he got out his waterproof over-trousers from the side pocket of his rucksack and undid the zips so that he could put them on over his boots. With legs and body well protected from the elements he pulled up his hood and secured the draw strings. He put his mitts on and started out on the short climb to the summit of Meall Garbh.

The wind, although still strong, was relatively constant in velocity and not gusting, which would have made it much more dangerous. This was a factor which decided him to go on across the ridge. He looked out from behind the cairn at the narrow stretch ahead. Although it was only fifty metres long at most there were steep drops on both sides and he could see the small town of Killin far below at the west end of the loch. The fact that the wind was coming from the north, making a fall on that side of the ridge unlikely, was reassuring. The north side was steeper than the south; a fall from there would almost certainly be fatal.

Bannerman turned away from the wind to make a final adjustment to his rucksack straps and hood fastenings before venturing out from the shelter of the cairn. He was surprised to see a figure coming up behind him. The tall figure of a man clad in dark waterproof clothing was about seventy metres below him and approaching the summit on the same path he had used himself. The fact that he was not alone on the hill gave Bannerman's confidence a boost. Although he liked solitude in the mountains, it was sometimes nice to know that there were other people around.

With a final tug at his straps to ensure tightness he came out from behind the cairn and moved out on to the narrow ridge. He moved gingerly at first, in order to gauge the strength of the wind, and then he moved steadily along the ridge until he reached the one obstacle in his way – a rocky little step which he would have to negotiate before being able to proceed. As he reached it, the heavens above him opened up and icy rain was driven into the right side of his face. He put his hands down on the rock to steady himself, and wedged his right boot into a small crevice to seek stability as he prepared to swing his left leg over the obstruction.

The crevice was not as secure as he had imagined. The rain had made it slippery, and as he put all his weight on to his right foot his boot slipped out of the crack and he fell heavily, his body straddling the ridge and the sharp edge of the rock catching him in the stomach. Fear and pain mounted a synchronous assault on him as he frantically sought to secure hand holds on the rock, which was streaming with water. He quelled the sudden rush of panic in his head and steeled himself to do nothing until he could get his breath back and think more clearly.

He was quite safe, he reasoned. He had fallen across the ridge, not off it. He had simply been winded hadn't he? He inhaled slowly and cautiously to see if there was any associated pain that might indicate damaged ribs, but there was none; he was all right. He turned his head to the left to avoid a sharp piece of rock that had been cutting into his cheek and saw that the climber who had been coming up behind him was now at the start of the narrow section and was edging his way out towards him. Bannerman signalled with his hand that he was all right, in case the man thought he was in trouble, but the man kept coming anyway.

Bannerman pulled himself up into a kneeling position but kept his hands on the ground for stability until he felt well enough to continue. The other climber stopped a few metres from him and Bannerman yelled against the wind that he was OK. The other climber looked at him over his ski mask but as Bannerman got up into a crouching position he suddenly realized that the man was intent on passing him. There was clearly not enough room to allow this to happen.

'For Christ's sake!' yelled Bannerman, but the other man just kept coming. Bannerman, still a bit unsteady, braced himself and prepared as best he could. 'There's no room!' he almost screamed, but the other man kept coming along the ridge as if there was nothing in his way. He barged into Bannerman, pushed him aside. Bannerman felt himself lose balance.

There was an awful moment when Bannerman felt himself topple over backwards in slow motion, losing all contact with the mountain. His hands reached up as if to grasp the clouds and a scream started to leave his lips, but it was short-lived as his head came down into contact with a rocky outcrop and he was knocked unconscious.

When he eventually opened his eyes, Bannerman was groggily surprised to find that he was still alive. He knew he was alive because he was in pain. His head felt as though it had played host to a nuclear explosion and his right arm was being pulled out of its socket. He was soaking wet and bitterly cold and his face was being grazed against sharp rock. His legs felt free, however. He looked down slowly and saw in one nightmarish moment that there was nothing below him! He was hanging over an abyss.

Bannerman closed his eyes, trying to shut out the nightmare, but he knew it was real. He turned his face slowly upwards to confim what he now suspected and saw that his ice axe, attached by a loop round his wrist had caught in a crevice between two small rocks and prevented him from falling completely off the ridge. He was suspended over a fall of three thousand feet by a quirk of fate and a thin strap round his right wrist.

Bannerman could not see how secure the axe was but he had no choice; he had to move. He tried to turn his right hand to grip the handle of the axe but there was no feeling in it. He would have to try turning on his rocky fulcrum to attain some kind of hold with his other hand. Summoning up every precious ounce of energy he had left, he took a deep breath and turned over. He heard the metal axe move against rock above him and he froze, but it held firm. He was now able to grip it with his other hand. He pulled himself painfully up on to the outcrop and knelt there to take the strain off his arms. A sudden rush of fear made him vomit as he thought how close he had come to death.

He was still not out of danger. His life-saving outcrop was some thirty metres below the ridge and to get off the mountain he had to get back up on to it. He was faced with a climb he would not have relished on a sunny afternoon, let alone in a state of exhaustion in a rain storm. He rubbed at his right arm until the circulation was restored and flexed his fingers until he felt they could be trusted. He had to fight off an inner surge of panic that made him want to rush at the climb and get it over and done with. That was not the way, he reasoned. If he was to make it he would have to consider every single move and do everything slowly.

It took twenty minutes to get back up on to the ridge, but he did so without further incident. He made his way back to Meall Tarmachan and came down off the mountain with pained slowness. He felt ill but he knew that the light was fading fast. There was no question of resting.

Fear was replaced by anger when he thought about the man who had jostled him off the ridge. He thought it beyond belief that anyone could have been so stupid and thoughtless. Perhaps in time he might become charitable enough to believe that the man had been overcome by panic at being caught on the ridge in such atrocious weather and had barged through without considering the consequences. But for the moment Bannerman was furious. The clown should have realized that there hadn't been enough room to get past.

When he reached the car, he tumbled his gear into the back in an ungainly heap. He got into the driving seat and closed the door, rejoicing that at last he was safe from the great outdoors. Right now the great indoors was all he ever wanted. He started the engine and made his way slowly along the shore road to the Ben Lawers Hotel. He hadn't had the energy to change out of his boots and had to concentrate hard on the pedals. He made it to the car-park at the hotel and almost fell out of the car with exhaustion.

'What on earth?' exclaimed the owner, when she saw the state he was in.

'I had a bit of an accident on the hill,' said Bannerman weakly.

The woman called her son Euan to help Bannerman into the bar where there was a roaring fire. She herself went to run him a hot bath. Euan handed Bannerman a glass of whisky and smiled at his reaction to the burning sensation as the spirit trickled down his throat. Bannerman handed him the glass and nodded at the suggestion of another.

When he finally eased himself out of the bath water to towel himself down – somewhat less than vigorously, Bannerman felt the back of his head where it had struck the rock. There was a lump but nothing serious, he reckoned. Amazingly that seemed to be his only injury apart from a sore right arm and a weal on his right wrist where he had been suspended from the loop on the ice axe. He rubbed it gently, knowing that a few hours ago it had been his only link with the land of the living. He shuddered and put on dry clothes.

'I really think we should call the doctor from Killin,' said Vera, the owner, but Bannerman insisted that it was unnecessary, thanking her for her kindness. 'All the treatment I need is in there,' he smiled, nodding at the bar.

'Well, if you're sure . . .'

'I'm sure,' said Bannerman.

Bannerman had another whisky, then ate the biggest mixed grill he had ever seen. There were only two other guests staying at the hotel, an English couple from Carlisle who planned on climbing Ben Lawers on the following day.

'I hear you had a rough day,' said the man.

'I had a fall,' said Bannerman, his mind rebelling at how innocuous the words sounded. All that fear, all that terror, all that living nightmare, dismissed as 'a fall'.

'Happens to the best of us,' said the man.

Bannerman smiled weakly and nodded. He didn't want to continue the conversation. He left the dining-room and returned to the bar to sit down by the fire. Filled with warmth and well-being, he felt himself quickly become sleepy. After one more drink he thanked the owner and her son for their kindness and went up to bed. As he pulled the covers up round his ears he was aware that rain was battering off the window. He remembered the weather forecast for the day . . . fine settled weather. 'Incompetent bastards,' he murmured before drifting off into a deep sleep.

'A deep depression centred off Iceland has moved south to bring rain and . . .' Bannerman clicked off the car radio. He didn't need anyone to tell him that it was raining cats and dogs as he headed for Kyle of Lochalsh and the ferry to Skye. Being on his own, he could indulge himself in the soothing sounds of Gregorian chant. The sonorous sound from the cassette player seemed appropriate for the forbidding darkness of the mountains and was only interrupted by the occasional slap of water against the floor pan as the Sierra's wheels hit puddles at speed.

There was only one unscheduled interruption in the journey, when traffic was held up by a landslide near Glen Garry for about forty minutes. Eventually, lumbering yellow mechanical diggers cleared the road and policemen, wearing fluorescent waistcoats, waved the traffic on.

Bannerman constantly found himself thinking back to what had happened up on the Tarmachan ridge. The fact that he had neither reported the affair to the police nor consulted a doctor afterwards had acted in a positive sense to minimise the seriousness of the incident in his subconscious, but he still felt the need to analyse it in terms of his personal behaviour. Very few people are tested to the limit in their lives. Consequently, many die without ever finding out how they would behave under extreme pressure. Bannerman found himself examining his behaviour in relationship to the very reason for his getting away from the hospital for a while. He had been worried about his performance under stress.

When seen in this light, he found that he had reason to be pleased. True, he had been physically sick with fear but this had happened *after* he had coped with the situation, not during it. This in turn reminded him that the shake in his hands at the hospital had happened after he had made his decision on the emergency section, not before it. Maybe his mental condition was better than he feared.

It was six in the evening when he reached the village of Ralsay on North Uist. He had crossed on the ferry from the Kyle of Lochalsh to Kyleakin on Skye and caught another from Uig, in the north of the island, to Lochmaddy on North Uist. An ancient saloon car, masquerading as a taxi, had brought him to Ralsay.

'Can you drop me at the hotel?' Bannerman asked the driver.

'There's no hotel,' said the driver.

'The pub then.'

'No pub,' said the driver.

'Where do visitors stay in Ralsay then?'

'They don't get many.'

Bannerman, who was tired after a long journey, found himself irritated at the driver's unhelpful attitude. 'There must be somebody who takes in visitors,' he ventured.

'You could try Mistress Ferguson along there on the left,' said the driver, who had decided that, as far as he was concerned, the journey was over.

'On the left?'

'The house has lions at the door,' said the driver, holding out his hand. Bannerman had a mind not to tip him but relented and gave him an extra pound. 'Have a drink on me,' he said. The driver smiled wanly and drove off. 'And please God it chokes you,' added Bannerman. He walked along the dark street until he came to the door with the lions. There was a sign saying 'Accommodation' in the window. It was a welcome sight.

'Eleven pounds fifty including breakfast,' said the severe woman who answered the door. 'One pound extra if you want tea and biscuits at bed time.'

'Sounds like heaven,' smiled Bannerman.

The woman looked at him as if he had blasphemed. 'Does that mean you will be wanting tea and biscuits?' she asked.

'Yes please,' answered Bannerman meekly. He followed the woman up a narrow flight of stairs and into a room where the slope of the roof prevented him standing upright anywhere other than on a one-metre wide strip of carpet at the foot of an old brass bed. The room felt cold and smelt musty, but it was a landlord's market. Bannerman said it would be fine.

'In advance,' said the woman holding out her hand.

'Of course,' smiled Bannerman getting out his wallet and paying her. The woman examined the English ten pound note with a look of mild disdain.

'Actually, I'm a bit hungry at the moment,' began Bannerman tentatively. 'I don't suppose you could . . . ?'

'I could do you bacon and eggs.'

Bannerman waited for the mention of an alternative but none came. 'That would be wonderful,' he said. 'I'm most grateful.'

'Not at all,' said the woman. 'We like to make people feel welcome.'

Bannerman's attempts at holding a conversation with Mrs Ferguson, during his meal, all failed. It wasn't that she was hostile, just uncommunicative. She did it in such a natural way that Bannerman concluded that he should take nothing personally from the monosyllabic replies. This was the way the woman must behave towards everyone. Tiring of fruitless attempts at small-talk, he got round to the purpose of his visit. 'I'm looking for a woman called Shona MacLean,' he confessed. 'Have you any idea where I might find her?'

'Follow the crowd, I should think,' snapped the woman.

'I'm sorry?' replied Bannerman.

'That woman is never short of visitors.' Mrs Ferguson swept

crumbs from the table as if they were an invading swarm of killer ants.

Bannerman felt uncomfortable, as he always did in close proximity to domestic frenzy. 'Does she stay near here?' he ventured.

'The white house with the red door. Appropriate if you ask me.'

'Thank you,' said Bannerman, excusing himself and going upstairs. He tried to see outside from the small window but inky blackness cloaked the village. He would have to wait until morning.

A cold, uncomfortable night was followed by a shave in tepid water and a greasy breakfast of more bacon and eggs. Bannerman packed his bag and said his goodbyes to Mrs Ferguson.

'I trust we'll be seeing you here again some time,' said the woman with as near as she ever came to a smile.

'I hope so,' smiled Bannerman, thinking it would be shortly after hell froze over. He walked down the street to the white house with the red door. His knock was answered by a good looking woman in her late twenties; she was wearing jeans, which emphasised her narrow waist and rounded hips, and a shapeless grey tee shirt with a dolphin on it. Her fair hair tumbled round a smiling face that made Bannerman want to smile in return.

'Hello,' she said, 'You're a new face round here.'

'I'm looking for Shona MacLean,' said Bannerman.

'You've found her,' replied the woman. 'What can I do for you?'

'I hope you can help me find Lawrence Gill,' said Bannerman.

The smile faded, and the woman said, 'I haven't seen Lawrence for years. Who are you?'

'I'm Ian Bannerman. I'm a pathologist and I'm trying to pick up the pieces of what Gill was working on when he ran off.'

'Ran off?' exclaimed Shona MacLean.

'Frankly, Miss MacLean, Gill's wife told me that he had run off to be with you.'

Shona MacLean's mouth fell open and she looked genuinely

shocked. This came as a surprise to Bannerman. Up till now he thought that Shona MacLean was lying.

'You'd better come in,' she said.

Bannerman was shown into a pleasant room that was furnished brightly with an emphasis on pine and chintz. He sat down on a long sofa that lay along the window wall. Shona perched herself on the arm of a large matching chair.

'Can you prove you are who you say you are?' asked Shona MacLean.

Bannerman took out his wallet and extracted credit cards, his driving licence and his hospital ID card, which carried a photograph of him. Shona MacLean leaned forward to examine them and handed them back. 'Do you have a connection with the Medical Research Council?' she asked.

Bannerman was surprised at the question. 'It was they who asked me to carry out this investigation,' he said. 'Why do you ask?' He could see that Shona MacLean was hiding something. 'You have seen Lawrence Gill recently haven't you?' he said.

Shona MacLean nodded.

'He did come here?'

'Yes, but not for the reason you suppose. Lawrence and I had an affair years ago, but that was all over. He came here because he needed a place to hide.'

'To hide?' exclaimed Bannerman.

'He was terrified. He said that people were after him and that they would kill him if they caught him.'

'But why?'

'He wouldn't say.'

'But he's on the island?'

'No.'

'Do you know where he is?'

Shona nodded. 'He's hiding on a neighbouring island. It's uninhabited.'

'But surely he can't stay there for ever,' exclaimed Bannerman. 'Won't he be in just as much danger again when he comes off the island?'

'Lawrence said not. He gave me a parcel to send to the Medical Research Council in London. He said that once they had it, the game would be over and there would be no point in hounding him any more.'

'A parcel?'

'Yes.'

'Did he say what was in it?'

Shona shook her head.

'Describe it.'

Shona indicated a squarish box with her hands. 'About a foot square I'd say.'

'And you sent this parcel off?'

'I took it to the post office in Cairnish.'

'When?'

'The nineteenth.'

'Can I use your phone?'

'Of course.'

Bannerman called the MRC in London and asked to speak to Milne. He asked about the parcel.

'It hasn't arrived,' said Milne. 'What was in it?'

'I don't know,' replied Bannerman. He put down the phone and said, 'It's had plenty of time to get there.'

'I'll check with the post office,' said Shona.

Bannerman sat down again while Shona called the post office in Cairnish. She began by exchanging pleasantries with someone called Kirstie. 'It's about the parcel I brought in on the nineteenth,' said Shona. 'The one for London.'

Bannerman watched the expression on Shona's face change to one of concern. 'Dr Gill did?' she exclaimed. 'But that's impossible . . . No, no, nothing wrong Kirstie. I must have misunderstood something. Don't worry about it. See you soon.' Shona put down the phone slowly and Bannerman waited with baited breath for her to speak.

'The post office say that Lawrence came in later that day to recover the parcel. He showed them proper identification and Kirstie returned the parcel to him.'

'Is that possible?' asked Bannerman.

Shona shook her head and said, 'Lawrence went to the island that day and he's still there. The boat hasn't come back, so it couldn't have been him . . . but whoever asked for the return of the parcel had Lawrence's ID . . . How could that happen?'

Bannerman felt sure that Shona was as capable as he of answering that question.

The implications of what they had just learned hung above Bannerman and Shona like a guillotine. Whoever had been after Gill had found him.

'You know what was in that parcel don't you?' said Shona, thinking she could read the look in Bannerman's eyes.

'No,' replied Bannerman, truthfully, but his mind was lingering over the missing brains. Is that what had happened to them? Had Gill tried to send them to the MRC in London? But why? And who had stopped the parcel being collected? And why, again? All of a sudden he felt afraid. The questions were coming thick and fast and he could think of none of the answers.

SIX

Bannerman followed Shona down the stone steps leading from the harbour wall to the water. He held the little white boat while she got on board and clambered up to the stern to prime the outboard engine.

'I hope you're a decent sailor,' she said. 'It might be a bit rough out there.'

'I'll do,' replied Bannerman.

Shona pulled the cord for the fourth time and the engine spluttered into life. She gave it a moment or two to warm up and settle down into an even rhythm, then cast off the securing ropes. Bannerman pushed the boat clear of the side and they were off. Gulls wheeled overhead as they cleared the harbour mouth and headed for the open sea with the boat picking up motion as its bow took the waves head on.

'I didn't ask you what you did for a living,' said Bannerman, raising his voice to be heard above the sound of the engine and the sea.

'I'm an artist,' Shona replied, using her free hand to keep her hair from her eyes.

'An artist?'

'Why so surprised?'

'I suppose I assumed you had some connection with medicine or science,' said Bannerman.

'Because of Lawrence,' said Shona. 'In a way you're right. I trained as a physiotherapist before chucking it up to go to art college in Dundee. I met Lawrence when we were both working in a hospital there.'

'And you had an affair.'

'That's what the world would call it,' said Shona.

'What would you call it?'

'We loved each other, but he was married,' replied Shona.

'So why didn't he leave his wife?'

'Are you married?' asked Shona.

'No.'

'I didn't think so, somehow,' said Shona.

'What does that mean?'

'Some things aren't as simple as other people imagine. Lawrence had two small children and a wife who was entirely dependent on him. He simply married the wrong person. Lots of people do and they don't all rush off to the divorce courts. People like Lawrence grin and bear it; it's in their nature.'

'People like Lawrence?'

'Nice people, but weak. Lawrence wouldn't have hurt a sparrow let alone another human being.'

'Who ended the affair?'

'I did, but we stayed friends. We write once or twice a year and if he needs a soul mate, he calls me.'

Bannerman nodded. He changed the subject. 'Can you make a living as an artist?' he asked.

'Depends what you call a living,' smiled Shona. 'I illustrate children's books and get the odd commission from *Mammon*. It's a bit erratic but it allows me to do what I want to do.'

'Which is?'

'To live on the island, paint, take the boat out when I want to, feel the wind, see the sky.'

'Sounds all right,' said Bannerman.

'What about you?'

'What about me?'

'Are you doing what you want to do?'

Bannerman found himself caught unawares at the question. 'I suppose so,' he said, 'I've never really thought about it.'

'You should,' said Shona, steering the boat head on to the shingle beach they were approaching. At the last moment she swung the motor out of the water so that it wouldn't foul the bottom and waited until the boat had grounded before leaping out into the shallows and pulling on the bow rope. Bannerman got out with a deal less elegance and helped her pull the boat up on to the shore.

'The cottage is up at the top on the western edge,' said Shona as they looked up at the cliff towering broodily above them.

The wind, which had been quite strong at ground level, increased as they made their way up the narrow cliff path, and was positively fierce at the top. They kept well away from the edge as they battled up to the cottage to find the back door flapping open and banging against the wall. They entered, discovering the groceries that Gill had brought to the island lying on the floor. They appeared to be untouched. A search of the cottage yielded no signs of Gill or any indication that he had been staying there.

Bannerman found some footprints in the grime on the kitchen floor and deduced that more than one person had walked on it recently. 'I think someone must have been waiting for him when he arrived,' he said.

'Maybe they took him back to the mainland,' suggested Shona.

'Maybe,' agreed Bannerman, but the doubt he felt showed in his voice. If Gill had been caught by his pursuers near the top of a cliff . . . He said that he was going to take a look around outside.

Bannerman crawled up further to the very western edge of the cliff top and looked down. He saw what he had almost expected to see, a man's broken body lying draped over the rocks below at an unnatural angle because of broken bones. Plumes of spray were breaking over it. Bannerman, who was lying on his stomach, brought his arms round in front of his face and rested his head on them for a moment. There was a hollow feeling in his stomach that he didn't like at all. He wondered just what he had got himself into.

Bannerman broke the news to Shona in the cottage. She stood before him with moistness in her eyes and an air of beguiling vulnerability. She said, 'I suppose I knew. As soon as Kirstie told me about the man using Lawrence's ID and the business of the parcel . . .' Her voice trailed off in sadness.

'I'm sorry,' said Bannerman, seeing that she was hurting.

Shona took a deep breath and recovered her composure. 'What now?' she asked, dabbing her eyes dry.

'We'll have to tell the authorities when we get back. They can recover the body and do what they have to do in such cases.'

Neither of them spoke much on the trip back to North Uist but just before they entered the harbour at Ralsay, Shona said, 'You will make sure his wife knows that he did not run away to be with me won't you?'

Bannerman agreed that he would.

Shona tied up the boat and they both climbed up onto the harbour wall. She looked at her watch and said, 'You're too late to get back to the mainland.'

'One more night at Mrs Ferguson's,' said Bannerman, inwardly cringing at the thought of more bacon and egg.

'Stay at my place,' said Shona.

'Won't that give the neighbours cause to talk?' asked Bannerman.

'Yes,' said Shona.

'I think we could both do with a drink,' said Shona as she closed the door of the white house and shut out the sound of the sea. 'Whisky?'

'Please.'

'And then we'll call the police?'

Bannerman hesitated with his response.

'We won't call the police?' asked Shona.

'I'd prefer it if *you* were to call the police . . . tomorrow, after I've left,' said Bannerman. 'My being here isn't going to help and I have a job to do.'

'What exactly is this job?' asked Shona. 'Do you know why Lawrence was killed?'

'I genuinely don't,' said Bannerman. 'But it has something to do with the deaths of three men up in Achnagelloch. Gill was looking into the cause of death and I think he must have found out something that certain people didn't want him talking about.'

'And it was worth killing him for?'

'Apparently,' shrugged Bannerman.

'What was special about the deaths? How did these men die?' asked Shona.

'They died of brain disease.'

'There's more to it, isn't there?' said Shona.

'What do you mean?'

'There's something you're not telling me,' said Shona.

Bannerman looked down at his feet, then confessed, 'There is a bit more, not that it helps in understanding why Lawrence Gill was killed.'

'Will you tell me anyway?' asked Shona.

Bannerman nodded. He said, 'Have you ever heard of a disease called *Scrapie*?'

Shona shook her head.

'It's a disease of sheep, a brain disease. It's been around for a long time but we thought it only affected sheep, so nobody paid it that much attention, until fairly recently.'

'What happened?'

'The disease crossed what we thought was a species barrier. It caused a condition in cattle called Bovine Spongioform Encephalopathy.'

'Mad Cow Disease?' said Shona.

'Yes. It turned out that there was no species barrier between sheep and cows after all.'

'Oh dear,' said Shona.

'We think that the three men up in Achnagelloch died of *Scrapie*.'

'It crossed to humans?' exclaimed Shona.

'Yes, and we have to find out how and why.'

'I see,' said Shona. 'Thank you for telling me.'

'I'd rather you didn't tell all your friends,' said Bannerman.

Shona gave a slight smile and nodded. 'Will you be going back to Edinburgh now?' she asked.

'No, Achnagelloch.'

'But won't you be in danger too?' asked Shona.

'I genuinely don't know anything,' said Bannerman.

'But you'll be doing the same thing Lawrence was doing, asking questions, poking your nose in.'

'I suppose . . .' said Bannerman thoughtfully.

'Please be careful.'

Bannerman saw the look of concern in Shona's eyes and nodded.

'I won't call the police until you've left,' said Shona.

'Thanks. One more thing,' said Bannerman. 'I'd be grateful if you'd just report the finding of the body. Don't tell them about the parcel or the man at the post office.'

'If you say so, but won't they think it was an accident in that case?'

'I'll make sure the authorities get to know what really happened. They'll deal with it without the newspapers getting hold of it.'

Shona prepared a meal for them that Bannerman thought a good London restaurant would have had trouble matching. He purred appreciatively as he sipped his coffee afterwards.

'I'm glad you enjoyed it,' said Shona. 'I like cooking, so I quite look forward to visits from authors and publishers when they come to see me about illustrations.'

The 'visitors' thought Bannerman, remembering what Mrs Ferguson had said. Malicious old cow. 'Can I help with the washing up?'

'Yes if you like,' said Shona.

When they'd finished, Shona manoeuvred another log on to the fire and they sat down to enjoy the warmth and the afterglow of well-being that the meal had bestowed on them. Shona asked Bannerman what he did when he wasn't investigating things. He confessed that this was the first time he had ever been asked to 'investigate' anything. He was a consultant pathologist at a London hospital.

'Then why ask you?' said Shona.

'I suppose because I'm a bit of an expert on brain disease.'

'I see. And do you like being "a bit of an expert on brain disease"?'

Once again Bannerman felt uncomfortable about the question. It was the same feeling he had experienced earlier on the boat. 'I suppose so,' he replied without conviction.

'It must be very interesting,' said Shona, getting up to put some music on. She sat down again and reaching behind her brought a cushion round to place it on the floor at her feet. 'Sit down there,' she said.

Bannerman opened his mouth to say something but closed it again and sat down between Shona's feet with his back to the chair.

'I noticed ealier that you have an injured right shoulder,' she said. 'You've been favouring it all day.' She kneaded her fingers into the muscles at the right side of Bannerman's neck and he let out a moan that was part pain, part pleasure. 'I hurt it yesterday,' he confessed.

'It's not often I get to practise as a physiotherapist,' said Shona.

'Why did you give it up?'

'It wasn't what I wanted to do.'

'That simple?'

'That simple. We only get once chance in this life.'

'Do you mind if I smoke?'

'Feel free.'

Shona stopped her massage until Bannerman had lit a cigarette with a burning wooden splinter from the fire.

'I thought doctors didn't smoke,' said Shona.

'This one does.'

'You find it as difficult as the rest of us to give up eh?'

'I haven't tried,' said Bannerman.

Shona sensed there was something behind the comment. 'Why not?' she asked, 'if it's as dangerous as you chaps are always telling us?'

'There's a belief around that death is a curable condition. My profession is responsible for creating it. They seem to suggest that if you eat the right things, take the right amount of exercise, avoid alcohol, tobacco, stay out of the sun and God knows what else, you'll increase your chances of living for ever. Not so.'

'No?'

'It will only seem like it. No heed is given to the quality of life on offer. It could be argued that by doing all these things you'll increase your chances of surviving long enough to lose all your faculties and end up as a blind, deaf, incontinent, doo-lally geriatric. I decided some time ago that that wasn't for me.'

'I bet you eat butter too,' smiled Shona.

'And I like caffeine in my coffee.'

'I hope you don't go around saying things like that to the patients,' said Shona.

'I've never told anyone that before,' said Bannerman, wondering why he was doing so now.

Bannerman became silent as Shona's fingers brought relief from the nagging pain, but Gill's death was uppermost in his mind.

Shona made up a *futon* bed for Bannerman in the room upstairs she used as a studio. The room had a large angled window set in the roof, which meant that he could lie on his back and look up at the stars set in a crisp, clear sky. The frost in the air made a halo round the brightest ones. There was a smell of oil paint in the room but it was not strong enough to be unpleasant and it reminded Bannerman of school days and the chaos of the art classroom. The sound of the waves breaking on the shore outside prolonged thoughts of childhood and conjured up images of family holidays and the elusive happiness that went with them.

At any other time such a pleasant ambience would have ensured that he drift off into a comfortable sleep, but not tonight. The thought of Gill's body lying broken on the rocks, with the waves breaking over it, kept returning to haunt him. Gill must have found out something about the deaths that no one else knew. Something so important that he was murdered to keep him quiet. It didn't seem to make any sense. He had already made known his suspicions about the involvement of the *Scrapie* agent in the affair and had forwarded sections of the brains to the MRC for examination. What more was there to know? What was the point of sending the brains to London, if that really was what was in the parcel.

After some further thought, Bannerman decided that there was one major difference between the sections of brain that Gill had sent to London and the actual missing brains themelves. The sections could be considered 'dead' material; the fixing procedure during the preparation would have killed off any live virus. The brains themselves however, would comprise a source of live virus. Was that the reason Gill had tried to send the parcel to the MRC? Because it contained *live* virus material? Bannerman felt a chill run up his spine as he thought about the interception of the parcel. He wondered why anyone would want to get their hands on such a deadly thing.

A whole range of nightmares queued up for consideration, ranging from criminal blackmail to the use of the virus as the ultimate biological weapon. Deranging large numbers of one's enemies could be a good deal more effective than killing them. A SCUD missile full of brain destroying virus falling in the streets of Tel Aviv was not a pretty thought and, unlike nuclear weaponry, it would be cheap. Bannerman decided that he was letting his imagination run away with him. Apart from anything else the 'new virus' was still a matter of conjecture. Who knew about the possibility outside the Medical Research Council . . . and Her Majesty's Government? This thought made Bannerman change tack. Maybe whoever had intercepted the parcel had not been interested in obtaining the live infecting agent at all? . . . Maybe they had simply wanted to destroy all evidence of it . . . to stop any further investigation?

When he woke, Bannerman took a leisurely shower in Shona MacLean's bright, modern bathroom and looked out at the early morning sunshine as he towelled himself down. It was so pleasant to be in a bathroom that had no need of frosted glass. He could watch the waves break on the shore. The smell of coffee brewing gave his appetite an edge as he dressed and went downstairs to find Shona in the kitchen.

'Did you sleep all right?' she asked.

'Eventually,' said Bannerman. 'How about you?'

'Eventually,' agreed Shona. 'I couldn't stop thinking about Lawrence. He was such a gentle man. I just can't believe that anyone would have wanted to murder him.'

Bannerman nodded sympathetically but couldn't think of anything to add.

'You've had no new ideas?' asked Shona.

Bannerman shrugged and shook his head. 'Not really, but somehow I'm more than ever convinced that the answer lies in Achnagelloch.'

'Don't you think that maybe it would be a good idea to tell the police everything after all?'

'Not just yet,' said Bannerman.

'I hope you know what you're doing,' said Shona.

Shona phoned for a taxi for Bannerman while he packed his things. He hoped it wouldn't be the same driver who had brought him to the village and his heart sank when he recognized the car as it pulled up outside. The same unsmiling man knocked at the door.

'Take care,' smiled Shona.

'Thanks for everything,' said Bannerman. 'Not least for saving me from another night at Mrs Ferguson's place!'

'Keep in touch,' said Shona.

'I'd like that,' said Bannerman, opening the door.

'Oh it's you,' said the driver.

'Correct,' replied Bannerman.

'I thought you were staying with Mrs Ferguson?'

'Did you?' replied Bannerman, getting into the car.

The first mile passed in silence and Bannerman would have preferred that the pattern continue, but the driver's curiosity got the better of him. 'Would your visit have been business or pleasure then?' he asked, with an attempt at what he considered a friendly smile.

'Business,' said Bannerman curtly, turning to look out the window again.

'And what exactly would your line of business be?'

They had almost reached the end of the journey. Bannerman

97

waited until the car had stopped before replying. He brought out his wallet and said, 'I'm an inspector of taxes. I work for the Inland Revenue.' He handed over the fare and a pound extra and said as a parting shot, 'Don't forget to declare the tip, will you?'

The journey back to the mainland was uneventful and the Sierra started first time when he turned the key. With a last wistful look over the water Bannerman said a silent farewell to Shona MacLean and set out for Achnagelloch.

For the first three hours the weather was kind and Bannerman felt quite relaxed when he stopped for lunch at a small village pub. The owner turned out to be an Englishman from Surrey who, after a lifetime in Insurance, had sold up everything down south and moved to the north of Scotland to run the hotel.

'How long have you been here?' Bannerman asked.

'This is our third winter,' replied the man.

'Does the reality match the dream?'

'I wish to Christ I'd never moved,' replied the man as he cleared away the dishes and bumped open the kitchen door with his backside.

Bannerman did not inquire further.

The rain started just south of Loch Shin and got progressively heavier until the wipers found it hard to cope. Bannerman had to slow to a crawl when he found the road along the west side of Loch Mor badly flooded. At times it was hard to tell where the loch ended and where the highway began. He prayed that the Sierra's electrics would survive the deluge of water from both above and below the car and purposely kept it in low gear to keep the revs high. After more than one heart stopping moment he was relieved to find the road climbing to higher ground. He lit a cigarette and began to relax a little but the feeling was short lived: it stopped when the signposts directed him to leave the main A 838 road and start out on the tortuous trail along minor B roads to Achnagelloch.

He had travelled barely a mile before he was brought to a halt by rocks on the road. They had been swept down from the barren hillside by the torrents of rain water. There was no alternative but to get out and clear a passage through them. Luckily none of the rocks were too big or too heavy to move, he managed most of them with his feet but he still got very wet in the process. 'Bloody country,' he mumbled as he got back in the car and slammed the door. It was seven o'clock when he reached Achnagelloch and found it as welcoming as a writ.

On his first traverse along the main street he did not see a single living soul. He turned and came back to where he had seen a hotel sign and this time he caught a brief glimpse of a figure flitting out of one doorway and into another. There was no one in the small hotel reception area when he entered, clutching his bag and brushing the rain off his shoulders. He read some of the notices that were pinned up on a wall by the door while he waited, hoping to get a feel for the place.

They were typical small town notices; one concerning the progress of the darts team, some adverts for properties owned by the National Trust in the area – all depicting gloriously sunny days, and a couple of receipts from local charities for collections made at Christmas in the bar. One notice in particular caught Bannerman's eye. It said that the sum of one hundred and eighty-three pounds had been raised for the fund for Mrs May Buchan. Bannerman recognized the name; one of the dead farm labourers had been called Buchan. The woman must be his widow.

'Can I be helping you?' inquired a soft highland voice behind him. He turned to find a man in his fifites wearing a heavy-knit cardigan over corduroy trousers, looking at him through thick-rimmed spectacles that sat beneath an unruly mop of grey hair.

'I'd like a room,' said Bannerman.

'Would you, now,' replied the man, almost absent mindedly as he appraised Bannerman virtually to the pont of embarrassing him with his stare. 'And what kjnd would you be wanting?'

'Ideally a warm, dry comfortable one with its own bathroom,' said Bannerman.

'Well two out of three isn't bad, as the Americans say,' replied the man. 'We don't have rooms with bathrooms but as you're the only guest you'll not be having much bother with queueing.'

'Sounds fine,' agreed Bannerman, who was so tired after his drive that he would have taken a stable. 'I'd like to go up right away if that's all right.'

'I'm afraid not,' said the man softly.

'No?'

'I'll have to have Agnes make the room up first. We don't get much in the way of passing trade at this time of year. Perhaps you'd like to wait in the bar?'

Bannerman said that he would. He opened the door that the man pointed to and found himself in a small, smokey bar with a coal fire at one end. There were three men seated at the counter and a boy in his late teens was serving behind it. They looked at Bannerman as he entered. 'It's a rough night out there,' said one of the men.

'Certainly is,' agreed Bannerman. The men looked to be local, two were wearing caps, one of whom was resting his elbow on a shepherd's crook, the head of which had been carved out of horn. The third man was wearing dungarees and a woollen hat. He was considerably younger than the other two and smiled a welcome.

'You're English?' said the younger man who had commented on the weather.

''Fraid so,' said Bannerman with a smile.

The smile was returned. 'We won't hold it against you,' said the man.

'In that case perhaps I might buy you a drink?' said Bannerman.

All three opted for whisky. Bannerman invited the barman to join them and the boy said he'd have a beer. The ice had been broken and faces relaxed into smiles.

'What brings you to Achnagelloch?' asked the man with the crook.

'I'm a doctor,' said Bannerman. 'I've come to talk to the local health authorities . . . about the three men who died.'

There was very little reaction from the men. One of them did shake his head and say. 'Bad business, meningitis. My sister's boy died of it.'

100

'Did you know the men?' Bannerman asked.

'It's a small place, most folks know everybody,' said the man with the crook.

'You look as if you work out on the hills yourself,' said Bannerman.

The man nodded.

'You too?' Bannerman asked the other man wearing a flat cap.

'Aye.'

'How about you?' Bannerman asked the younger man.

'I'm in the quarry,' replied the man.

'The quarry?'

'The stone quarry.'

'I didn't realize there was a quarry near here,' said Bannerman.

'There wasn't until the Dutchman bought the Invergelloch estate. Everyone thought he was mad buying a barren wasteland, but next thing we know he's got himself a licence to quarry roadstone and is making a fortune.'

'Bloody foreigners,' grumbled one of the farmworkers. 'The Scottish highlands have got more bloody Dutchmen in them than Amsterdam.'

'I'm not complaining,' said the quarry worker. 'I've got a good job and one that doesn't involve bloody sheep!'

Bannerman smiled, and the quarry man warmed to his theme. He said, 'I'm telling you without a word of a lie, if you removed sheep as a topic of conversation from this town there would be a great silence.'

'Get away with you!' exclaimed one of the farmworkers with a lazy swing of his arm, but there was no malice in it. The man's face wore the smile of the old tolerating the foibles of the young.

'Did the quarry bring many jobs?' asked Bannerman.

'About fifty,' replied the quarryman, 'between men from here and Stobmor.'

'Coolies,' said one of the shepherds. 'The Dutch keep all the cushy jobs for themselves. The workers are just coolies.'

The quarryman shrugged but didn't rise to the bait.

'Are there many Dutchmen?' asked Bannerman.

'Ten or twelve.'

'Making a fat living out of Scotland,' growled one of the others.

'Maybe a Scotsman should have thought of it first?' said the quarryman.

The topic of the quarry died out and Bannerman asked the farm workers if they knew the farm where the three men had died. Maybe they even worked there themselves?

Both men shook their heads. 'We work the Liddell estate,' said one. 'That's well to the south of Inverladdie.'

'I hear Inverladdie had trouble with *Scrapie*,' said Bannerman. 'Have you had any bother?'

'No, touch wood,' said the man with the crook. 'We're clear.'

Bannerman watched to see if any tell-tale glances would pass between the two farmhands but saw none. He knew that sheep farmers were often reluctant to admit to the presence of *Scrapie* in their flocks.

The landlord came into the bar and told Bannerman that his room was ready. 'Would you be wanting anything to eat?' he asked.

Bannerman found his eyes straying to the dried tomato stain on the front of the man's cardigan. 'What have you got?' he asked.

'We could do you, bacon and eggs?'

Bannerman fought off notions of homicide and was relieved to hear the man continue with alternatives. He ordered a steak and wished goodnight to his new-found companions in the bar before taking his bag upstairs. Bannerman noticed a distinctive smell as he climbed the stairs. It was the smell of small hotels all over the country, a mixture of dust, dampness and carpeting.

He supposed that it had something to do with the fact that so many of these places had lain empty for quite long periods in their history. They had not been built as hotels of course, but had been large family houses at one time and had become too expensive to continue in that role. As a consequence, they had suffered neglect and decline, before eventually being rescued for sub-division or, as in the case of this one, conversion for use as a hotel. Bannerman suspected that during the times when such buildings had lain empty the cold and damp had crept into their floors and walls like ink spreading through blotting paper and had remained there ever since.

His own room appeared to be warm enough, thanks to an electric radiator that had been turned on to FULL, but it was surface warmth, a cosmetic warmth. He sat on the bed and found it firm and comfortable. There was a picture hanging above it depicting a trawler with waves breaking over its bow, which held the caption, 'Heading for Home' written below it in ornate writing. A gust of wind drove rain hard into the window pane and made Bannerman smile. 'What a bloody good idea,' he murmured.

The telephone rang and startled him. It was the owner announcing that his steak was ready.

SEVEN

Bannerman telephoned the Medicial Research Council in the morning. It seemed to take an age before he was put through to Hugh Milne.

'I tried calling you in Edinburgh; I was told you had gone north,' said Milne.

'Something awful has happened,' said Bannerman. 'Lawrence Gill has been murdered.'

'Murdered?' exclaimed Milne.

'I don't know who did it or why, but I do know that it had something to do with this brain disease business.'

'But this is incredible. Why would anyone want to murder a pathologist who was simply trying to establish a cause of death?'

Bannerman took a deep breath and said, 'I know it sounds stupid, but I'm convinced that someone or some . . .' Bannerman searched for a word, 'faction, does not want the true cause of death discovered.' He told Milne about the brains having been removed from the cadavers in Edinburgh.

'Where exactly are you?' asked Milne.

'There wasn't much point in staying in Edinburgh with no pathological material to work on, so I came up to Achnagelloch. I found out from Gill's wife about the island he had run off to, so I tried to find him to ask about the missing brains. Instead I found him at the bottom of a cliff.'

'I suppose there's no chance it was an accident?'

'None at all. Gill was hiding on the island because he knew

someone was after him. He tried sending a parcel to you which I think contained the missing brains.'

'But why send it to us when we had already seen the slides he had prepared?'

'I wish I knew.'

There was a pause in the conversation. Bannerman guessed that Milne was having difficulty coming to terms with what he had heard. He suspected that the introduction of possible criminal involvement in what was thought to be a purely medical mystery was having the same unsettling effect on Milne as it was on himself. Both of them were getting out of their depth.

Milne broke the silence, 'Perhaps you should return to London immediately,' he said. 'There may be danger in pursuing the investigation.'

'I've thought about that,' said Bannerman, 'but I'm here now, so I may as well ask around a bit. It would be a help though if Gill's death were played down for the moment. I don't want the newspapers making connections between Gill's murder and the problems up here. I thought your colleague, Mr Allison, from the Prime Minister's office might help in that direction.'

'I'll alert him. I'm sure he has no wish to see this develop into a media circus.'

'I'm sure he hasn't,' agreed Bannerman with just the merest hint of sarcasm, thinking about the cover-up of the radiation leak at Invermaddoch.

As a first step, Bannerman set out to find the vet's surgery in Achnagelloch. He hadn't bothered to ask at the hotel for directions because he thought the place small enough for him to find it on his own and he wanted to take a look at the town. He liked small towns; he liked their manageable proportions, the fact that you could see how everything worked and fitted together, unlike big cities which were anonymous places, their workings hidden inside bland concrete boxes.

After twenty minutes of searching he admitted defeat and asked directions from a woman who was coming out of a shop, carrying bread and milk. The bell attached to the shop door jangled loudly as she closed it, obliging him to begin his question over again. 'I'm looking for Mr Finlay, the vet,' he said. 'Can you tell me where his surgery is please?'

The woman looked at Bannerman as if he had arrived from a strange planet. She stared at him so long without expression that he felt himself become embarrassed. The smile died on his lips.

'You're not from round here,' said the woman.

'No I'm not,' agreed Bannerman, declining to add details.

'Finlay lives in the old manse.'

'The old manse.'

The woman nodded as if this were enough.

'How do I find the old manse?' asked Bannerman.

'Just outside the town,' said the woman.

'This way?' asked Bannerman, pointing with his finger to the east.

The woman nodded and looked at him as if there were no other way out of town.

'Thank you. You've been most helpful.'

The old manse stood about a hundred metres back from the main road and was hidden from view by a stone wall which was topped by green lichen. Several yew trees formed a secondary screen and cast a shadow over the house. Bannerman walked up the drive to the dark building which looked as if it had been built to the design of a primary-school class drawing. It was a simple stone box, two storeys high with regularly placed windows, all the same size. The door was placed exactly in the middle and there was a single chimney in the centre of the roof. Outside, on a semi-circular apron of gravel, stood a Land Rover and a dark green Jaguar with a number plate on it that told Bannerman it was as new as it looked. He paused to admire the gleaming paintwork and the fat sports tyres. He rang the doorbell.

The presence of the Land Rover had cheered Bannerman. It suggested that he had caught Finlay before he set out on his rounds. This was confirmed by a woman who answered the door, eating a piece of toast. She pressed her hand to her chest and gave an exaggerated swallow to empty her mouth before saying, 'Excuse me, I'm just finishing my breakfast.'

Bannerman asked if he might speak to Finlay. He was invited in and shown into a front room, where he stood looking at the pictures on the wall until he heard someone come into the room behind him.

'You're not from round here,' said the short, balding man that Bannerman found before him. He had a fair, ruddy complexion and was running to fat despite the fact that Bannerman reckoned he could not have been more than thirty. His lips had a moist quality about them which Bannerman thought unpleasant in a man. He wore baggy corduroy trousers and a navy blue Guernsey sweater.

'No, I'm not,' agreed Bannerman, thinking that the next person to make that observation might well push him over the edge. He announced who he was and added, 'I'm looking into the deaths of the three farm workers at Inverladdie.'

'Most unfortunate,' said Finlay. 'Meningitis, I believe.'

Bannerman nodded. 'A particularly virulent form,' he said, 'hence our interest.'

'How can I help?' asked Finlay.

'I understand that there was an outbreak of *Scrapie* on the farm where the men worked?'

'Yes, that's right,' agreed Finlay, quietly. His expression betrayed the fact that he was trying to work out the connection.

'You made the diagnosis in the animals?'

'Yes . . . I'm sorry, I don't see what this has to do with . . .'

Bannerman made a dismissive gesture with his hands and said, 'At this stage I'm just gathering together all the facts I can about the dead men's lives.' He added what he hoped was a reassuring smile.

'Again?' asked Finlay with a suggestion of irritation.

'I'm sorry?'

'A pathologist named Gill came to see me and asked the same sort of questions. I just don't see what the *Scrapie* outbreak has to do with the deaths.'

Bannerman thought it strange that a vet could not follow

such a line of questioning with ease. He had been prepared to ask for Finlay's discretion in not mentioning the possibility of a link between *Scrapie* and the deaths, but now it did not seem necessary. 'Did you send brain samples from the sheep to the vet lab?' he asked.

'No I didn't,' said Finlay.

'Why not?' asked Bannerman, as pleasantly as he could ask that sort of question.

'Because I didn't have to. It was quite obvious what was wrong with the animals. I've seen it before. Apart from that, *Scrapie* is not a notifiable disease and it costs money to have lab tests done. The farmers don't like it.'

Bannerman nodded. 'What exactly happened to the carcasses?'

'They were buried on the farm in a lime pit.'

'Immediately?'

'As far as I know.'

'Why on the farm?'

'What do you mean, why?'

'Why do it themselves? Isn't it more usual to have renderers take carcasses away?'

'No any more,' replied the vet. 'Firms of renderers used to pay farmers for diseased carcasses and then prepare cattle feed from them, but since it was shown that that was how cows got BSE the government has put a stop to it. The firms now charge the farmers for taking the carcasses away. It's cheaper to dispose of them themselves.'

'Thanks for the information,' said Bannerman.

'Don't mention it,' said Finlay, coldly.

'Have there been any further cases of *Scrapie* on local farms?' asked Bannerman.

'None.'

'None that you've heard of?'

'I keep my ear to the ground. It's hard to keep a secret in a small community like Achnagelloch. I would know if there had been any other animal problems.'

'How about the nuclear power station? Have there been any problems with that?'

Finlay smiled and said, 'Of course. Every time a ewe aborts, a child coughs or a cake fails to rise in the oven, the station gets the blame. People are people and we all need something to blame for our misfortunes.'

'So you haven't come across any veterinary problems associated with it?'

'None that I could ascribe to the station with any degree of certainty, but then that's always the problem with radiation isn't it? You can't see it, you can't smell it and its effects take some time to show up. Usually by that time you can't prove it any longer.'

Bannerman sympathized with Finlay's assessment. 'One last question,' he said.

'What?'

'How do I get to Inverladdie Farm?'

'Why do you want to go there?' exclaimed Finlay.

'I told you. I want to know everything about the dead men's lives.'

'There doesn't seem to be much point in wasting time on a sheep farm when . . .'

'I've plenty of time, Mr Finlay,' replied Bannerman, evenly.

Finlay gave him directions and showed him to the door.

'Nice car,' said Bannerman, referring to the Jaguar.

Finlay nodded and closed the door. Bannerman traced his finger lovingly along the line of the Jag as he passed and thought to himself that country vets must do a lot better than he had ever imagined.

Bannerman had to run the gauntlet of two labrador puppies on his way down the drive. Finlay's wife, who had been down to the mail box at the entrance, tried to control them with one hand while carrying newspapers and mail with the other. He smiled and made a fuss of them for a few moments before saying goodbye and walking back to the hotel where his car was parked in a small courtyard at the back. When he got there, he found his way barred by two men dressed in leather aprons; they were unloading metal beer canisters from a brewery lorry parked across the entrance. The kegs were being rolled across the cobbles and down a ramp to the hotel's cellar.

'They won't be long,' said the hotel owner, appearing at the

109

back door of the hotel. 'Do you want something while you're waiting?'

'Coffee,' replied Bannerman. He left the car and went inside. He almost immediately regretted his decision when he was met by a woman armed with a vacuum cleaner. She was attacking the hall carpet and his feet had the temerity to be on it. He side-stepped into the lounge and closed the glass door in a vain attempt to escape the noise. A few minutes later, coffee appeared and the owner asked what his plans were for the day.

'I'm going up to Inverladdie Farm,' replied Bannerman. 'After that I'm going to try having a chat with the local GP.'

'Angus MacLeod? A fine man,' said the hotelier. 'Some would say he's getting a bit long in the tooth for the job, but I'm not one of them. The man has a wealth of experience. He's been our doctor for nearly thirty years now.'

'Really,' said Bannerman, putting a possible age of seventy on the man. In his book, doing the same thing year in, year out did not amount to 'a wealth of experience' but he kept his thoughts to himself. He finished his coffee and set off for Inverladdie.

There was a contractor's van parked in front of the whitewashed farmhouse. It bore the name of an Inverness firm of heating engineers and, as if to prove the point, there were several radiators of varying size and a pile of copper piping stacked outside the door. Next to that was a contractor's skip piled high with what looked like bits of old plumbing.

Bannerman picked his way through the jumble and knocked on the door. There was no answer until he had knocked a second time. A plump woman in her early fifties with a shock of hair that could not make up its mind whether it was fair or grey appeared at the door; she was drying her hands on a tea towel. The towel had 'Great Bridges of the World' printed on it. Bannerman recognized the Forth Bridge near the bottom.

'Yes?'

'Good morning, my name's Bannerman. I work for the Medical Research Council. I wonder if I might have a few words with you and your husband?'

110

'Medical Research Council? We've already had university people here asking questions. What more is there to say?'

'It won't take long,' said Bannerman with a smile.

'John's down in the town and we're having a new heating system installed . . .'

'So I see,' said Bannerman. 'John's your husband?'

'Yes, John Sproat. I'm Mrs Sproat.'

'Will he be long?'

'We're still a man short on the farm. He went down to see if he could recruit someone.'

'I see,' said Bannerman, reluctant to leave. He stood his ground until the woman was embarrassed into saying, 'You'd best come in and have a cup of tea. He might be back by then.'

Agnes Sproat shut the kitchen door and Bannerman was pleased to find that much of the metallic hammering noise from the room next door was muted by it. She put on the kettle and bade Bannerman take a seat at the large scrubbed pine table in the middle of the room. It was a comfortable farmhouse kitchen, light, spacious and a large Aga stove made the room warm and welcoming. 'We've been promising ourselves a new heating system for years,' said Agnes Sproat.

'You really need it up here,' said Bannerman.

'You're from London?'

'Yes.'

'I went there once, about ten years ago,' said Agnes Sproat. 'It was too muggy for me. I couldn't breathe.'

The sound of a car outside made her lean over the sink to look out of the window. 'It's John,' she said. 'You're in luck.'

Bannerman stood up and saw that a white Mercedes saloon had parked outside beside the skip. A tall, gaunt man was getting out; a few moments later he appeared in the kitchen doorway.

By no stretch of the imagination could John Sproat have been called handsome. His skin was sallow, his features sharp and angular and grey hair seemed to sprout from his head at odd angles. Spikes of it stuck up at the back and at both sides.

111

He wore a tweed jacket and trousers. In his hand he carried a deerstalker hat.

'John, this is Dr Bannerman from the Medical Research Council,' said Agnes Sproat.

'What do *they* want?' asked Sproat to his wife, as if Bannerman wasn't there.

'I've come about the three men who died,' said Bannerman.

Sproat shook his head to signify exasperation. 'Another one,' he said.

'I've told him a doctor from the university was here,' said Agnes Sproat.

'And the police, and the area medical officer,' added Sproat. 'Maybe I should turn the place into a bloody safari park and charge admission.'

'I'm sorry you've been troubled,' said Bannerman evenly, 'but it's important we investigate this thoroughly.'

'What do you want?' asked Sproat.

'Ideally, I'd like you to show me round your farm. I'd like to see the terrain and the boundaries.'

'And then you'll leave us in peace?'

'Probably,' said Bannerman.

Sproat put on his hat and said, 'Right then. Follow me.'

Bannerman smiled at Agnes Sproat and followed her husband out into the yard where they climbed into a Land Rover that seemed to have been buried up to its wheel hubs in manure at some point in the recent past. A black and white collie dog stood by the side of the vehicle until Sproat signalled to it to climb on board. It leapt up on to the rear platform and lay down as Sproat started the engine. They jolted off up the track leading to the hills.

'I farm both sides of the glen,' said Sproat.

Bannerman could see sheep spread over the slopes of the hills on both sides. The Land Rover growled as Sproat dropped down through the gears in deference to the ever steepening slope. Stones were thrown out from the wheels as the tyres fought for grip on the loose surface of the track.

They reached the head of the glen and came to a halt with the vehicle perched at an angle on the crest of a hillock. The land from there spread out in a gentle slope that led down to the sea. To the east, Bannerman could see the somehow threatening outline of the Invermaddoch power station. It seemed incongruous in the rugged landscape. 'Does your land go right up to the station?' he asked Sproat.

'To the fence,' replied Sprot. 'There's a two hundred yard boundary with a double fence.

'So the sheep are confined to the west of the station?'

'Yes.'

'There's no way the animals could stray further?'

'No. We have to maintain the fences on the east side of the farm because the ground to the south and east of the station is so rough. If we didn't, we'd lose animals in the gulleys and crevices and shepherding is impossible on that terrain. Not even the balloon trikes can cope with it.'

'Do you have much contact with the people at the station?' asked Bannerman.

'Not much.'

'Is there a contingency plan for the area if there should be a problem?'

'Search me,' said Sproat. 'If there is, no one told me.'

'I just thought there might be evacuation plans should an emergency arise,' said Bannerman.

'There's not much to evacuate round here,' said Sproat.

Bannerman smiled ruefully and said, 'I suppose you're right . . . just a few sheep.'

'I think we'll get a warning just the same,' volunteered Sproat.'

'How so?'

'One day, about eight or nine months ago, they must have had a problem down there. I've never heard such a racket in all my life; klaxons, sirens, the lot. It sounded like a major air raid.'

'Did you find out what the problem was?' asked Bannerman.

Sproat shook his head. 'Not a word,' he said.

'Would you mind if I were to take a look around the boundary on my own, maybe tomorrow?'

'Feel free,' said Sproat. 'Although I don't see what that has

113

to do with anything. Just don't underestimate the terrain down there, it's a long walk up from the road. I can't let you have a vehicle.'

'No problem,' said Bannerman. 'I could use the exercise.'

Bannerman looked towards the sea and saw that there was a railway track tracing the shore line. 'What's that?' he asked.

'It's the line for the stone quarry,' said Sproat. 'The roads around here won't accommodate the size of vehicle the quarry needs, so the Dutchman built a railway line to take out the stone to the sea terminal at Inchmad.'

'Is the quarry near here?' asked Bannerman.

Sproat raised his left arm and pointed to the north-west. 'About half a mile,' he said.

'Doesn't the noise worry you?' asked Bannerman.

'They only blast once a month. Any other noise is carried away on the wind and with all the stone going out by rail there's no extra traffic to speak of. You'd hardly know they're there.'

'The best kind of neighbours to have,' said Bannerman.

'Aye,' agreed Sproat. 'Is there anything else you'd like to see?'

'Maybe you could show me where you buried the infected sheep and then where you store chemicals on the farm?'

Sproat didn't reply. He just got back in the Land Rover and started the engine. They drove laboriously round the head of the glen and down into the next one, where they came to a halt. Bannerman was glad they did; his spine was beginning to protest at all the jarring.

'We dug the pit over there,' said Sproat, nodding to his right.

Bannerman could see where the ground had been disturbed. He got out and walked over to the mound. Sproat joined him.

'I understand from the vet that no brain samples were taken from the sheep?' said Bannerman.

'That's right. It was obvious what was wrong with them.'

Bannerman looked down at his feet.

'If you're thinking what I think you're thinking, you can forget it,' said Sproat. 'We didn't skimp on the lime.'

Bannerman smiled. He had indeed been wondering whether there was any chance of the virus having survived in the sheep burial pit but he had no wish to start digging and decided to accept Sproat's assurance. 'I'm sure,' he said.

They passed a small cottage on the way back to the farmhouse. Bannerman asked about it.

'That's where Gordon Buchan lived with his wife,' said Sproat quietly.

'Maybe I could have a word with Mrs Buchan,' said Bannerman.

'No,' said Sproat quickly. 'She's away at the moment.'

'Away?' asked Bannerman.

'On holiday. She needed to get away for a bit.'

Bannerman nodded. 'And then what?' he asked. 'I presume it's a tied cottage?'

'It is,' agreed Sproat. 'She'll probably move back to live with her family in Stobmor.'

The pulled into the farmyard as the first spots of rain began to dapple the windscreen. 'More rain,' complained Bannerman.

'At least it's not snow,' said Sproat. 'We store chemicals and fuel in the barn.'

Bannerman took a look round the barn and found nothing out of the ordinary. It was a sheep farm, so there wasn't much call for the wide range of chemicals that might be found in arable farming. What there was seemed to be stored well and the labels were well known proprietary brands.

'What exactly is it you're looking for?' asked Sproat.

'I'm not sure myself,' replied Bannerman.

Later on that afternoon, Bannerman telephoned Angus MacLeod's surgery from the hotel. He thought that that might be the best time to contact him, in the lull between morning and evening surgeries and when the house calls should be over for the day. His housekeeper answered and told him that MacLeod was having a nap.

'Is it an emergency?' she asked.

Bannerman said that it wasn't but that he would like to speak to the doctor.

115

'He only sees reps by prior appointment,' said the house-keeper defensively.

'I'm from the Medical Research Council,' replied Bannerman.

'I see, well if you give me your name I'll tell the doctor you called.'

'I'm staying at the hotel,' said Bannerman. 'Perhaps you would ask him to give me a ring when he wakes up?'

'I'll do that, Doctor . . . ?'

'Bannerman.'

Bannerman filled in the time with phone calls to London. He spoke to Olive at the lab and then to the chief technician, Charlie Simmons, who told him that everything was going smoothly and that there was nothing to worry about.

'How about the locum?' asked Bannerman.

'He's about fourteen years old,' replied Simmons. 'We should have him trained by the time you get back.'

Bannerman smiled. It was pretty much the reply he had expected. He asked to speak to Leeman but was told that he was carrying out an autopsy. Bannerman said not to disturb him but to tell him that he had called and to pass on his regards. He asked to be transferred to Stella's extension but the hospital switchboard cut him off somewhere in the proceedings and he had to call again simply to be told that Stella was in theatre. He had barely replaced the receiver when the phone rang. It was Angus MacLeod.

'How can I help you, Dr Bannerman?' asked MacLeod, in clear, measured tones.

'I'm looking into the deaths of the three men from Inverladdie, Doctor,' replied Bannerman. 'I understand you were their doctor.'

'Yes, indeed,' replied MacLeod. 'There's no other practitioner in Achnagelloch.'

'Perhaps we could talk?'

'Come on over,' said MacLeod. 'When you leave the hotel turn left. Take the first right after the post office and my surgery is on your left, half way up the hill.'

* * *

Despite his name and, albeit refined, Scottish accent, there was nothing about Angus MacLeod's dress to suggest Scottishness. Bannerman found this surprising. For some reason he had expected a tweed jacket at the very least, or perhaps a tartan tie, but no, MacLeod was wearing a dark, three piece suit with a gold watch chain disappearing into his waistcoat pocket. His white shirt was crisp and his tie was a muted dark blue. It went well with his silver hair. Bannerman reckoned that he could not have been far short of seventy but, despite the apparent frailty of his thin body, his voice was strong and his intellect seemed quick and unimpaired.

'Good of you to see me Doctor,' said Bannerman, stretching out his hand. He found MacLeod's grasp firm and free of masonic information. He was shown into what was obviously MacLeod's consulting room and invited to sit down.

'There's really not much I can tell you,' said MacLeod, placing his elbows on the desk and resting his chin on folded hands.

Bannerman could imagine him adopting this posture in front of generations of patients . . . Tell me all about it Mrs Macpherson, when did you first notice the swelling . . .

'The condition came on so quickly that there was very little I could do, except provide some relief from the pain and give them sedation. One of the men was dead of course when they found him and another was raving mad in the streets. Gordon Buchan was the only one I managed to attend, simply because he had a wife to call me in.'

'What were your thoughts when you first saw him?' asked Bannerman.

MacLeod grimaced slightly at the memory. He said, 'I once saw a man die of rabies in North Africa. That's the only thing I could compare the condition to. Progression into complete dementia with the patient experiencing the most horrible nightmares.'

'I wonder if I might see your case notes on the men?' asked Bannerman. 'I'm trying to collect together every single detail.'

'Of course,' replied MacLeod, getting up stiffly from his chair and opening a three-drawered filing cabinet. He brought out the relevant files and placed them on the desk in front of Bannerman.

'I understand that some kind of viral meningitis is being blamed for the deaths,' said MacLeod, as Bannerman worked his way through the slim files.

Bannerman met MacLeod's eyes briefly and said, 'That's what I understand too.'

'Did you know that the men were employed on burying dead sheep when they fell ill?'

'I had heard,' said Bannerman without raising his eyes this time, although his pulse rate rose a little.

'The sheep died of *Scrapie* . . . Did you know that?'

This time Bannerman felt he could no longer avoid MacLeod's clever probing. He lifted his head and said, 'Yes Doctor.'

'Just so as you know,' said MacLeod gently with a vaguely amused look on his face.

Bannerman closed the files and stacked them together on the desk. He said, 'Yes Doctor, you are perfectly right in your suspicions. The *Scrapie* connection is why I'm here. I apologise for not having come clean with you right away.'

MacLeod shook his head slightly and made a gesture with his hands to signify that no offence had been taken. 'Then you believe it's a real possibility?'

'I'm afraid so,' replied Bannerman. 'All the evidence seems to point to the men having contracted sheep *Scrapie*. I'm trying to prove it and find out just how it happened.'

'A breach of the species barrier would be no joke,' said MacLeod.

Bannerman nodded. He had taken a liking to MacLeod. He felt guilty about having misjudged the man when he first heard about the length of his service in the area. He asked, 'What happened after the men's deaths?'

'I requested that post-mortems be carried out by the MRC instead of the area pathologist.'

'Why?'

'The symptoms displayed by the men suggested acute brain disease to me and I was aware of the MRC's national survey. I called Stoddart in Edinburgh and he sent up a chap named Gill and his research assistant, Dr Napier. I must confess I was quite surprised to get George's letter saying that meningitis was being blamed but I didn't say anything.'

'Why not?'

'I know my place,' grinned MacLeod. 'GPs are the equivalent of village idiots as far as the medical establishment are concerned.'

Bannerman smiled and asked, 'Do you know Stoddart personally?'

'I once taught him basic anatomy,' said MacLeod.

'I think he forgot,' said Bannerman and MacLeod's face broke into a huge grin.

'I didn't realize you had taught medicine,' said Bannerman.

'Just for three years,' replied MacLeod, 'I had a spell in Africa in the fifties, playing at being the saviour of the dark continent and then a lectureship at Edinburgh – a different sort of jungle.'

'And that's where you met Stoddart?'

'He was one of my students. In fact I think I can say that I was responsible for directing Stoddart towards a career in pathology.'

'Really?'

'I didn't want him getting his hands on any *live* patients,' smiled MacLeod.

Both men laughed.

'It hasn't stopped him getting to the top,' said Bannerman.

'Intellectual short-coming seldom does in my experience,' said MacLeod.

'So academia wasn't for you?' said Bannerman.

'It certainly wasn't,' agreed MacLeod. 'Academics are more institutionalized than prisoners in jail, only they don't realize it.'

'Why general practice?' asked Bannerman.

'I wanted to be part of a community, not something outside it. As a GP I'm at the heart of things. I'm in at the beginning and I'm there at the end. It was what I wanted to do and I've never regretted it.'

'There's not too many people can say that about their lives,' said Bannerman.

'On the contrary, Doctor,' said MacLeod. 'A lot of people *say* it but whether or not it's true is an entirely different matter.'

'Point taken,' conceded Bannerman.

'Would you join me in a drink, Doctor?' asked MacLeod, opening his desk drawer and taking out a bottle. 'But first be warned that if you should happen to say, "It's a little early for me" I may be inspired to violence.'

Bannerman smiled and said, 'I would be honoured.'

MacLeod poured the whisky and Bannerman asked, 'What happened about the examination of the bodies?'

'They were taken to the small cottage hospital facility we have at Stobmor. Dr Gill performed elementary examinations and then Dr Napier took over the brunt of the laboratory work while Gill went around asking questions. After a few days it was decided that the bodies would be taken to Edinburgh for full autopsy.'

'I didn't realize you had a hospital in the area,' said Bannerman.

'It's more of a clinic, really,' replied MacLeod. 'But we have a nursing sister and it's somewhere where small or emergency operations can be carried out, should the need arise.'

Bannerman wondered about MacLeod's ability to operate at his age but did not say anything. MacLeod smiled as he read his mind and said, 'We can call on a surgical rota from Inverness and Glasgow.'

'I see,' said Bannerman.

'And now you are going to ask me about the power station,' said MacLeod.

'I am?'

'Yes.'

'How did you know that?' asked Bannerman who was increasingly enjoying MacLeod's company.

'If you are looking for a likely cause of mutation in a virus, you could hardly ignore the presence of a nuclear power station next door could you?'

'Once again I have to take my hat off to you Doctor,' said Bannerman, with a smile. 'Has the presence of the station caused any health problems in the area?'

'It's hard to be objective,' replied MacLeod. 'The population is so small up here that it's difficult to gather meaningful statistics.'

'You have a higher than average childhood leukaemia incidence,' said Bannerman. 'I've had a look at the figures for the area.'

'That's a good example,' said MacLeod. 'Two years ago our figures were slightly below the national average. Two cases last year, one in Stobmor and another in one of the outlying farms, were enough to push us into the "statistically higher than average" category. It could have been chance.'

Bannerman nodded and said, 'I thought that might be the case.'

'Lies, damned lies and statistics,' sighed MacLeod. 'But that's not to say that the children didn't get it from the presence of the station. We just can't prove it one way or the other.'

'That brings me to my next question,' said Bannerman. 'Do you have any radiation monitoring equipment?'

MacLeod said that he had, adding, 'I was given it when they opened the station, a battery operated Geiger counter and calibration kit.'

'I'd like to borrow it,' said Bannerman. 'I want to take a look at the boundary land between the station and Inverladdie Farm.'

'By all means,' said MacLeod. He got out of his chair and slid open the bottom cupboard door of a bookcase that held volumes of medical text books. He brought out a wooden box fitted with brass catches, which he unclasped. 'There we are,' he said, removing the cylindrical monitoring probe. 'Better check the batteries.'

EIGHT

Bannerman decided that it was about time that he took a look at Stobmor, Achnagelloch's neighbouring community. He ascertained that it boasted a hotel, then arranged by phone to have dinner there at eight o'clock. He left his own hotel at six and drove the seven miles over to Stobmor, leaving himself plenty of time to look round.

In many ways Stobmor was little different from Achnagelloch, although it did possess a small office block, an unimaginative concrete box with signs saying that it was the headquarters of the Dutch quarry company, Joop van Gelder. Further along the road Bannerman found the cottage hospital that MacLeod had mentioned although, at the moment, it seemed empty and showed no lights. There was a board outside giving emergency telephone numbers. In the main street he found the local job centre with a lighted window and looked at the cards for a while to see what was on offer in the area.

There were ten vacancies. There was a post for an electrician at the quarry – preferably with knowledge of electric motors. Three further jobs at the quarry were for labourers. There were openings for two security guards at the power station – ideally with a services background – and there was a lab technician's job in the monitoring section. The remaining positions were for domestic help and for a shop assistant's post in the local mini-market. There was one farm job on the board: it was for a sheep worker at Inverladdie.

As he walked the streets Bannerman passed the primary school with its child paintings stuck up proudly in the windows.

Road safety appeared to have been the theme, with traffic lights and Zebra crossings well to the fore. One window was entirely taken over by a cardboard cut-out policeman holding up traffic with a hand that appeared to have sausages for fingers.

Bannerman noticed that there was no shortage of cars parked in the streets, many with registrations younger than three years old. He took this as a barometer of the prosperity of the town. The quarry and the power station had ensured full employment in the area. He wondered how long Inverladdie might have to wait before a man opted for a farm labourer's wage instead of the more lucrative alternatives.

Bannerman's theory of general prosperity seemed to be reinforced by the fact that the houses seemed well-cared for and the gardens tidy and meticulously tended. Many of the houses appeared to have undergone recent upgrading; their doors and windows had been replaced. This was a working community, well ordered and probably quite content, thought Bannerman. He made his way towards the Highland Lodge Hotel in Main Street and a dinner he was now ready for.

The dining-room of the hotel was empty when Bannerman went in, although he noticed that another table had been set for half a dozen people. It was cold in the room and he rubbed his hands together and shivered as he sat down and took the menu from the girl who had showed him in. Happily she took the hint and lit a butane gas fire that stood in front of the fireplace with its empty and cheerless grate. The butane burner made a noise like a propellor driven aircraft approaching from afar. It made Bannerman think of the war film, *The Dambusters*.

'You're not from round here,' said the girl when she came back to hover, with her pad and pen at the ready.

'Does that mean that local people wouldn't dream of eating here?' asked Bannerman, immediately regretting his mischief-making when he saw the girl blush deeply.

'Oh no,' she exclaimed. 'I just meant that it was unusual to see a tourist at this time of year. Lots of people eat here, honestly.'

'I'm sorry,' said Bannerman. 'I'm sure it will be very nice.'

'Mr van Gelder, himself, is giving a dinner party here later,' said the girl, indicating to the set table.

'A more than good enough recommendation I'm sure,' said Bannerman, wishing that he hadn't upset the girl in the first place and resolving to give her a big tip whatever the food was like. He guessed that she was a high-school girl making some money with an evening job. She had an openness and innocence about her that made him feel old.

'Would you like a drink while you're deciding?' she asked.

'I'd love a gin and tonic,' replied Bannerman with a distant smile.

The meal proved far better than Bannerman had dared hope and was without doubt the best meal he had eaten since the one Shona MacLean had cooked. He found himself reluctant to leave the dining-room, which had warmed up considerably, and gladly accepted the offer of a second refill to his coffee cup to go with another cigarette. He was thinking about Shona MacLean when the all male dinner party arrived. He found that he recognized one of them. Jack Sproat, the owner of Inverladdie Farm was the second man to come into the room.

The newcomers were all laughing at something but the smile faded from Sproat's face when he saw Bannerman sitting there. He detached himself from the party and came over.

'I didn't expect to find *you* here Doctor,' he said.

'I fancied a change,' replied Bannerman, evenly.

'How is your investigation going?'

'It's not really an investigation,' replied Bannerman. 'I'm just checking to see if anything was overlooked at the time.'

'Who is your friend, John?' asked a voice with a pronounced accent.

'This is Dr Bannerman, Joop,' replied Sproat. 'He's from the Medical Research Council. He's looking into the deaths of my workers.'

'Won't you join us, Doctor?' asked the man with the accent.

'Thank you but I've just eaten,' replied Bannerman, looking at the smiling man with the short, cropped fair hair. Bannerman thought him to be in his early fifties, although he looked younger at first glance because of his good teeth and a smooth, slightly tanned skin. It was a complexion he associated with wealth.

'Just for a drink perhaps?'

'All right, thank you,' replied Bannerman, and he got up to join the others.

'I'm Joop van Gelder,' said the smiling man, getting up to shake Bannerman's hand and bring another seat for him. Bannerman was introduced to the others in turn. Two of the remaining men were Dutch; the other three local farmers and land-owners.

'That was a terrible business at Inverladdie,' said van Gelder. 'Meningitis seems to be on the increase these days.'

'I think Dr Bannerman believes my sheep killed them,' interrupted Sproat. There was an embarrassing pause before the others laughed.

'Surely not?' said van Gelder, who hadn't joined in the laughter.

'The truth is that we don't know where the bug came from Mr van Gelder, something my profession is always reluctant to admit. In the end we will probably call it a virus infection; we usually do in these cases, and then the public thinks how clever we are.'

The men laughed again and this time van Gelder joined them. 'How refreshing to find a doctor who doesn't take himself too seriously,' he said. 'We must have another drink.'

Bannerman declined this time, saying that he had to be going and that they must all be hungry. He wouldn't delay them any longer. 'I recommend the fish,' he said, getting up from the table.

'Then I will have it on your recommendation,' said van Gelder, getting up and shaking Bannerman's hand again. 'Nice to have met you Doctor.'

Bannerman turned to Sproat and asked, 'If it's all right with you, I'd like to visit Inverladdie again tomorrow?'

'You're welcome,' said Sproat.

*   *   *

Bannerman had a night cap back in the bar of his hotel. The quarry worker he had met on the previous evening was sitting at the counter and he chatted to him for a while before going upstairs. He looked at his watch and dithered for a moment before deciding to phone Shona MacLean. She replied after the third ring and sounded sleepy.

'Sorry, did I wake you?'

'Oh it's you!' exclaimed Shona.

'I thought I'd better check that you didn't have any problems with the police?'

'No, not at all. I called them when you left and told them about finding Lawrence's body at the foot of the cliffs. They arranged for it to be taken back to the mainland.'

'They treated it as an accident?'

'I think so.'

'I've told the people in London that it wasn't.'

'Good,' said Shona. 'He didn't deserve to die like that. How is the investigation going?'

'All right, I suppose,' said Bannerman. 'I had a talk with the local vet who seemed . . . *thick*.'

'Thick?'

'The more I think about it the curiouser it becomes. I'm the second investigator from the MRC who has been up here to ask him questions about the *Scrapie* outbreak at Inverladdie Farm where the men died and he still hasn't twigged to what we're getting at.'

'Maybe he's being deliberately obtuse?'

'But why?'

'Can't help you there,' said Shona.

'The local GP was quick enough to figure it out. He's a wily old bird. I liked him a lot. I think he twigged to some kind of *Scrapie* involvement from the first time he was called out to the patients.'

'What's the next move?'

'Tomorrow I'm going to examine the land between Inverladdie Farm and the nuclear power station, to see if I can find any trace of a radiation leak having occurred.'

'That sounds dangerous.'

'It only *sounds* dangerous,' said Bannerman. 'Actually it involves little more than going for a walk with a torch-like thing in your hand.'

'All the same, I think you should be very careful.'

'I will,' said Bannerman.

'You will let me know how you get on?'

'If you want me to,' said Bannerman.

'I do,' said Shona.

Bannerman lay back on the pillow and reflected on how nice it had been to talk to Shona again and how good it was to know that they would be in touch again. All in all it hadn't been a bad day. On the bedside table lay the Geiger counter that Angus MacLeod had loaned him for examining the boundary area tomorrow. He moved it slightly to one side and switched out the light. The room wasn't completely in darkness; light from a street lamp across the way made patterns on the ceiling as it shone through the waving branches of a tree outside the window. He thought about Shona's plea that he should be careful, and a cloud crossed his mind as he remembered the broken body of Lawrence Gill lying on the rocks.

Bannerman drove the Sierra as far up the Inverladdie Farm track as possible and then parked it out of the way of any vehicle that might want to pass. He had hoped for good weather but the fates had other ideas. There was a strong westerly wind and the sky promised rain in the not too distant future. Bannerman changed his shoes for his climbing boots and zipped himself into his shell jacket and waterproof trousers, before protecting his face with a woollen balaclava and pulling up his hood. He collected the rucksack containing MacLeod's Geiger counter from the boot, before locking up the car and setting off up the east side of the glen. He was breathing hard by the time he reached the head of the glen and could see the power station away to his right.

Sproat had been correct about the terrain on this side of the glen. The ground fell away steeply and was riddled with cracks, gulleys and peat bog. It looked as if at some time in the past the

127

ground had breathed deeply and caused a general upheaval in the landscape. This was not the kind of place to break an ankle in, he reminded himself as he went over slightly on his left one. He was going downhill but the effort required seemed greater than on the climb up the glen.

Although the power station was probably not more than a mile away, as the crow flew, the need for constant detour and climbing down into and up out of craters meant that Bannerman had covered nearly three times that distance before he reached the area around the perimeter fence. After a break of a few minutes to get his breath back, he had a cigarette in the shelter of a large rock before starting out to follow the line of the fence down to the railway track and beyond to the sea where he planned to begin his examination of the ground.

He got out the Geiger counter from his rucksack and checked the condition of its battery, despite having inserted a new one that morning. He turned the sensitivity switch on the side to B-CHECK. The needle rose well past the red minimum mark, so he turned the switch to its most sensitive setting to start a rough scan of the area. With his back to the sea, he crossed the single-track railway line leading to the quarry and began to walk slowly back up the line of the fence. He held the sensor in front of him and swung it slowly backwards and forwards to cover as wide an area as possible.

Apart from an occasional click from the instrument as it received natural radiation from the atmosphere the pointer hovered quietly on the base line. Bannerman pushed his hood back a little so as not to miss any sounds coming from the small speaker in the side of the instrument. Suddenly he heard a loud rasping sound, but it came from behind him. He turned round to see an inflatable boat, its bow bouncing over the waves, coming straight for the shore. It's outboard engine was buzzing angrily.

As he watched, Bannerman grew alarmed when he realized that he was the object of attention for the men on board. The three of them jumped out into the shallows below him and waded quickly to the shore to start running towards him. They were carrying automatic weapons. He soon found himself being gripped firmly on both sides by the arms.

'What's your game, then?' demanded the third man who stood in front of him with sea-water dripping from his oil-skins.

'I think I might ask the same of you,' said Bannerman, with more courage than he felt. 'I am on Inverladdie Farm property and I have permission to be here.'

'A smartarse, eh?' sneered the man. 'Let's get him back.'

Bannerman protested loudly but he was manhandled down to the beach and forced into the boat. Once on the move, he sat quietly. The sound of the engine and the heavy sea made conversation impossible and, for the moment, there was no place else to go. He looked at the three men who seemed to be doing their best to ignore him. All were dressed in the same weatherproof uniforms with a badge above their left breast which said, SECURITY. Their boots were of the commando type which laced up well above their ankles. They sat with the butts of their automatic rifles on the wooden floor of the boat.

The boat traced a large circle out of Inverladdie territory and round to the back of the power station where it was brought in to a small bay. The man at the tiller left it to the last moment to cut the engine, with the result that the boat coasted on to the shingle by virtue of its own momentum and slid to a halt on the shore.

'Get out!' rasped the first man out to Bannerman.

Bannerman complied, introducing an air of resigned lethargy to his movements in an attempt to salvage his dignity.

'Move,' another man ordered, punctuating his request with the muzzle of his weapon in Bannerman's back.

Bannerman was marched up the beach and through the gates of the station. He was directed into a long low building and put in a room devoid of furnishings, save for a table and two chairs. One of the armed men remained in the room with him until a new face appeared. The newcomer was in his thirties, clean shaven and dressed in a dark suit with what looked to be a college tie. Judging from the stiffening of his guard when the man entered, Bannerman guessed that the new man might be in charge of security.

The man seated himself opposite Bannerman at the table and said, 'Name?'

'Who wants to know?' replied Bannerman.

The man leaned across the table and said, 'Me.'

'And who are you?' said Bannerman, evenly.

The man stared at Bannerman for a moment then brought out an ID wallet and put it down on the table in front of Bannerman.

Bannerman looked down at it and read that the bearer was 'C. J. Mitchell, Head of Security.'

'Bannerman.'

'First name?'

'Ian.'

'Well, Ian Bannerman,' said Mitchell sitting back in his chair. 'You are in trouble.'

'One of us is,' replied Bannerman.

Mitchell sized up Bannerman in silence for a few moments before saying, 'What were you doing at the fence?'

'I was on Inverladdie Farm property. I had permission to be there and what I was doing is none of your business.'

'Is that where you left the Citroen?' asked Mitchell.

'What Citroen?' asked Bannerman.

'The 2CV with "Save the Whales" in the back window and "Nuclear Power No Thanks" along the back bumper. That's what all you buggers drive isn't it?'

'Who exactly are "all us buggers"?' asked Bannerman.

'The club,' Mitchell sneered. 'The lentil eaters, the organic turnip heads, the gay, vegan, lesbian, whale saving, league against nuclear power brigade.'

'Oh I see, you thought I was trying to blow up the station,' said Bannerman, making the notion sound so ridiculous that Mitchell's mouth quivered in anger. 'I'll ask you again, what were you doing by the fence?'

'And I'll tell you again, it's none of your business,' said Bannerman meeting the security man's eyes with a level stare.

The impasse was broken by one of the men from the boat coming in and placing Bannerman's Geiger counter on the table. 'He had this with him, sir,' the man announced before leaving.

'Well, well, well,' purred the security man. 'What do you know, the boys' own radiation monitoring kit. Just what the hell did you hope to find?'

'I didn't *hope* to find anything,' replied Bannerman. 'I wanted to know if there had been any leakage of radioactive material to the west of the station.'

The security man seemed intrigued. He leaned towards Bannerman and asked, 'Why?'

'That's my business.'

'Your business?' said Mitchell, putting a different inflection on the word.

'Yes.'

'A journalist? Is that it? A crusading investigative journalist. Isn't that what you scaremongering busybodies call yourselves? Is that it Bannerman?'

'You really have a problem don't you,' said Bannerman, quietly. 'Have you ever thought about a career more suited to your personality, say, lighthouse keeper in the Arctic Ocean?'

Without warning, Mitchell swung his fist at Bannerman and caught him high on his left cheek bone. The force of the blow knocked him backwards and his chair toppled over to send him sprawling to the floor.

Bannerman sat up slowly holding his hand to his face and breathing erratically, partly through surprise and partly through shock. Mitchell got up to stand over him. 'Wait outside,' he rasped to the guard by the door. The man, who Bannerman could see was uneasy about what he was witnessing, complied immediately.

'What now?' asked Bannerman. 'Electrodes on my testicles?'

'You lot make me sick,' sneered Mitchell. 'Get up.'

Bannerman got to his feet. He had recovered from the blow and was holding his temper firmly in check. He said, 'I'd like to see the station manager please.'

'He's a busy man,' said Mitchell.

'So am I,' said Bannerman. He enunciated every syllable with arctic coldness. 'I am Dr Ian Bannerman, consultant pathologist at St Luke's Hospital London, currently investigating the deaths of three local men at the request of the Medical Research Council and Her Majesty's Government.'

Mitchell looked as if he was about to lay an egg. His eyes suggested his brain was asking his ears for a recap on what they'd just heard. 'ID?' he croaked.

Bannerman showed him identification.

Mitchell looked down at the table surface as if it were to blame for everything. 'Why didn't you say so in the first place?'

'Because I didn't choose to,' snapped Bannerman. 'I was on private property when your men abducted me and brought me here. I pointed this out to them at the time and to you when I got here but you took no notice. Now get me the station manager.'

Mitchell left the room and Bannerman lit a cigarette. His fingers were trembling slightly.

Some ten minutes passed before the door opened and Bannerman was politely invited to follow one of the security men. He had suddenly become 'sir'. He was taken to the main building of the power station and then by elevator to the top floor where he was shown into the station manager's office. Mitchell was with the manager and Bannerman could see that the man had been fully briefed about what had happened.

'Leave us, Mitchell,' said the manager curtly and Mitchell walked past Bannerman with a small, uneasy smile.

'My dear Doctor I don't quite know what to say,' said the station manager, coming round from behind his desk to usher Bannerman to a chair. 'I'm John Rossman. I can only offer my most profuse apologies and ask you to understand some of the pressures my people have to cope with. Nuclear power stations are natural targets for every inadequate misfit in society who's looking for a cause to crucify himself for. Constant vigilance is a must.'

'Beating up anyone who comes within yards of your perimeter fence is a bit more than being vigilant,' said Bannerman.

'Well, yes but . . .'

'And being against nuclear power doesn't automatically make you an "inadequate misfit".'

132

'Well, no but we get so much negative publicity that perhaps we're all just a bit paranoid in the industry. We are constantly portrayed as harbingers of danger rather than suppliers of cheap, clean power,' said Rossman.

'Perhaps,' said Bannerman.

'I understand you were monitoring the ground outside the west fence,' said Rossman.

'That's right. I wanted to see if there had been a radiation leak in the recent past.'

'But if there had been we would have . . .'

'Covered it up like last time,' interrupted Bannerman.

Rossman looked at Bannerman in silence for a long moment before saying, 'I don't think I understand what . . .'

'My information came from the Cabinet Office,' said Bannerman.

'I see,' said the manager, obviously wondering how to deal with him. He got up from his desk and walked over to a large map of the station which was mounted on the back wall of his office. 'If I might ask you to join me, Doctor?'

Bannerman walked over to the map and Rossman pointed to an area on the east side of the station. He said, 'We had a problem with a pipe carrying cooling water from the reactor suite. There was a crack in it and we suffered a slight loss of fluid before it was discovered.'

'How slight?'

'About a hundred gallons.'

'How big an area was affected?'

'We think not more than two hundred square metres,' said the manager.

'You think?'

'You've seen the ground round here. It's hard to say for sure.'

'You seem pretty complacent about it,' said Bannerman.

'On the contrary,' said Rossman. 'We cordoned off an area twice that size and dug trenches along the perimeter. Contaminated earth was removed and constant monitoring of the area was maintained for several months after the incident. Apart from that Doctor, no one lives to the east of the station. There was never any danger to anyone.'

133

'Then why cover it up?' asked Bannerman.

Rossman adopted an exasperated air and said, 'It wasn't a question of covering anything up. We just didn't publicize the affair and for the reasons I spoke of earlier. We would have been pilloried by those anxious to destroy the nuclear industry.'

'Have there been other incidents that you didn't publicize?' asked Bannerman.

'No. None at all. This station is perfectly safe, I assure you.'

'Until a hundred gallons of radioactive cooling water goes for a walk,' said Bannerman.

'That is exactly the kind of scaremongering we can do without in this industry!' said the manager, going slightly red in the face. 'We provide a lot of jobs in the area. You should think twice before putting them in jeopardy with that kind of talk.'

'What I said was the truth,' said Bannerman. 'Not scaremongering.'

'It was a one-off incident,' insisted the manager.

'But it happened! You can't dismiss it as if it never really had!'

'I don't think you fully understand the benefits that nuclear power can bring to our country Doctor,' said Rossman.

'Oh but I do,' insisted Bannerman. 'I understand the benefits perfectly. What really gets up my nose is your industry's reluctance to face up to the problems. You pretend that there aren't any. You maintain that accidents won't happen when everyone else knows that they will. You keep generating waste that you can't deal with because it's going to be dangerous for thousands of years and the best you can do is bury it in holes in the ground and keep looking for more holes.'

'It's not like that at all,' said Rossman.

'I think it is,' said Bannerman.

'Then I think we must agree to differ,' said Rossman.

Bannerman looked at his watch and said, 'Time I was going.'

'I will have someone drive you home,' said the manager.

'No you won't!' exclaimed Bannerman. 'It took me three hours to get to the perimeter fence from Inverladdie, I'm not doing that hike all over again. I want to get on with monitoring the ground I was working on when your men got "vigilant".'

'But I've told you we've had no problem on that side of the station,' said the manager.

'That you know of,' added Bannerman.

The manager took a deep breath and then exhaled slowly. 'Very well,' he said. 'I'll have Mitchell's men take you back there.'

'Good.'

'I have also instructed Mitchell to make a personal apology to you before you leave.'

'Thank you,' said Bannerman.

Bannerman was led away from Rossman's office by a security man who had been waiting outside the door. Half-way along the corridor he paused at a window to look down at the huge generating hall and the figures clad in white plastic suits tending to the machinery. The constant whine from the turbines seemed to pervade every part of the building, despite the extensive use of soundproof double glazing. There was a surgical cleanliness about the whole operation, no coal dust or oil or furnaces, just silent, invisible power sealed in concrete silos, its presence only advertised by the constant yellow and black radioactivity symbols.

Mitchell stood up when Bannerman was shown into his room. He had recovered his aplomb and his eyes were filled once again with self confidence. 'I'm sorry for our little misunderstanding, Doctor,' he said, 'but I'm sure you appreciate just how careful we have to be.' He held out his hand and said, 'Shall we let bygones by bygones?'

The self-satisfied look on Mitchell's face was too much for Bannerman. He swung his right fist in a short sharp hook to Mitchell's jaw and the man went down like a sack of potatoes. 'If we're going to do that,' he said, 'then let's start even.'

Mitchell sat on the floor holding his jaw with an expression of dazed bewilderment on his face. The security man who had brought Bannerman back moved in to grip Bannerman's arms but Mitchell held up a hand. 'Let him go,' he said. 'Take him where he wants to go.'

*   *   *

135

Once outside the fence, Bannerman cursed himself for his lack of self control. Of all the stupid things to do! You had to go and behave like a headstrong schoolboy! You had to throw away the moral high ground and hit him! You're no better than he is! Why do you do these things Bannerman? Are you ever going to act your age? His self reproach was total; he couldn't find one redeeming factor in his behaviour; he felt utterly disgusted with himself. He stubbed out his cigarette and got up from the boulder he had been sitting on. Perhaps if he threw himself into the job at hand he might block out some of the bad feelings.

During the course of the next three hours Bannerman moved up and down the ground between Inverladdie and the power station, meticulously scanning a two-metre wide strip each time. He was aware that he was being watched from the power station but no attempt was made to interfere with what he was doing. By the time he decided to call it a day his fingers were numb with cold and rain water had sought out several weak points in his waterproof clothing. He packed the Geiger counter back into his rucksack and set out on the long trek back. He had found no evidence of radioactive contamination of the soil at all.

Back at the hotel, Bannerman lowered himself gingerly into a hot bath and slipped slowly beneath the suds. He breathed a sigh of appreciation as the warm water covered him up to his chin and started to work on the aches and pains. The fact that he had achieved nothing positive for all his efforts did not help the recovery process, but the prospect of a hot meal and several whiskys to follow counteracted any notions of failure for the moment.

As he nursed his second glass of malt whisky in front of the fire in the bar, Bannerman wondered whether or not it would be worthwhile to continue examining the ground between Inverladdie and the power station. He had carried out a pretty exhaustive scan of the border strip – about sixty metres wide, he reckoned, but there were still other possibilities to take account of. He had gone for the obvious scenario of a leak occurring in the station and contamination spreading outside the wire through the soil but there were other possibilities.

Contamination could have occurred from the sea. The station

would have discharge pipes which would empty into the sea. Officially the discharge would be monitored and kept within agreed and legally enforced limits of radioactivity but what if an accidental discharge of high level waste had gone into the sea? Conceivably the tide could have brought it back on to the shore along the Inverladdie coastal strip. Alternatively there could have been aerial contamination from a discharge of radioactive gas.

Bannerman decided that it was worth him checking out the coastal strip of Inverladdie because a two-metre scan along three hundred metres or so of beach should reveal any tide borne contamination. Checking for contamination from the air, however, was a different matter. A gas cloud could have come down anywhere and he couldn't possibly hope to monitor the whole farm on his own.

His decision to examine the coastline at Inverladdie meant that he had sentenced himself to another hard day. He pondered on whether or not to have a day off before going back but decided that that would be giving in to his age. The landlord had agreed to dry off his wet clothing and boots, so he decided he would have one more whisky and then have an early night. As he went to the bar to get his drink the quarry worker he had come to know entered the bar and Bannerman bought him a drink.

As they sat down together at the fire the quarry man, now introduced as Colin Turnbull, said, 'The word is that you think the nuclear station had something to do with the meningitis deaths.'

'Silly gossip,' replied Bannerman, but he was unpleasantly surprised at how fast it had travelled. 'I met your boss last night,' he said. 'He seemed a nice enough chap.'

'Mr van Gelder? He's OK and the job pays well. The only drawback is that there are no prospects.'

'Why not?' asked Bannerman.

'Search me,' replied Turnbull. 'The company seems pretty enlightened in every other way, good pay, conditions, health care etc. but absolutely no prospects of promotion. Senior posts are strictly for the Dutch.'

'Strange,' said Bannerman.

'I'm thinking of taking them to the Race Relations Board,' smiled Turnbull.

Bannerman laughed and said, 'What sort of post were you hoping for?'

'I've been doing an Open University degree in geology. I should get my BA this summer. I was hoping for a job I could use it in but it's no go.'

'A pity,' said Bannerman. 'Maybe they'll change their minds if you keep on at them.'

'That's what I'm hoping,' agreed Turnbull. 'I've been doing a bit of survey work on my own in the hope that I can impress them.'

'That sounds exactly like the kind of initiative they couldn't ignore,' said Bannerman, draining his glass.

'Can I get you another?' asked Turnbull.

Bannerman shook his head and said that he was having an early night. He had another hard day ahead of him tomorrow. As he got up, Turnbull looked up at him and said, 'I hope you don't mind me saying this Doc but I think you should be a bit careful.'

The words chilled Bannerman. He looked at Turnbull and saw embarrassment more than threat in his eyes. 'I don't understand,' he said.

'The power station has local support. It provides a lot of jobs round here. Criticism isn't welcome, if you get my meaning?'

'I do,' replied Bannerman. 'Thanks for the warning.'

NINE

Despite the soothing effects of the whisky, Bannerman had a restless night, plagued by thoughts of the warning given to him by Turnbull and what he saw as the stupidity of his actions at the power station. He would not now be sorry to leave Achnagelloch. Whether or not he found evidence of contamination that day he was resolved to return to Edinburgh on the following day. There was nothing else to be done here for the moment. He felt sure that the only source of the rogue virus was in the experimental mice at the university.

The rain of the previous day had cleared away to leave a bright blue sky but looking nice was about as far as it went. It was bitterly cold and the wind was strong enough to make the chill factor a significant problem up on the exposed sides of the glen. The landlord had done a good job in drying out his clothing and had also offered to provide him with two thermos flasks, one filled with soup, the other with sweet coffee, an offer Bannerman readily accepted.

As a matter of courtesy Bannerman telephoned John Sproat at Inverladdie to ask for permission to spend another day on his land. It was granted without comment. Bannerman had half hoped for an offer of a rough terrain vehicle so that he would not have to trek all the way up the glen again, but this was not forthcoming. He steeled himself for the hike.

Although numbingly cold as expected, Bannerman found the going easier than the day before because the overnight plunge in temperature had caused the earth to freeze hard, providing a firmer footing than the slippery mud of yesterday. This was

139

a positive advantage in climbing up to the head of the glen but on the descent over the rough, broken ground to the shore it presented a new danger in the form of ice filled gulleys and steep, slippery rock falls with little or no sure footing to be had.

Bannerman was relieved to make it to the railway line by the shore without causing himself any more injury than the bad bruising to his left knee caused when he had slipped and gone down heavily on it while negotiating one of the rock falls. He found a hollow to shelter in and had the soup from the Thermos, cupping both hands round the mug so as to make as much use of the heat as possible. The soup was followed by a Mars bar and a cigarette.

With his back against a rock, Bannerman propped his rucksack between his knees and got out the Geiger counter. MacLeod had also given him a few specimen containers which he could use to take soil samples back if necessary. He brought these out and stuffed them into one of his jacket pockets where they would be more readily accessible. He had already decided that the sensible thing to do would be to walk as far west along the shore as he intended to monitor and then turn round and carry out a slow sweep with the counter on the way back. That way he would have the wind behind him on the actual slow monitoring leg.

Making sure that all his zips and toggles were properly closed and tightened he leaned forward, bowed his head and set off into the wind. He had barely gone a hundred metres when a sudden loud noise penetrated his hood and startled him so much that he lost his footing; he stumbled and fell to the ground. A freight train, which he hadn't heard because of the wind, rolled past on the single-track line. Its driver looked out of the cab but did not acknowledge him.

Bannerman got slowly to his feet and watched the trucks trundle by. The train seemed to consist mainly of fuel wagons and empty hoppers on their way up to the quarry. Bannerman silently gave thanks that he hadn't been walking on the line at the time. The locomotive would have hit him before he had heard it. He reached what he thought was a reasonable point to start working back from. If there had been any contamination of Inverladdie from the sea he would be bound to pick up signs of radioactivity in the four hundred metres or so of the shore that he planned to scan. He knelt down to take the lens cap off the Geiger counter's sensor.

The cap was a bit tight because the cold had made the plastic hard and unyielding so he laid down the meter by his side while he wrestled with it. Suddenly the glass on the meter shattered and the whole box jumped up into the air.

Bannerman looked at the instrument stupidly as if it had been subject to the attentions of a poltergeist. 'What the . . .' he exclaimed before realizing in a searing flash of panic what had really happened. A high velocity bullet had hit the Geiger counter! Someone had shot at him!

It seemed that his capacity to coordinate his limb movements was deserting him just when he needed it most. His arms and legs insisted on trying to behave independently as he half ran, half stumbled his way up the shore and over the railway line to tumble down into the first gulley that presented itself. It was his misfortune that it happened to have a puddle of water in the foot of it. There was a layer of ice on its surface but it gave way when he crashed down on it and he found himself kneeling in icy water. It was deep enough to cover his calf muscles and he felt them contract and threaten cramp in protest as he pressed his face to the muddy wall of his refuge.

As the seconds passed in silence, apart from the sound of his breathing, Bannerman became aware of the pain and discomfort afflicting him. These had been ignored as secondary considerations in his desperation to get out of sight of the gunman but now they screamed for his attention. He had come down heavily on his already bruised left knee and it was throbbing. Both his legs from the knees down had become numb with cold and his back was aching through holding himself against the wall of the gulley at an uncomfortable angle. He couldn't stay like this for ever but, on the other hand, he would be a sitting target for the gunman if he broke cover.

Perhaps the gunman wasn't there any more, thought Bannerman as what seemed like an eternity passed without any further shooting. His breathing quietened and he became aware of gulls wheeling above him in the wind. The analogy with vultures circling a dying man was inescapable, although he could only have been hiding for four or five minutes. His body was insisting that he move, so, very slowly, he edged himself up on the frozen mud wall and looked over the lip of the gulley. He was rewarded with a face full of grit as a bullet slammed into the ground less than a metre in front of him. He tumbled back down into the icy puddle and let out a cry of anguish as his injured knee took yet another knock.

Bannerman could hardly see through tears of frustration and pain but he fought to get a grip on himself and tried to consider his position as logically as he could in the circumstances. It was a crisis and he had to deal with it. At the time of the first bullet he had no idea where it had come from; the Geiger meter had just exploded and jumped up before his eyes. The second bullet had, however, given away the gunman's position because of the way the grit had flown up from the impact point. His attacker was almost due west of him. Big deal, thought Bannerman cynically. The truth was that if his attacker wanted to come down and finish him off there and then there was nothing he could do to stop him. The question was, did he?

Bannerman looked at his watch and had cause to rue his disdain for modern digital watches and their shockproof, waterproof casings. His own stylish, traditional watch had stopped. The blob of water under the cover glass told him why. He swore, looked up at the sky and tried to guess the time. Somewhere around two in the afternoon, he reckoned. In a couple of hours it would start to get dark. That was his only hope of escape. But if he were to have any chance at all of getting out under cover of dark he would have to get himself out of the icy puddle and get his circulation going. At the moment hypothermia and frostbite seemed a more likely scenario than escape.

It occurred to Bannerman that his attacker might have had that in mind. If he were to die of exposure it would look like an accident. There would be no inconvenient bullet holes to be explained away. Was that the reason the gunman did not appear to be interested in advancing on him? Was his plan to keep him pinned down until nature took its course?

Bannerman put his theory to the test by raising himself cautiously, once more, to the rim of the gulley. He was rewarded with a bullet a couple of metres away. The sound of the report was no nearer and the direction of the grit spurt had not changed; the gunman hadn't moved.

Survival against the elements was now the name of the game. He had to get through the next couple of hours as best he could and still be fit enough for a trek back to Inverladdie in darkness. As a start, he crawled along the bottom of the gulley and pulled himself out of the water and up on to a small rocky ledge where, if he kept himself bent over, he could still be out of sight of his attacker. With great difficulty he managed to loosen the straps of his rucksack with numb fingers and got out the unopened coffee Thermos. He removed the cap slowly so that he wouldn't spill any and poured some steaming coffee into it. Each burning sip was like a life-giving transfusion.

As soon as he had finished, Bannerman took off his boots and peeled off his wet socks. He put them to one side and replaced them with his spare pair from the rucksack, then he emptied the water out of his boots and laced them back on. He spent the next few minutes massaging his calves vigorously until the circulation returned to his legs bringing with it an agonising pain which made him throw his head back against the wall of the gulley and screw his face up tight until the pain began to subside.

Bannerman instigated a programme of wriggling his toes non-stop, for periods of thirty seconds, every few minutes. At the same time he would swing his arms across his chest and move his fingers in synchronous exercise. After an hour of this regime he permitted himself the luxury of the last of the coffee and a cigarette. After another hour he prepared to leave. He tied the wet socks he had taken off round his injured knee to provide some protection against accidental knocks and tried to psych himself up for the coming test.

Bannerman's new problem was in deciding just when it would

be dark enough for him to make a move. He desperately wanted there to be some light left so that he could make reasonable progress over the worst part of the journey, the stretch between the shore and the head of the glen, but, of course, this part came first and he would be hopelessly exposed if he just made a run for it. He looked anxiously at the sky. It was definitely getting dark but there was no cloud cover. It would be a clear and bitterly cold night.

Bannerman could feel his heart pounding as he tensed himself to move out of the gulley. He had decided on his first gambit. He vaguely remembered seeing another rock gulley about twenty metres to the left when he ran from the shore. When the moment came, he would pull himself out of his present hole and make a run for it.

With a last rub at his legs to make sure that they would support him, he placed his hands on the rim of the gulley and concentrated hard. He took three deep breaths to steady his nerves and then pulled himself strongly upwards to roll over the parapet. Fuelled by panic and adrenalin, he scrambled to his feet and made for the next gulley in a crouching zig zag run. He had almost started to think there was no need for this precaution when a crack rang out behind him and the whine of a ricochetting bullet sent him tumbling down into the safety of the new trench. 'Bastard!' he cursed, his nerves threatening to fray at the edges.

He had seen where his next run was to take him. Without waiting to consider, in case courage failed him or his adrenalin surge dropped, he crawled along to the end of his present cover and pulled himself up again. Another crouching run and he was into cover again. This time there was no accompanying shot and twilight was beginning to give way to darkness. Yet another zig zag run, and this time Bannerman made it a priority to get a good view of the general direction he wanted to head in. Safe in his next cover he got out his compass from his jacket pocket and made a mental note of the bearing of the head of the glen and the path back to Inverladdie.

*   *   *

The temperature was falling; the ground felt like concrete beneath his feet and every scrape or fall brought new agonies. The air was so cold that it pained him to take the deep breaths that his level of effort dictated he must if he were to fight off hypothermia. More and more his feet began to lose grip as he gained height and frost coated everything. As he hit his injured knee once more on a sharp rock – the wet sock protection kept slipping – he cried out and sank to the ground in helpless frustration. He wanted to scream and curse but the intake of icy breath made his throat contract, denying him even that release.

Discipline and coordination were all but gone by the time he made it to the head of the glen and he was reduced to making progress on all fours. Even this was lop-sided because of a reluctance to put all of his weight on his damaged knee. His efforts over the first stage of the journey had brought him to the point of exhaustion and he had been forced to slow down, which was causing him to become even colder. It was a vicious circle which was getting the better of him.

There was a plus side to it. The coldness was numbing the pain. He was actually beginning to feel better. The gnawing soreness was slipping away to be replaced by an almost pleasant sensation of nothingness, a feeling of lightness, a pleasant tiredness . . . He would stop for a while, have a cigarette and then think about going on . . . Bannerman reached into his pocket feeling distinctly light-headed and deliciously tired. There was a vague warning signal at the back of his mind but he was in no mood to heed it. He needed a rest. The small voice telling him that he mustn't stop would have to wait.

He found his cigarettes and matches and managed to open the pack with his tongue and teeth. He extracted a cigarette with his lips and then removed one of his gloves to light a match. Trying to shield the match with cupped hands which also contained the match box proved to be a disaster. The match ignited but fell into the half open box and the whole thing flared up in front of his face. Bannerman shied back stupidly from the firework, thinking how pretty it was, but

then darkness returned and he was tired again, oh so very
tired . . .

Bannerman opened his eyes and saw the face of an old man
smiling down at him. Was there a god after all?

'How are you feeling?' asked the old man.

'Where?' . . .

'You're in the Achnagelloch Hotel and you're quite safe,' said
the voice.

The mention of the decidedly earthly sound of 'Achnagelloch'
cleared Bannerman's head of all ethereal thoughts. He even
recognized the voice. It was Angus MacLeod.

'How did I get here?' he asked as consciousness and pain
sought to re-inhabit his body at an alarming rate. He remembered everything at once, except how he came to be in bed at
the Achnagelloch Hotel.

'The search party found you,' said MacLeod, 'thanks to your
brilliantly improvised flare.'

'Flare?'

'The matches,' said MacLeod.

'Oh the matches,' repeated Bannerman, none the wiser.

'Another few hours and it might have been a different story,'
said MacLeod. 'You have the young lady to thank for insisting
on a search party.'

'Young lady,' repeated Bannerman, feeling that he was a
distinct outsider in what was going on.

'Me,' said a female voice.

Bannerman looked in the direction of the voice and saw Shona
MacLean standing there. She was smiling the same smile he
remembered when she had opened the door to him on North
Uist. It was all too much for him; he allowed his head to fall
back on to the pillow in bemusement. Shona came to the side
of the bed and said, 'Don't worry, there's a perfectly logical
explanation for everything. I had to go to Inverness to discuss
some illustrations for the Highland craft fair so I thought I
would look you up. Seeing as how there is only one hotel in
Achnagelloch it wasn't that difficult. The landlord told me that
you had gone off into the hills this morning, so I decided to wait.

When you weren't back by nightfall I started to get worried. The landlord agreed that if you didn't turn up by seven we would raise the alarm. That's what happened.'

'How did they know where to look?' asked Bannerman.

'I told them,' said MacLeod. 'The police called to warn me of a possible emergency on the hills. They said a man was missing and when they said it was you I was able to give them a fair idea of where you had gone. They found you at the head of Inverladdie Glen.'

Bannerman digested this information in silence for a moment then he suddenly began to think about his medical condition. Frostbite! He wriggled his toes and fingers in unison and found that they all moved. MacLeod saw what he was doing and said, 'You're fine. You'll be right as rain in the morning apart from your knee, which I suspect caused all the trouble in the first place?'

Bannerman looked at him and suddenly saw the easy way out of all the explanations he feared he might have to make. 'Yes, I fell and hurt it. It slowed me up so much that I got caught out by darkness and wandered around in circles I suppose.'

'Easily done,' said MacLeod. 'Now if you'll excuse me I'll be getting to my bed.'

'Thanks Doctor,' said Bannerman sincerely.

'You're welcome,' replied MacLeod.

Shona reached out her hand and smoothed the hair away from Bannerman's forehead. 'What really happened out there?' she asked.

For some reason, Bannerman did not even consider lying to her. 'Someone took a shot at me.'

'The same someone who killed Lawrence?'

'I don't know,' replied Bannerman.

'Do you know why?'

'They obviously didn't want me poking around that area of Inverladdie Farm.'

'Because it's contaminated with radioactivity?' said Shona.

'I suppose so,' agreed Bannerman. 'But the truth is that I had found no evidence of that at all.'

147

'What if you had?' asked Shona.

'I would have reported it to the authorities and presumably action would have been taken.'

'The station would be closed?'

'I suppose that's a possibility.'

'Then it's not difficult to see who wouldn't want that,' said Shona.

'I suppose you're right,' said Bannerman, with an attempt at a smile. 'Half the workforce of Achnagelloch for a start.'

'But finding radiation wouldn't have cleared up the mystery of the cause of the men's deaths would it?' asked Shona.

'No. I need the results of lab tests in Edinburgh for that, but if I'd found radiation then almost certainly that would have been specified as the cause for a mutation occurring in the virus.'

'It seems that someone is going to extraordinary lengths to see that the nuclear industry doesn't get the blame for that.'

Bannerman shrugged but didn't say anything. They were both considering whether or not these lengths included murder.

'What are you going to do now?' asked Shona.

'I'm going back to Edinburgh. Lawrence Gill inoculated some experimental mice with brain material taken from the dead farm workers.'

'Why?' asked Shona.

'To grow the infecting agent so that we would have a source of it to test and identify.'

'You'll be able to tell if it's a new form of the virus?'

'Yes. We'll be able to find out everything about it. Its host range, its incubation time, its virulence, everything. It's important to know your enemy.'

'Will you be fit to drive back to Edinburgh?' asked Shona.

Bannerman had been wondering this himself. The thought of changing gear several hundred times with his injured left leg did not fill him with pleasurable anticipation. He moved his knee under the blankets and winced. 'I'll manage,' he said.

Shona smiled and said, 'I'll make a deal with you.'

'What?'

'If we can go to Inverness first, I'll do the driving and take you back to Edinburgh.'

'You're serious?' said Bannerman.

'Of course.'

'But why?'

'Because I want to,' said Shona. 'It's ages since I've been in Edinburgh. What do you say?'

Bannerman didn't know what to say.

'Of course, if you don't want my company . . .'

'Oh no, far from it,' insisted Bannerman. He took Shona's hand and said, 'I think that would be absolutely great and thank you. Apart from that, I understand that I owe you my life.'

'Nonsense,' scoffed Shona. 'I'm sure the landlord would have raised the alarm on his own without any prompting from me.'

Bannerman smiled. 'Maybe,' he said, 'but the fact remains that we'll never know that for sure. You were the one who did it. Thanks.'

'You're welcome,' smiled Shona. 'See you in the morning.'

Bannerman felt his eyelids become heavy. The feeling of warmth, after having been so cold, was still a sensation to be savoured and relished. Angus MacLeod had given him some analgesic for his aches and pains, so they did not interfere with the feeling of well-being which was now being joined by another pleasurable thought; Shona MacLean was just next door.

'Good morning,' said Shona when Bannerman came down to the dining-room for breakfast. She was wearing a tight-fitting navy blue sweater with a white scarf at her throat and a pair of light blue ski pants. They were the only two guests in the hotel and there was a slight chill about the room at this time in the morning. This was partially off-set by the fact that the weather was bright and sunlight was streaming into the room through French windows. 'I didn't think you'd be up for ages yet.'

'Good morning,' said Bannerman, returning the smile and moving slowly across the floor to join her. 'I never could lie in bed.'

'Sore?' Shona asked.

'You name it, it hurts,' replied Bannerman, easing himself painfully down into a chair.

'Are you sure you want to leave today? Maybe you should take it easy. I can get the bus to Inverness.'

Bannerman insisted that he felt well enough. 'There is one problem however,' he added.

'What?'

'My car. I left it up at Inverladdie Farm yesterday. It's still there.'

'I could collect it?' suggested Shona. 'You don't look as if you are in any fit state for a hike.'

'Perish the thought,' said Bannerman, rolling his eyes upwards.

The phone rang in the hall and they heard the landlord answer it. Bannerman heard his name being mentioned so he wasn't surprised when the man came into the room and said, 'That was the police Dr Bannerman. They're bringing your car down from Inverladdie.'

'That's good of them,' said Bannerman. 'We were just discussing how we were going to deal with that problem.'

The landlord moved his head uneasily as if embarrassed and said, 'I think there's some problem, sir.' Without waiting to be quizzed on what he meant he made an excuse to leave the room.

'I wonder what that's all about?' said Bannerman.

Shona shrugged her shoulders.

Bannerman's car was not driven back from Inverladdie; it was delivered on the back of a police car transporter. When Bannerman and Shona went outside to meet it they could see why. The car's tyres had been slashed and the bodywork had been defaced by copious amounts of red and black spray paint. There was a message to be extracted from the mess which Bannerman, by leaning his head this way and that, managed to read out a word at a time. 'Fuck off . . . bastard . . . leave . . . our jobs . . . alone . . .'

Two policemen from an accompanying Panda car came to join Bannerman. 'Sorry about this Doctor,' said one of them. 'If it's any comfort we've got the pair who did it.'

'You have?'

'It's a small place. It didn't take us long to find out who's been buying spray paint recently. They still had it on their hands.'

'Who are they?' asked Bannerman.

'Couple of local lads, Turner and Ferguson. They work at the power station. The story's been going around that you are trying to close it down.'

'I wonder who started that,' said Bannerman, thinking of C. J. Mitchell.

'These two cretins thought they would take matters into their own hands, make their own protest so to speak. I take it you'll be pressing charges?'

'It's not my car,' said Bannerman. 'Ask Hertz.'

'I see, sir, then presumably you won't want it left here.'

Bannerman shook his head, looking at the sorry state of the Sierra. He was wondering how far disgruntled workers would go to see off a threat to their jobs. Was that what was behind the shooting up on the shore yesterday? he wondered. 'I'll call the car company, Officer, and ask them to deal with it.'

'Very good, sir. It'll be in the police station yard at Stobmor.'

Bannerman called the rental company and was pleased to hear that they weren't at all put out by his tale. Would he like them to deliver another car to him from Inverness? Bannerman consulted Shona and they decided that they would travel down to Inverness by bus and pick up the new car there after Shona had completed her business. 'I'll have it waiting,' said the clerk.

'The bus will be here at ten thirty,' volunteered the landlord. 'If you miss that you'll be here another day.'

This was a threat that Bannerman took notice of. He was packed and waiting at the stop with Shona shortly before twenty-five past the hour. Three other people boarded the bus at Achnagelloch bringing the total aboard to eight. Two more were picked up from outlying farms on the twisting roundabout route the bus followed to reach the A838 before heading south.

*   *   *

151

Bannerman collected his new car from the rental company while Shona visited the offices of the people responsible for promoting the craft fair she wanted to participate in. He gave her an hour before driving to the pick up point, where he waited a further fifteen minutes before she appeared.

'How did it go?' he asked.

'Very well I think,' said Shona. 'They'll let me know by the end of the week.'

'Does that mean you won't be coming to Edinburgh?' Bannerman asked.

'Of course I will,' insisted Shona.

'Good,' smiled Bannerman, and he meant it.

They had missed lunch by being on the bus and they had made do with a snack when they finally got to Inverness. Bannerman asked if Shona was hungry or should they make a start and eat on the way south to Edinburgh.

'Let's get started,' said Shona. 'Move over.'

Bannerman relinquished the driving seat to her and settled down to enjoy the journey. He had always preferred being a passenger in a car to driving it. That way he never lost his temper. Thinking about that reminded him that he had forgotten to collect his tape of Gregorian chant from the damaged Sierra in Achnagelloch.

TEN

They stopped at Aviemore to eat and chose a restaurant which appeared inviting by virtue of its orange lighting which suggested warmth. Inside, people in ski-wear were bemoaning the fact that there had been no snow. They were complaining about how much money it was costing them to find alternative things to do.

'Last bloody time,' said one man with a pronounced north of England accent. 'I could have gone to bloody Zermatt for half of what it cost me to visit bonnie bloody Scotland.'

'Maybe it'll snow tomorrow, love,' suggested his wife.

'Piss wi' bloody rain more like,' said her husband.

The general consensus agreed with the husband.

'I've not had a single chance to try out my new skis,' complained another woman clad in what appeared to be a purple-coloured second skin. It clashed violently with her pink lipstick. Sunglasses, perched high up in her hair, seemed as incongruous as sandals in Siberia.

The northern man leaned towards her and said, 'I tell you what, love, if that silly bloody tour guide comes round once more with his silly bloody talk about going for a nice walk in the hills, I'll try out your new skis for you on him . . . sideways.'

The skiers laughed and Bannerman noted that the Dunkirk spirit, so beloved by politicians, was still alive and well.

'Do you ski?' Shona asked.

Bannerman said not. 'You?'

Shona shook her head.

*   *   *

153

Despite the fact that it had rained for most of the way and the wind was forcing high-sided vehicles to double-up on the Forth Road Bridge, Bannerman was sorry that the journey was coming to an end. He and Shona had spoken practically non-stop and he had enjoyed every minute of it. There was something about Shona's philosophy of life which he found intriguing and appealing. On the surface it appeared to be straightforward and uncomplicated – people should do what they want to do. It was only when you considered the difficulties of putting this into practice that the degree of achievement in actually doing it became apparent. As Angus MacLeod had pointed out, people liked to pretend that they were doing things their way, but it was seldom true.

'What are you thinking about?' asked Shona.

'Life,' smiled Bannerman.

'Life is what happens to you while you're thinking about it,' said Shona.

Bannerman turned his head to look at her. She was concentrating on the road ahead but there was no sign of stress or strain on her face, despite the appalling driving conditions. She seemed vibrantly alive and enjoying every minute of it. What was more, she looked beautiful.

'What are you thinking now?'

'I was thinking I would have to phone the Medical Research Council in the morning,' lied Bannerman.

As they cleared the brow of a hill the darkness ahead was suddenly speckled by a carpet of amber lights in the distance, denoting the outskirts of the city. Shona asked, 'Where are you staying?'

'In the Royal Mile but drive to where you want to go and I can drive from there, really. How long are you staying?'

'I'll have a wander round tomorrow and look up some old friends. I'll probably head back the day after tomorrow,' said Shona.

'You're not staying with friends then?' asked Bannerman.

'No.'

Bannerman felt awkward. He said, 'I don't want you to get

154

the wrong idea, but the apartment they've given me has two bedrooms and if you would care to stay there while you're here, you'd be most welcome.'

Shona smiled at Bannerman's awkwardness, thinking it belonged to another generation. Remembering what Bannerman had said to her on North Uist about the neighbours, she said, 'Wouldn't the good people of the university be outraged?'

'Probably,' said Bannerman.

'Then I accept,' said Shona.

'Welcome back Doctor,' said George Stoddart, when he saw Bannerman walk into the common-room at the medical school.

Bannerman collected some coffee from the machine and joined him.

'You have a limp,' said Stoddart.

'I hurt my knee,' said Bannerman.

'I understand that you were instrumental in discovering poor Lawerence's body?'

Bannerman wondered whether or not the MRC had informed Stoddart about the real fate of 'poor Lawrence'. He was relieved to find, as the conversation progressed, that Stoddart was under the impression that Gill's death had been an accident. This was good. Stoddart could contribute nothing useful to the investigation. The less he knew the better.

'Such a promising career,' crooned Stoddart, 'and all sacrificed on the alter of Venus.'

Bannerman looked at Stoddart sideways, wondering if he'd heard right. 'Professor,' he said, 'Lawrence Gill's running off had nothing to do with "Venus". He did not run off to be with another woman as you all thought.'

'Then why?'

'I don't know.'

'Most peculiar,' mumbled Stoddart.

'I don't see Doctor Napier,' said Bannerman looking about him.

'No,' said Stoddart. 'She took the news of Lawrence's death very hard I'm afraid. I suggested she have a couple of days off.'

Damn, thought Bannerman. He had hoped to hear news of the animal experiments from Morag Napier. Now he would have to glean what he could for himself.

Bannerman was surprised to find the door to the animal lab unlocked. He opened it and knocked gently on the glass portion of the half open door; there was no reply, so he went inside. He followed the sound of music coming from one of the back rooms until he found signs of life. The animal technician on duty was not the same girl that he had seen on his last visit with Morag Napier. This was an older woman and she was carrying out a post-mortem examination on a rabbit. The animal was spreadeagled on a wooden board, its limbs secured to nails at the four corners by strong elastic bands. The first incision had been made, opening the animal from neck to crotch and the technician was presently taking samples of lung tissue. Music was coming from a small portable radio propped up on a corner of the table.

Bannerman coughed quietly to attract attention.

The woman dropped the scalpel she had been holding and caught her breath. The instrument bounced off the edge of the table and clattered to the floor. 'God, you gave me a fright,' she exclaimed. 'Who are you?'

'My name's Bannerman. We haven't met.'

'Bannerman?' repeated the woman, the tone of her voice indicating that the name meant nothing to her. Her whole demeanour suggested fear and uncertainty.

Bannerman smiled in an effort to put her at ease. 'From the MRC,' he said. 'I'm working on Dr Gill's project. I'm sorry I startled you.'

The woman relaxed. 'My fault,' she said. 'The door should have been locked but I forgot again. The Prof will have my hide if he finds out; you won't tell him will you?'

Bannerman shook his head. 'No. Why the preoccupation with locked doors?'

'The animal rights people,' replied the woman. 'They've been active around Edinburgh recently.'

Bannerman watched as the woman used lysol to swab the

156

areas of the table and floor that the dropped scalpel had come into contact with. She discarded the used swabs in a sterilizer bin.

'Something nasty?' asked Bannerman, noticing the meticulous care she was taking.

'TB,' replied the woman. 'It's making a come-back in AIDS patients.'

'Why the rabbit?'

'There was some question about this particular patient's strain being bovine or human in origin so we did a guinea pig and rabbit inoculation. If it's bovine it'll infect both, if it's human it'll only go for the guinea pig, but I suppose you knew that?'

'If I ever did, I've long since forgotten,' smiled Bannerman. 'I haven't come across a case of TB in years.'

'Lots of things are making a come-back in AIDS patients,' said the woman. 'People with no immune system are just what a whole lot of bugs have been waiting for.'

'Not a happy thought Miss . . . ?' said Bannerman.

'Cullen, Lorna Cullen. Have a look at the lungs on this animal. They're riddled.'

Bannerman took a closer look and saw the rash of buff coloured nodules over the rabbit's lungs. 'I see what you mean.'

'How can I help you, Doctor?'

'Lawrence Gill inoculated some mice before he disappeared. I just wondered how they were getting on. They were up here if I remember rightly,' said Bannerman, moving to where the relevant mice boxes were on his last visit. He brought down the first one and looked inside. In contrast to the last time when he had seen nothing but healthy animals the two mice inside had lost condition and had little sense of balance or coordination. It was the same story in the other two boxes.

'How are they?' asked Lorna Cullen, continuing with her post-mortem. The words were muffled by her protective mask.

'Sick.'

'What do you want done with them?'

'Nothing. I'm going to check with the Neurobiology Unit first to make sure they are prepared to receive samples, then either myself or Morag Napier will kill the animals and remove their brains.'

'Something nasty?' asked Lorna Cullen, using Bannerman's own expression.

'Very,' replied Bannerman.

Bannerman phoned Morag Napier from upstairs. She sounded very subdued when she answered, saying, 'I didn't realize you were back.'

'Last night,' said Bannerman. 'I'm sorry about Gill.'

'He was a nice man,' said Morag.

'I've just been down to the animal lab,' said Bannerman. 'The mice that Gill inoculated are looking very sick. I think they should be killed soon and brain samples sent to Hector Munro's lab.'

'Did you find out anything about the deaths while you were up north?' asked Morag.

'Very little, but I think the mice results will tell us for sure. I'm going to kill them tomorrow.'

'Would you like me to do it?' asked Morag.

'Are you coming back soon?' asked Bannerman.

'I'll be in tomorrow,' said Morag.

'Why don't we both do it. We'll be able to get the samples to Munro's lab by lunch-time and I thought we could make a few microscope preps for ourselves? If we see evidence of degenerative disease we'll *virtually* have the answer. Munro's people can fill in the technical details about incubation times and infectivity titres later.'

'Very good,' said Morag. 'See you tomorrow.'

Bannerman called Milne at the Medical Research Council to say that he was back in Edinburgh and to give a progress report.

After initial pleasantries Milne asked Bannerman how the investigation was going.

'Before he died Lawrence Gill inoculated some experimental mice with brain material taken from the three men who died. I'm going to kill them tomorrow, if they're not already dead, and give the brains to Hector Munro for full *Scrapie* testing. That should prove beyond all doubt whether or not the men died of *Scrapie* and we can get started on characterizing the agent fully. The circumstantial evidence that *Scrapie* was involved is already overwhelming.'

'Is there anything we can do at our end?'

'You can arrange for radioactivity monitoring along the foreshore of Inverladdie Farm. I tried to do it myself but I ran into some opposition.'

'Opposition?'

'I was seen as a threat to jobs in the area.'

'No violence I hope?'

'A little,' said Bannerman. 'My car was vandalized and somebody took pot shots at me on the beach.'

'Good God, Bannerman. You've had an exciting time.'

'I managed to monitor the boundary ground between Inverladdie and the nuclear station and it was clear, but there is a chance that contamination came in from the sea further along the shore. If so, that might have caused the sheep virus to mutate.'

'There has been no further incidence of brain disease in the area I take it?'

'None,' agreed Bannerman.

'So there's a chance that this may have been a single isolated incident which may never happen again,' said Milne.

'It's possible,' agreed Bannerman, thinking that it was also possible that the new virus had already been spread to every corner of the country and was waiting to infect new flocks before slipping through the food chain to the Sunday lunch tables of the land. He had a mental picture of a crow on the wing, its beak dripping with blood from the sheep carcass it had just gorged itself on.

'I'll ask Allison to brief the Health and Safety Executive. They'll carry out a full inspection,' said Milne.

'What about Gill's death?' asked Bannerman.

'Not much to report I'm afraid. I understand from Allison that the only lead they have is a description of the man who called at the post office in Cairnish pretending he was Gill, and it wasn't particularly helpful.'

'Not a one-legged Chinaman with a scar?' said Bannerman.

'Afraid not. Quite tall, medium build, fairish, good-looking, and the post mistress thought he had some kind of an accent but she couldn't place it.'

'As you say, not much to to on,' agreed Bannerman.

'What are your plans after tomorrow?' asked Milne.

'Once I've got the brain samples off to Munro and done the microscopy I'll return to London and get back to work at the hospital while we wait for the results.'

'We're very grateful to you Doctor,' said Milne.

'What is Mr Allison saying to all this?' asked Bannerman.

'I think the official line is to treat this whole affair as an isolated incident.'

'It's a bit early to conclude that,' said Bannerman. 'And if it should turn out that the men died of *Scrapie*, we will have to face up to the fact that the disease can pass to man.'

'Mr Allison and his colleagues are taking the view that if a *mutated Scrapie* virus is to blame then it is no longer a *Scrapie* virus.'

'That is outrageous!' said Bannerman.

'I think we must be positive Doctor, not alarmist. You said yourself that *Scrapie* has been around for a long time. If it had caused trouble before we would have been aware of it.'

'Not necessarily,' argued Bannerman. 'The reason you were carrying out the brain disease survey in the first place was because we have no real idea of its incidence in the population. A few deaths here and there don't get noticed. It's only when you know what you are looking for that things become clear.'

'I don't think we can realistically destroy our farming industry on the basis of a few unclassified deaths here and there which may or may not have been due to infected animals. Do you?' asked Milne.

'I don't think we should cover it up either,' said Bannerman.

Milne said, 'Mr Allison has assured me that generous government funds will be made immediately available to investigate brain disease in the population.'

'Right after you tell them what they want to hear,' mumbled Bannerman under his breath.

'Pardon? I didn't quite catch that,' said Milne.

'It wasn't important,' said Bannerman with resignation.

'Perhaps you would like to apply for an MRC project grant for your own department to carry out some of the work?' said Milne.

Bannerman closed his eyes and kept rein on his tongue.

'Perhaps,' he said and put down the phone.

Bannerman was still in a bad mood when Shona arrived back at the apartment early evening.

'Bad day?' she asked, noticing Bannerman's preoccupation.

'You could say that,' he smiled. 'How about you?'

'Oh, so-so,' said Shona. 'I seem to have spent most of my day listening to former friends speak of nothing but babies and mortgages and what Roger or Harry likes for his tea. They used to be interesting people!' complained Shona. 'Whatever happened to them?'

'The Age fairy,' said Bannerman.

'The what?'

'I have a theory. One night we go to bed and the Age Fairy comes and taps us on the shoulder. When we wake up we're old and boring.'

Shona smiled and asked, 'At what age does this Age fairy come to call?'

'No set age,' replied Bannerman. 'It can happen to some people when they're in their twenties or in some cases not even by their sixties.'

'Dare I ask . . . ?'

'I woke up one night and saw it there,' said Bannerman. 'It scared me.'

'But it didn't touch you. I can tell,' said Shona.

'I'm not so sure,' said Bannerman.

'What made your day so bad?' asked Shona.

'Dealing with the establishment.'

'What do you mean, "the establishment"?' asked Shona.

'People with power. The people who run things in this country. Sometimes their behaviour is little short of downright dishonest.'

161

'Never,' said Shona sarcastically.

Bannerman looked at her and said, 'Oh I know it's popular to suggest that everyone in power is corrupt and self-seeking but I never really believed it. A few maybe, but I thought that basically, truth, honesty and integrity prevailed and operated in our best interests.'

'And now you don't?'

'It's what they *perceive* to be in our best interests that worries me,' said Bannerman.

'Such disillusionment calls for large quantities of medicinal alcohol,' said Shona. 'It's my last night. Let me buy you a drink?'

'No, no,' protested Bannerman. 'I'm indebted to you for driving me down here. I don't think I could have made it otherwise. I insist on taking you out to dinner, unless you've made other arrangements?'

Shona smiled and said, 'No, no other arrangements.'

Shona and Bannerman were on the verge of leaving the apartment; Bannerman was checking his pocket for the keys, when the doorbell rang. 'Who on earth . . .' he muttered, pulling open the door. Lawrence Gill's wife was standing there.

'The department gave me your address; I hope you don't mind, I understand you were the one who found Lawrence's body?'

'Er, yes, that's so Mrs Gill and I'm very sorry, you have my deepest sympathy. I was actually going to come and see you before I left . . .'

Vera Gill was obviously waiting to be asked inside and Bannerman was acutely aware that Shona was standing just to the left of the door in the hallway. He felt embarrassed. 'I was just on the point of going out,' he said, uncomfortably aware of how callous he must appear.

'I just wanted to know something about the place where he died,' said Vera Gill. 'I know it must sound silly but I'd like you to describe it to me, so I could picture it in my mind.'

'Hello Vera,' said Shona quietly coming out from behind Bannerman.

'You!' exclaimed Vera Gill, her eyes filling with suspicion. 'What the . . . Oh I see, you've lost Lawrence, you're after him now!'

'Nothing like that,' said Shona, with what Bannerman thought was admirable calmness. 'It's true I was once in love with your husband and I did have an affair with him, but that was many years ago. Lawrence did not run away to be with me. He didn't leave you Vera; he loved you; that's why he broke it off with me.'

Vera Gill stared wild-eyed at Shona and said, 'Lying bitch! He was overheard on the phone making arrangements to come to you just before he disappeared!'

Bannerman tensed himself, preparing to intervene between the two women should it become necessary.

'He did phone,' said Shona, 'and he did come to the island, but it was because he wanted a place to hide! Lawrence didn't leave you Vera. He ran away because he was frightened. He was in great danger.'

'Frightened? Danger?' scoffed Vera Gill. 'What rubbish!'

'It's true,' said Bannerman. 'Your husband thought someone was trying to kill him.'

Vera Gill's initial anger subsided and was replaced by confusion. 'I don't understand,' she said. 'Lawrence was a doctor, why would anyone want to kill him?'

'You had better come in Mrs Gill,' said Bannerman, putting an arm round Vera Gill's shoulders and guiding her gently inside. Shona went to the kitchen to make tea.

'When your husband disappeared, Mrs Gill, he was looking into the deaths of three farm workers. We think that he found out something about their deaths that someone else was prepared to kill to keep secret. Somehow Lawrence knew that his life was in danger, so he contacted Shona and asked for her help in providing him with a place to hide out for a while.'

Vera Gill took a moment or two to digest what she'd heard and to consider the implications. Making an obvious effort to control her emotions, she said, 'Are you saying that my husband's death was not an accident?'

'Lawrence fell to his death from the cliffs on Barasay Mrs

Gill. That's what we know for sure, but we have reason to think that he may have been pushed. We have no proof of this but the authorities are aware of our suspicions and will investigate.'

Shona came back into the room carrying tea on a tray. Vera Gill accepted a cup with a look that signalled peace between the two women. She sipped it slowly and deliberately, her eyes betraying that her mind was still reeling. 'I don't know whether to laugh or cry,' she said, half apologetically. 'Lawrence didn't leave me after all.'

'No he didn't,' said Shona.

'Who told you about your husband's call to Shona?' asked Bannerman.

'Morag Napier.'

Bannerman nodded.

By the time she had finished her tea Vera Gill had regained her composure and was ready to leave. She thanked Bannerman and Shona and even shook hands with them both, although she diverted her eyes when taking Shona's hand.

Shona let out a long sigh when Bannerman returned from seeing Vera Gill to the door. 'I didn't reckon on that,' she said.

'Me neither,' agreed Bannerman. 'I thought you said that it was you who broke up the affair with Gill?'

'It was,' said Shona.

'You're a nice person.'

'Can we eat?'

The confrontation with Vera Gill put a bit of a damper on the evening for Bannerman and Shona. Up until Vera's arrival it had seemed that the pair of them might be able to forget the deaths for a while to relax and enjoy each other's company, but now the subject of Gill's death and those of the men of Inverladdie was again uppermost in their minds.

'Have you still no idea at all why Lawrence was murdered?' asked Shona.

'I've thought about it a lot,' said Bannerman. 'But I end up going round in the same circles. Gill was desperate to send off the package which we presume contained the missing, infected brains. From what he told you, he thought he would be safe as soon as that happened. That must mean that whoever received the package would know all there was to know about the deaths. It was addressed to the MRC, so presumably he meant the MRC to analyse them. But he'd already sent samples of the brains to the MRC! And they had already been analysed! We knew about the *Scrapie* involvement!'

'And he knew that you knew,' added Shona.

'Exactly,' said Bannerman.

'So there must have been something else in the brains that wouldn't have appeared on the slides,' suggested Shona. 'Something else that he wanted you to know about.'

'Like what?' said Bannerman slowly. He was addressing the question to himself.

'If radiation had caused the virus to change, would that show up in the brain samples?' asked Shona.

'No,' replied Bannerman, shaking his head. 'No it wouldn't.' Did that mean that any connection between the nuclear industry and Gill's death could be discounted? he wondered.

'So the people at the power station would have nothing to gain by stopping any further analysis on the brains?' said Shona as if she had read Bannerman's mind.

'Agreed,' said Bannerman.

'I think you're up against something much bigger than a few bully-boy workers afraid for their jobs,' said Shona.

Bannerman who suddenly felt afraid said, 'I think you're right.'

Shona put her hand on top of Bannerman's and said, 'It'll be out of your hands after tomorrow. You can go back to your hospital and this will all be just a bad dream.'

Bannerman looked at her and gave a little nod. 'It's not all been such a bad dream,' he said. 'Some of it has been very nice.' He took Shona's hand and held it to his lips.

'Come on,' said Shona softly, 'Drink up, let's go home.'

* * *

165

In the morning Bannerman drove Shona to the station where she would catch the train to Inverness, on the first leg of her journey home. He found himself very reluctant to say goodbye and insisted on seeing her on to the platform where they stopped by an open carriage door.

'I can't thank you enough for driving me down,' said Bannerman.

'It was nothing,' said Shona. 'It's been ages since I've been in Edinburgh and it was nice to see how my friends were getting on.'

'I've enjoyed being with you,' said Bannerman, his eyes saying more than the awkward words.

'I've enjoyed it too,' said Shona. 'I wish you luck.'

'You too,' said Bannerman. 'Safe journey.'

Shona climbed on board as the guard blew his whistle and doors began to slam along the line. 'Keep in touch. Let me know what happens.'

'I will,' said Bannerman. He waved as the train slid away from the platform and waited until it was out of sight. Feeling strangely vulnerable, he turned and walked to his car. The last time he had felt like this was, he recalled, when he had been fourteen years old and a holiday romance in the Lake District had come to an end.

As he walked up the hill out of the station he felt full of impotent anger; it was directed at himself. Why hadn't he said what he felt to Shona instead of coming out with guarded little phrases that were designed not to leave him exposed. Fear of rejection? Reluctance to make a fool of himself? He had wanted to tell Shona that for whatever reason – and he didn't understand it himself – he felt hopelessly attracted to her and wanted to see her again. But he couldn't do that could he? That would be totally out of keeping with his job, his circumstances and his age.

Bannerman got into the car and drove away without looking behind him. A red saloon announced its presence with a long blast on its horn. 'Shit!' said Bannerman, thumping down on both feet on brake and clutch and getting an agonizing reminder from his left knee that it would rather he didn't do that too often.

He raised his hand in apology to the driver of the red car and shrugged off the tirade of abuse he saw being mouthed.

As he neared the medical school, the traffic came to a halt in a long queue. The road up ahead for some reason had been reduced to a single carriageway and police were controlling the traffic flow. After a wait of three or four minutes the line started to move and Bannerman could see that several fire engines and police cars were parked outside the medical school quadrangle. Hoses snaked across the ground and firemen in yellow waterproof trousers were reeling them in. He signalled his intention to turn into the car-park but a policeman waved him past. He had to park nearly a quarter of a mile away and walk back.

Bannerman showed his ID to the policeman at the entrance who requested it. 'What happened?' he asked.

'Nasty fire, sir,' replied the officer. 'Bloody lunatics.' The policeman moved away to stop a car that looked as if it might be turning into the quadrangle.

Bannerman made his way through the clutter and found Stoddart talking to two men in plain clothes. They were taking notes and Bannerman could not make up his mind whether they were police or press. He saw Morag Napier nearby and went over to ask her about the drama.

'The Animal Rights People had a go at us last night,' said Morag.

'Good God, is there much damage?'

'The animal lab was completely gutted and the whole bottom floor is awash with water.'

'The animal lab?' repeated Bannerman. 'You mean the animals were . . .'

'Wiped out,' said Morag.

'Gill's mice?' asked Bannerman.

'Incinerated.'

Bannerman was devastated. 'I thought these damned people cared about animals!' he exclaimed.

'Care?' exclaimed Stoddart, who had come across to join them. 'They're just a bunch of terrorists. They don't care about anything!'

167

'Apparently they gained access to the building through the animal house because the door had been left unlocked,' said Morag. 'They couldn't get any further however, because the connecting door to the main building had been locked, so they tried to burn the place down by setting fire to the animal lab.'

The last of the firemen left the building and the quadrangle began to clear, leaving Bannerman feeling utterly dejected. His last chance of proving the relationship between *Scrapie* and the men's deaths in Achnagelloch had gone. He walked slowly round to the entrance to the animal lab and saw the blackened wall outside. There was broken glass underfoot and several slogans proclaiming the innocence of animals, and the evils of science had been daubed along the wall adjoining.

Although everything inside was dripping wet and there was at least two inches of water on the floor, the air smelled strongly of burning flesh. It grew stronger as Bannerman picked his way among the blackened cages with unrecognizable messes inside. The inner portion of the lab had been roped off because the ceiling above it had collapsed and there was a danger of further falls. Bannerman could see up into the room above where books and papers had fallen through the hole into puddles on the floor. Shafts of sunlight came in through the windows highlighting dust particles from the debris. There was an eerie silence about the place; it was how he imagined a battlefield might be when the fighting had stopped and the living had gone home. The land had been left to the dead.

ELEVEN

The clean-up operation was beginning in the building as Bannerman went upstairs to his room. It had been untouched by the fire; only the smell of burning told the tale. He called Milne at the MRC and told him what had happened.

'Damned people,' said Milne. 'As if we didn't have enough to contend with, we get a bunch of lunatics running around with fire bombs.'

'Unless the missing human brain material turns up the mice were our last chance of getting to grips with the infective agent,' said Bannerman.

'What do you think the chances are of recovering that material?' asked Milne.

'Practically nil,' replied Bannerman. 'I suspect it was all destroyed in order to stop any investigation of it.'

Milne sighed and said, 'Then I suppose we will just have to resign ourselves to the fact that we will never know for sure what caused the deaths in Achnagelloch.'

Bannerman could not help but feel that an awful lot of people might be quite happy with that state of affairs; the government, the nuclear lobby and maybe even Milne himself. It was never easy to tell people what they didn't want to hear, especially if they happened to control your purse strings. The Medical Rsearch Council were autonomous but they were funded from central government.

'Will you return to London today?' asked Milne.

'Tomorrow,' replied Bannerman.

*   *   *

Bannerman thought it right that he should lend a hand with the clean-up in the rooms affected by the fire. Many of the labs contained dangerous chemicals as well as stocks of bacteria and viruses which demanded skilled handling. Portering and domestic staff would work on the corridors and common-rooms. He put on protective clothing, borrowed from the post-mortem rooms, and asked Morag Napier where he could be most useful.

Morag looked at him as if she hadn't heard and he repeated his question.

'Sorry, I was thinking about something,' she said. 'The tissue culture suite is in a bit of a mess. Perhaps you'd care to salvage what you can?'

Bannerman said that he would do what he could.

A junior technician interrupted to ask Morag something and she almost snapped the girl's head off, then looked embarrassed when she realized that Bannerman had witnessed her behaviour. She made some excuse for leaving and walked quickly away.

'Doctor Napier is upset,' said Bannerman to the technician. 'Perhaps you could give me a hand in the tissue culture suite?'

With the mess cleared up from the tissue culture room floor and having thoroughly disinfected it, Bannerman and the technician set about salvaging what glassware they could and packed it into bins for washing and re-sterilizing. When they had filled the last of the bins Bannerman suggested, 'Why don't you go have a cup of tea?' The girl readily agreed.

Bannerman closed the door behind him and started walking along the corridor. Half way along he paused when he thought he heard the sound of a woman crying. There was no mistake. He looked into the room the sound was coming from, half expecting it to be Morag Napier because of her earlier nervous state, and found someone else. It was Lorna Cullen, the animal technician he had met yesterday.

Bannerman felt awkward. It wasn't a situation he felt comfortable dealing with but there was no one else around he could call on. He approached the woman and sat down beside her. 'It can't be that bad,' he said gently.

The woman looked up at him and said bitterly, 'Tell me about it. I've just been fired.'

'Why?'

'The professor blames me for all this.'

'What?'

'He says I left the door to the animal lab unlocked and that's how the terrorists got in.'

'Oh,' said Bannerman, remembering that the door had been unlocked yesterday.

'But I didn't!' protested the technician. 'That's what's so unfair!'

'But can you be sure?' asked Bannerman gently.

'Yes damn it! I can! You gave me such a fright yesterday when you walked in on me that it was fresh in my mind. I made very sure I locked the door when I left. I even remember trying the door after I had locked it to make certain.'

'I see,' said Bannerman. 'So how did they get in?'

The woman looked at him again, her face showing that she knew she would not be believed when she said, 'They must have used a key.'

Bannerman's face betrayed the fact that he found this unlikely and the woman conceded it herself. 'But that's the only explanation,' she said, wringing her hands helplessly. 'They must have. I locked the door. I know I did.'

'Do you live far from here?' asked Bannerman.

'Leith.'

'That's down by the sea isn't it?'

The woman nodded.

'Do you have a car?'

The woman shook her head.

'Get your coat. I'll take you home.'

Still holding her handkerchief to her face, Lorna Cullen went off to fetch her coat while Bannerman sought out Morag Napier and told her what he was going to do.

'Why?'

'Stoddart fired her.'

Bannerman walked off leaving Morag Napier staring after him, wide-eyed but silent.

By seven in the evening Bannerman had packed up all his belongings and was ready to return to London the next morning. He had taken the car back to the rental company, cleared his desk in the medical school and had thanked Stoddart for his hospitality. He couldn't find Morag Napier to say goodbye to her but had asked Stoddart to do it for him and to thank her for her help. He had tried to put in a good word for Lorna Cullen but Stoddart was unwilling to move on the subject. 'The damned woman was always leaving the place open,' he maintained.

Bannerman stood quietly at the window looking out over the lights of the city and noting for once that the wind had dropped. The dark silhouettes of the trees in Princes Street Gardens were motionless. The stars had come out in a clear sky and there was a suggestion of moonlight behind the castle rock. He wished that he could have felt better about his trip, but the truth was that he felt thoroughly dejected. His investigation had been thwarted at every turn, leaving him feeling empty and frustrated. There was only one thing he wanted to do now, and that was get drunk.

He was about to leave when the telephone rang. Fearing that it might be George Stoddart asking him to dinner, Bannerman prepared his excuse for not going and picked up the receiver. It was Shona MacLean.

'Hello, Ian. I'm back home on the island.'

'Oh God it's so good to hear your voice,' he blurted out.

'I'm glad you said that,' said Shona, 'because I don't have a good reason for calling. I just wanted to hear *your* voice.'

'That's good enough,' said Bannerman quickly, knowing that if he slowed down his response he would start considering his replies and editing them. If he answered quickly there was a chance that the truth might get out. 'There was so much I wanted to say this morning and didn't. I've got to see you again.'

'But how?'

'I don't know how,' said Bannerman. 'Just tell me that you want to see me?'

'Yes,' said Shona. 'I want that.'

'Then we'll work something out,' said Bannerman.

'I'm so glad I phoned,' said Shona.

'You're glad?' laughed Bannerman.

'Did you get your experiments finished today?' asked Shona.

Bannerman told her about the fire.

'That's awful!' exclaimed Shona. 'You won't be able to prove that *Scrapie* was to blame.'

'No,' agreed Bannerman. 'It's all been one big waste of time.'

'Maybe you should get drunk,' said Shona.

'That's exactly what I intend doing,' said Bannerman. 'You caught me just as I was about to leave.'

'Then I won't hold you back any more,' said Shona. 'Call me tomorrow?'

'You bet.'

After a couple of drinks Bannerman's euphoria over Shona's call and his relief at his honesty in telling her how he felt, began to subside. He had no doubts about his feelings for Shona but he began to see some of the problems he was creating. How could he hope to carry on a relationship with Shona when he worked in London and she lived on a remote island? One of them would have to move and he could imagine Shona's thoughts about a move to London. Bannerman's head started to protest under the relentless assault of his own questions. He dealt with them, temporarily, with a third drink and then decided to find something to eat.

There was a Greek restaurant not too far from the last pub he had been in, so he opted for that. He ordered a traditional dish and asked for a carafe of the house red. When it came, the wine wasn't good, but it didn't matter so long as it continued to dull the cutting edge of reality. He sipped it slowly while waiting for his food and amused himself by looking at the obligatory travel posters of Greece on the walls.

They'd make it seem a lot more like Greece if they'd heat the bloody place properly, he thought as the door opened and another blast of cold air swept in. He looked round at the new arrivals and was surprised to see Morag Napier standing there. She was with a man who Bannerman deduced must be her fiancé. He got a brief glimpse of a handsome man in his twenties before Morag walked over to his table and said, 'Dr Bannerman, what a surprise. I didn't think I'd get a chance to say goodbye. Professor Stoddart said that you'd left already.'

'I'm going back to London in the morning,' said Bannerman, hoping he wasn't slurring his words. 'Perhaps you and your young man would care to join me?'

'That's very kind but we just popped in on our way past to book a table for tomorrow,' said Morag. 'We're on our way out.'

'Well thank you for all your help, Dr Napier,' said Bannerman, making to get to his feet.

'Please don't get up Doctor,' insisted Morag. 'And *bon voyage.*'

'Thank you,' said Bannerman, watching her walk back over to her fiancé and take him by the arm to turn him round and usher him out of the door. A waiter was left looking bemused as the door closed behind the couple.

It was obvious to Bannerman that the story about them having come in to book a table had been a lie. Morag Napier had not wanted to stay in the restaurant when she had found out that he was there. Was he really that drunk? he wondered.

Bannerman finished his meal and left. Despite the fact that he had drunk a fair bit over the course of the evening he felt stone cold sober, yet had no desire to drink any more. That was the trouble with alcohol, he mused, it only exaggerated the mood you're in, and he was feeling low.

The temperature had fallen because of the clearness of the sky and there was a suggestion of frost in the air. He decided to walk for a bit before returning to the apartment. This would be his last chance to look at the city by night, unless he came back here at some time in the future. He walked to the head of the Mound, once literally a mound of earth that had been piled up to connect the old town of Edinburgh, high up on the back of the castle rock, to the Georgian new town lying below. Traffic formed strings of light on the steep hill.

Bannerman rested his hands on the railings near the top and looked at the lights spread out below. It was a beautiful city, he thought; when the weather allowed you to love it, when the wind dropped and allowed you to hear its heart beat. He could smell the earth in the gardens, feel the silence, sense the sharpness of the frost. A boy and girl were walking slowly up the hill with their arms wound round each other, totally absorbed in each other's company. They wore heavy coats and university scarves. A nice city to fall in love in, thought Bannerman. He pulled up his collar and silently wished them well. He walked slowly back to his apartment.

The phone was ringing inside but by the time he had unlocked the door and switched on the light it had stopped. Something else to wonder about, he thought, but it would have to take its place in the queue. At the moment it was well down the list of questions that kept niggling away at him. The question of why Morag Napier had been so anxious to get out of the restaurant earlier was near the top, but at the very top was the fact that the animal rights people had succeeded in murdering all the animals in their attack on the department.

There was a contradiction in that which worried Bannerman because it could not be argued that the animal deaths had been accidental. The terrorists had entered the building through the animal house itself so they had had every opportunity to release the animals before setting fire to the place . . . but they hadn't.

It was just conceivable that there had been an element of social responsibility in this. The terrorists just might have been bright enough to acknowledge that releasing experimental animals into the wild was an act fraught with danger. The animals might be carrying all kinds of diseases which they would spread into the community. On the other hand and despite frequent warnings, the animal liberation people had not taken much notice of this in the past.

The electric kettle came to the boil and Bannerman went into the kitchen to make coffee. He spooned coffee grounds into the cafetiere while he faced the fact that paranoia might be playing a part in his thoughts. It seemed such a cruel quirk of fate for a fire to destroy all Gill's experimental animals and with them, the Achnagelloch disease. Almost too cruel to be true.

Despite acknowledging this feeling, Bannerman was left with one simple but unanswered question: could such dedicated animal lovers, as the rights people claimed to be, have calmly set fire to a room full of animals and burned them alive? And if he thought that question was difficult, it was nothing to the can of worms he would open if the answer should turn out to be, 'No'.

'Shit!' he said out loud, as he put his head back on the couch and stared up at the ceiling, searching for inspiration. In his heart of hearts he knew that he wasn't angry with himself because he couldn't think of answers. He was angry because he could. It was facing up to them that was difficult! His mind baulked at the evil it was being invited to consider. But one subversive corner kept urging him on to do just that.

It said, Maybe the attack on the department had not been carried out by the animal liberation people at all? Maybe it had not even been an attack on the department! Maybe it had been a deliberate attack on the animal lab in order to destroy Gill's experimental animals and, with them, evidence of the new disease! According to his thinking, Gill had been murdered not only to stop him talking but to stop the authorities getting their hands on infected brain material. Perhaps the same motive had been behind the fire?

The water Bannerman was wading into was getting perilously deep and cold but there was no going back. Once again he asked himself who had the most to lose by having the true nature of the brain disease in Achnagelloch revealed? His experience at the nuclear power station had left him with little love for the place, but he simply could not bring himself to believe that the management and workers could be involved in a conspiracy involving arson and murder. But if they weren't, who was? Maybe he had been too localized in his thinking? True, the nuclear industry would take a bit of a bashing if it turned out that leaks from one of their stations had been responsible for the deaths in Achnagelloch. But wouldn't even larger bodies like the agricultural industry and perhaps the government itself, have even more to lose if it were revealed that animal brain diseases could spread to man! The thought did little to put Bannerman at his ease.

Bannerman arrived back in London on the following evening after spending the morning doing some last minute shopping in Edinburgh. He did not call anyone when he got back, not even Stella. The flat seemed strange and unwelcoming and his efforts at making it cosier through warmth and lighting only suceeded in making it seem claustrophobic. He tried going to bed early but that proved to be a mistake. He tossed and turned, switched the light on and off, picked up and laid down a book so many times he lost count.

He finally got up and rummaged through the bathroom cabinet for some chemical assistance. He didn't have any sleeping tablets but he did find a bottle of antihistamines. On their own they would have a very moderate sedative effect, but when taken in conjunction with a large gin a couple of tablets would let him sleep right through. He watched a little television while he drank the gin and then when he felt the windmills of his mind begin to slow, he turned off the set and went to bed.

Olive Meldrum broke into a broad smile when she saw Bannerman come through the door, collar up, briefcase in hand.

'I hope you didn't forget my haggis,' she said.

Bannerman put down a plastic bag on her desk and announced, 'One haggis, and may God have mercy on your digestion.'

'You remembered!' exclaimed Olive.

Bannerman smiled.

'It's nice to have you back,' said Olive.

177

'Nice to be back,' said Bannerman, but it wasn't how he felt. He said hello to everyone in the lab then made for the sanctuary of his office where he could let the mask slip. Olive brought in coffee then left him to read through a small mountain of mail. He managed to sort it first without opening anything. All obvious advertising literature went straight into the bucket *virgo intacta*. That left university and medical school material, which he felt obliged to read, and some letters which gave no outward clue as to their source. None proved to be interesting.

Bannerman ploughed through the university mail with a heavy heart and growing impatience. How could so many people spend so much time on so little? he wondered, as he had so often in the past. He reminded himself that if anyone could, academics could. They seemed to be blessed with an innate capacity to say absolutely nothing, at enormous length. 'Three pages!' he muttered angrily, 'three bloody pages on car-parking at the hospital.' And what was the bottom line? There wasn't one as far as he could discern, but that was par for the course. Actual conclusions were a grey area in academia; academics were happier with a range of possibilities. And decisions? Perish that fascist thought.

Bannerman screwed the missive into a ball and chucked it across the room just as Olive came in. He had to smile sheepishly in apology.

'Already?' she said. 'Your holiday hasn't done you much good.'

'It was no holiday,' said Bannerman, with a hint of bitterness. 'Would you get me the MRC please Olive.'

'Milne.'

'It's Ian Bannerman. I'm back at St Luke's.'

'Glad you made it back safely Doctor. What can I do for you?'

'I requested that the shore at Inverladdie Farm be monitored for signs of radioactivity?'

'Ah yes,' replied Milne, with what Bannerman thought was a hint of embarrassment. 'We did ask the Health and Safety Executive to do this . . .'

'And did they?' asked Bannerman.

'They did, and they found nothing.'

'Nothing,' repeated Bannerman, feeling that there was more to come.

'But . . . they did report that the area had been cleaned.'

'Cleaned?'

'Sprayed with detergent, recently.'

'Damnation,' said Bannerman. 'There was no trace of detergent when I was there. They must have treated the area after I left.'

'Unfortunately, there is no law against it,' said Milne cautiously, as if fearing Bannerman's response.

'So they get away with it!'

'I'm afraid so. There is no evidence that the shore was ever contaminated. I think we have to be philosophical about it Doctor.'

'Quite,' said Bannerman, and put down the phone. It rang again almost immediately. Bannerman snatched it and snapped, 'Yes?'

'Well hello to you too,' said Stella.

'Sorry Stella,' said Bannerman, 'I'm a bit . . .'

'I can tell you're a bit . . . ,' said Stella. 'I phoned to see if we could have lunch. I'm not in theatre this afternoon.'

'I see,' said Bannerman. He hesitated for a moment trying to assemble his thoughts into some kind of order, but failed. His mind was a maelstrom.

'Of course, if you're too busy . . .'

'No, no, I'm just a bit upset that's all. Lunch will be fine. I'll see you in the car-park at one?'

'Look forward to it,' said Stella and the line went dead.

Bannerman replaced the receiver slowly and tried to put thoughts of Achnagelloch out of his mind. He wondered what Stella would have to say about Shona when he told her. Would she be happy for him? Or would she see it as an opportunity for sophisticated sarcasm? He lit a cigarette and massaged his forehead with the tips of his fingers. He opened his desk drawer to see if that was where the cleaner had hidden the ash tray and his eyes alighted on three microscope slides propped up in the slide rack in the corner. They were the slides sent to the MRC by Lawrence Gill and forwarded by the MRC, to him, for his opinion. The slides that had started the whole furore. He hadn't returned them to the MRC. He decided to have another look and took them over to his microscope.

He focused on the first slide with a low power objective then swung the high power oil immersion lens into play. If anything it was even clearer than he had remembered it. A perfect illustration of the havoc wreaked on the human brain by Creutzfeld Jakob Disease. He read the little label on the end of the slide and saw that it had written on it in pencil, G. Buchan.

This information had been irrelevant the first time but now it meant something – as did the initials, MN on each of the slides. Morag Napier had prepared them. This section had been made from Gordon Buchan's brain. Buchan had been the married sheep worker. He remembered seeing the cottage on Inverladdie where he and his wife May had lived. He wondered if May Buchan had come back from holiday yet and whether or not she was living with her parents in Stobmor as Sproat suggested she would. He scanned the brain section, looking at the cells which had once made the decisions in Gordon Buchan's life.

A knock came to the door and Bannerman said, 'Come in,' without turning round.

'Nice to see you back,' said Charlie Simmons' voice.

'Hello Charlie, how are things?' asked Bannerman, still without turning round.

'No real problems. We had a bit of trouble with the freezing microtome but it's been sorted out.'

'What sort of trouble?'

'It was cutting tissue sections too thick. It's getting old. Maybe you could think about requesting a new one, or putting in a grant request to somebody?'

'I'll try Charlie,' said Bannerman. He knew that hospital equipment funds had been used up for the current financial year and any request would just go into the queue for next year beginning in April. A grant request was a possibility however.

Milne at the MRC had dangled that particular carrot before him, for whatever reason.

'Are you taking back control of the lab immediately?' asked Charlie.

Bannerman shook his head and said, 'No, I'll wait until Monday. I'll ease myself back in gently.'

'Karen's leaving,' said Charlie.

'Why?'

'She been offered a job in one of the private hospitals.'

'More money?'

'More money,' agreed Charlie.

'The hospital board will probably freeze the post,' said Bannerman.

'I was afraid of that,' said Charlie, 'but we'll manage. We always do.'

'I'll press for a replacement as hard as I can,' said Bannerman.

Charlie Simmons nodded and asked, 'Anything interesting?' He nodded in the direction of the microscope.

Bannerman got up and said, 'Take a look. Tell me what you see.'

Simmons adjusted the width of the eye-pieces and started to examine the slide. A few moments passed in silence then he said, 'Extensive spongioform vacuolation . . . senile decay . . . and fibrils which I think might be SA fibrils . . . I'd go for Creutzfeld Jakob.'

'Me too. This is the reason I went north. The slide was made from the brain of a thirty-year-old who died after a three week illness.'

'You're kidding.'

'That's what I said when they first told me,' said Bannerman. 'In fact I still can't get over it. That's why I'm looking again.'

'I'm glad it's not April the first,' said Charlie. 'I'd never have believed you. I would have said someone had switched the slides.'

Bannerman put down his knife and fork; everything tasted like cardboard and the restaurant was unpleasantly crowded.

'Not hungry?' asked Stella who seemed not to notice.

It told Bannerman that there was nothing wrong with the food or the restaurant. It was the way he was feeling. 'Not really,' he replied.

'You shouldn't let it get to you like this,' said Stella. 'You did your best to get evidence. The main thing is that this mutant virus or whatever it was is now dead and gone.'

'Like Lawrence Gill and the three men in Achnagelloch,' said Bannerman.

'From what you've told me, Gill could conceivably have slipped to his death. You don't know for sure that he was murdered. As for the three sheep workers, they were in the wrong place at the wrong time. It could happen to any of us.'

'But the missing brain samples, the fire at the medical school – doesn't that tell you something?' asked Bannerman.

'I agree that some skulduggery appears to have been going on but the fire could have been coincidence. Couldn't it?'

'I don't believe it,' replied Bannerman.

'Maybe you don't want to believe it,' said Stella.

'It's not that simple,' said Bannerman. 'I didn't imagine being assaulted. I didn't imagine being shot at. The fairies didn't slash the tyres on my car,' protested Bannerman.

'You said yourself that there was local feeling against you because of job fears,' said Stella.

'The local yobs wouldn't have mounted a clean-up operation on the beach,' said Bannerman. 'That would have required a management decision. You know the funny thing? I had almost written off any involvement of the power station until Milne told me about the clean-up this morning.'

'You can't read too much into that either,' said Stella. 'If the management at the power station thought you were going to make trouble they would be bound to clean up their act. That's human nature. It's like dusting before your mother-in-law arrives.'

'So you don't believe me,' said Bannerman.

'I believe, that you believe it,' said Stella. 'I'm just trying to get you to relax. It's over. You did your best and from what you've told me there doesn't seem to be a new disease to worry about, so why not let it drop?'

Bannerman nodded. He had no intention of letting it drop but he had no wish to continue talking about it.

'So what else is new?' asked Stella.

Bannerman smiled and said, 'I met someone while I was away, a girl.'

'Good for you,' said Stella. 'Is she special?'

'I think so,' replied Bannerman.

'Then I'm happy for you,' said Stella. 'Tell me about her. Is she young?'

'Youngish,' smiled Bannerman, thinking he detected a barb on the question. 'Her name is Shona MacLean; she's an artist. She makes me feel like I've never felt before. Alive, confident . . .'

'Young?' added Stella with an amused smile.

Bannerman shrugged his shoulders in disappointment at the question and Stella reached across the table to take both his hands. 'That was a joke silly,' she whispered. 'Really, I'm delighted for you. When do I get to meet her?'

'Soon, I hope,' said Bannerman. 'Very soon.'

Bannerman returned to his office and tried to stop thinking about Achnagelloch and its problems by concentrating on his work. Thinking it was about time that he make himself known to the locum the MRC had provided for the lab in his absence, he asked Olive about his whereabouts and was told that Dr Sherbourne was down in the PM room. 'That's where I'll be,' said Bannerman.

From what Charlie Simmons had said on a previous occasion, Bannerman expected Sherbourne to be young. He looked like a schoolboy. He seemed totally out of place at work in the mortuary, looking like a first-rate advertisement for the land of the living. He was tall, good-looking, animated and exuded *joie de vivre*. He instantly made Bannerman feel a hundred years old.

'Hello,' said Sherbourne. 'Who are you?'

'I'm Dr Bannerman.'

'Oh, I beg your pardon,' said Sherbourne, becoming flustered. 'Please excuse me. I heard you were back but I thought I would carry on until you said not to.'

'Please do,' said Bannerman. 'I just came to introduce myself and say thank you for your efforts in my absence.'

'A pleasure,' said Sherbourne, looking as if he meant it. 'It's been most interesting. I've enjoyed every moment of it and it's all been valuable experience.'

'You intend to make pathology your career then?'

'I certainly do,' smiled Sherbourne who was about to make the first incision in the cadaver he had on the table. 'I find it absolutely fascinating, but then you must feel that way too.'

Bannerman nodded without comment. He watched Sherbourne complete the cut and then change to rib shears to gain access to the internal organs. 'Actually I want to be a forensic pathologist,' said Sherbourne. 'That's my goal.'

His goal? thought Bannerman. He wants a life spent among mutilated corpses, headless torsos, semen stained clothing and last night's vomit? That's his goal? 'I see,' he said.

Sherbourne was about to drain the blood from the neck of the corpse when Bannerman stopped him. 'Not that way,' he said. 'If you want to be a forensic pathologist you have to remember that signs of injury can be very hard to detect even after strangulation. You have to be very careful how you drain the blood. Watch.' Bannerman took the knife from Sherbourne and made the incision for him.

'Thank you!' said Sherbourne enthusiastically. 'That's exactly the kind of tip I need.'

'Don't mention it,' said Bannerman. 'I'll leave you to it.'

Bannerman returned to his office upstairs wondering about the younger generation and why he himself had become a pathologist. He wasn't sure that he could remember clearly.

TWELVE

Stobmor February 4th.

'You'll be late again if you don't get a move on!' cried Kirstie Bell.

'So you've said!' retorted her husband. 'At least a hundred bloody times, woman.'

'Don't you swear at me Andrew Bell, I'm not one of these fish factory tarts. Just you mind your tongue around here.' Kirstie Bell moved away from the table but continued her diatribe while washing dishes. 'When I think of the men I could have married, I should have listened to my poor father. He always said you'd amount to nothing. He wanted me to marry Jock Croan, he did, and you know what? He was right. I saw Jock the other day and do you know what he was driving?'

Andrew Bell continued to eat his breakfast without heeding the question.

'A Volvo, that's what,' announced Kirstie in triumph. 'A "J" registered Volvo.'

'And what have we got? Answer me that.' demanded Kirstie.

Bell continued to eat, deliberately making a slurping sound with his spoon.

'A 1979 Vauxhall Viva, that's what, with more rust than paint!'

'You know what Kirstie?' said Andrew looking up from his plate.

'What?'

'I bet Jock Croan's wife has got an *en suite* bathroom as well as double glazing . . . and cavity wall insulation. Oh and patio

185

doors, mustn't forget patio doors must we? What would life be without patio doors? The neighbours can't see what you've got if you don't have patio doors.'

'Don't you sneer at me Andrew Bell,' raged Kirstie. 'You're just jealous. You just can't bear to see other people getting on in life, that's your trouble! I don't know why I bother. I work my fingers to the bone to make the place look nice and what thanks do I get? None, that's what.'

Andrew slurped his milk again.

'You are disgusting!' snarled Kirstie.

Andrew slurped all the louder.

Kirstie was suffused with anger. She took it out on the pot she was cleaning.

Andrew looked at her out of the corner of his eye and suddenly felt a mist of regret wash over him. Who was the snarling virago with the angry red face? She was so old. Whatever happened to the girl with the smiling face? The girl whose sexuality had captivated him thirty years ago, the girl whose pouting breasts and proud buttocks had fired his fantasies and kept him awake at night until she had finally brought them to fruition in his mother's back bedroom, one Saturday night, after a dance in the town hall. May had been born nine months to the day, six months after the wedding.

Could this shapeless mass in the faded towelling robe be the same Kirstie? he wondered. Even her voice was different. This creature made a harsh, low pitched noise from a thoat ravaged by cigarette smoke. She continually whined and sounded resentful. The real Kirstie had a sweet, soft voice, one that could tease and excite, one that could promise so much by saying so little. And her eyes! That was another thing. Kirstie had lovely clear eyes. This woman had nastly little pebbles set in crows' feet and underhung with folds of scrawny skin. This woman wasn't Kirstie! This woman was some kind of usurper who had taken Kirstie's place!

She was a witch. That's what she must be! An evil witch who had taken Kirstie's place and who was going to drive him mad unless he did something about it. She was the cause of all the headaches he'd been having! It was becoming clear now!

They weren't headaches at all! She had been putting spells on him, making his head hurt, driving him to distraction with her sorcery!

'Why are you looking at me like that?' asked Kirstie. An air of uncertainty had crept into her voice. 'Is it your head again? Are you ill or something?' she demanded, trying to regain the upper hand.

'Ill? Me? No I'm not ill . . .' said Andrew quietly, 'I've just realized . . .' He got up slowly from the table.

'Realized what?' snapped Kirstie. 'You're not making any sense, and if you don't get a move on . . .'

'You're not Kirstie.'

'What are you blabbering about. If I wasn't Kirstie I wouldn't be married to you and living in this pig sty would I? Stop looking at me like that. Did you hear what I said? I said stop it!'

Bell, who still had his porridge spoon in his hand suddenly jabbed it hard into Kirstie's face and she fell to the floor, her hand pressed to her cheek over a cut that had opened up under her left eye. Her eyes were wide with shock. 'You . . . hit me,' she stammered lamely. 'Have you gone raving mad?'

'You're not Kirstie,' breathed Andrew as he looked down at the figure on the floor with expressionless eyes. He picked up the milk bottle from the table and raised it above his head.

Kirstie covered her eyes and started to scream but it was cut short by the base of the bottle smashing down into her mouth. The force of the blow was enough to break most of her front teeth and impale her lips on the jagged stumps that were left. Andrew brought the bottle down hard again and it broke on Kirstie's skull.

Still holding the broken neck of the bottle. Bell swept the jagged edge of the glass back and forward across his wife's face until she was completely unrecognizable. 'You are not Kirstie,' he repeated in an urgent whisper. 'You are not . . . Kirstie.'

Finally exhausted by his efforts. Bell stood up and looked down at the featureless body on the floor that had been his wife. 'A witch!' he whispered. 'A witch! . . . must burn the witch!'

*   *   *

With a sense of purpose that never wavered, Bell set about building a funeral pyre for his wife. He removed the reservoir from a paraffin heater in the hall and poured the contents over her body. He soaked cushions taken from the settee in similar fashion and propped them up around her. A tablecloth and towels were added and then Bell broke up two dining chairs to provide wood for the bonfire. When he was satisfied with the size of the pyramid, he collected his jacket from the peg in the hall and put it on. 'Late for work,' he murmured. His last act before throwing a lighted match on to the bonfire was to turn on the gas in the kitchen.

The suddenness of the conflagration took Bell by surprise. One moment the little yellow flame was arcing through the air like a comet through space, the next the whole room seemed to erupt in yellow flame accompanied by thick, black, sooty smoke. He put up his arm to protect his face and backed out of the door, closing it behind him. 'Burn witch, burn!' he muttered as he set off down the stairs. He was going to be late. MacKinnon was going to go on at him again. Why didn't they understand about the headaches? Why didn't they?

'So you finally consented to turn up!' exclaimed a thick set man with sparse red hair as he saw Bell come through the front door of Stobmor Engineering. 'This is a garage not a holiday camp! This is the third time this week you've been late and George Duthie has just phoned to say that the new starter motor you put in his Escort yesterday won't start it this morning. He's screaming blue murder. What the hell's the matter with you?'

Bell brushed past the angry man as if he wasn't there. This only served to increase MacKinnon's anger. The harangue continued. 'I said you'd be out to the farm to fix it properly today. I also told Hamish Lochan that the welding job on his van would be done by noon so you'd better get a move on!'

Still without acknowledging the other man's presence, Bell continued about his business as if on automatic pilot. He walked to the back of the garage and released the chains that held a trolley, containing two gas cylinders, upright against the wall. MacKinnon watched him manoeuvre the trolley round and start wheeling it across the garage. He knew that something was wrong, but didn't know what. His anger began to be replaced by curiosity. 'Look if you have some kind of problem, tell me. Maybe we can sort something out . . .'

Bell ignored him and set up the welding set beside an old Bedford van. He unwound the hoses from the heads of the cylinders and opened the valve on the acetylene cylinder; he ignited the torch flame and it started to burn with a slow licking yellow flame. Bell stared at it and smiled as if remembering something. MacKinnon came to stand by his side. He said, 'I don't like having to bawl you out every morning. Why can't we talk this thing out?'

Bell ignored him and reached up to turn on the oxygen supply. The yellow flame turned to intense blue as oxygen entered the flow. It made MacKinnon angry because neither man was wearing protective goggles. 'What the hell do you think you're doing?' he stormed, covering his eyes.

Bell turned round as if in a trance. He smiled, distantly, and without further hestitation pushed the torch flame right into MacKinnon's face. MacKinnon's features were transformed into a blackened crater within seconds and he fell to the floor, his head wreathed in smoke which drifted slowly upwards. Bell stepped over the body and started to work on the van as if nothing had happened. He hoisted it up on the hydraulic lift and positioned himself underneath. He was welding the chassis when the postman came into the garage and saw MacKinnon's body. The man let out a cry of horror.

Bell looked out from under the van and smiled at him. 'Hello Neil,' he said with a smile. 'How are things?'

The postman backed away; he thought the smile on Bell's face the most terrifying thing he had ever seen. There was something disturbingly unnatural about it. Bell stood there as if waiting for an answer, the welding torch still burning in his hand, its flame now cutting through the petrol tank of the van. The postman turned on his heel and ran screaming to the door.

An ear-splitting blast behind him helped him on his way and sent him sprawling out into the street.

Neil Campbell struggled to his knees and looked back in through the maw of the doorway. He saw the flaming figure of Andrew Bell, hands raised in the air, pirouetting slowly to the floor in his death throes. The postman's eyes didn't blink. It took another explosion to break the spell. He didn't know it at the time but it was a gas explosion from a neighbouring street.

Bannerman was thinking about going to bed when the phone rang. These days when the phone rang at night it was usually Shona but he had spoken to her already this evening, less than an hour ago.

'Bannerman.'

'Doctor Bannerman? This is Angus MacLeod in Achnagelloch.'

Bannerman was taken aback, but hid it well. He inquired after the GP's health and asked, 'What can I do for you, Doctor?'

'It's more what I can do for you,' replied MacLeod. 'There was an incident in Stobmor today which I thought you would be interested in.'

'Really? What sort of an incident?'

'A man went berserk.'

'Berserk,' repeated Bannerman. He could feel himself going cold.

'A garage worker named Andrew Bell went totally out of control. It appears that he murdered his wife and his employer before immolating himself. In view of the deaths in Achnagelloch a few weeks ago, I thought you might be interested.'

Bannerman saw the awful implications of the news immediately. If this death was due to the same cause as the others it meant that the source of disease had not been contained after all! A mixture of fear and excitement welled up in his throat. 'What happened to the man's body?' he asked in a voice that was almost a croak.

'There was very little of it left,' replied MacLeod. 'He was doused in burning petrol and fell on to a lit welding torch.'

'What are the chances of getting pathology samples?' asked Bannerman.

'Zero, I'm afraid,' answered MacLeod. 'We are not talking about burns Doctor. We are talking cremation.'

'Damnation,' said Bannerman as he realized he had been thwarted again. It suddenly registered what MacLeod had said about the man's occupation. 'You said he worked in a garage?' he asked.

'As a mechanic,' replied MacLeod.

'That doesn't fit,' said Bannerman. 'How long has he been doing that?'

'About fifteen years and before that he worked in a fish factory over on the east coast.'

'But surely there must be some link with the others?'

'There's a familial connection,' said MacLeod.

'Go on,' said Bannerman.

'His daughter, May Bell. She is, or was, married to Gordon Buchan.'

'Bell was May Buchan's father?' exclaimed Bannerman.

'Yes. Does that help?'

'I don't know,' confessed Bannerman. 'I'll let you know if I think of anything, and Doctor?'

'Yes?'

'I appreciate your call. If there should happen to be any other incidents . . .'

'I'll let you know,' promised MacLeod.

'How the hell? . . .' complained Bannerman as he thought it through. How could Gordon Buchan's father-in-law contract the disease? He had nothing to do with sheep! He had worked in a garage for fifteen years. But surely it was too much of a coincidence to be due to anything else. The overwhelming priority for the moment was that the killer disease had not been wiped out. It was alive in Stobmor. It was too late to call the MRC; he would call Milne first thing in the morning.

Bannerman got to the hospital a little after eight-thirty to find that Milne had already called him. Bannerman phoned him back and lit a cigarette while he waited for an answer.

191

'Bad news I'm afraid,' said Milne.

'You're going to tell me that there has been another case,' said Bannerman.

'How did you know?'

'MacLeod, the local GP, phoned me last night.'

'I just don't understand it,' said Milne. 'The man is a garage mechanic.'

'Me neither,' agreed Bannerman.

'I'm calling a special meeting for ten-thirty. Can you make it?'

Bannerman said that he could.

Cecil Allison from the Prime Minister's office was the last to arrive at the meeting. Bannerman was looking out of the window at the rain while the only other two, Hugh Milne and the secretary of the MRC, Sir John Flowers, discussed some internal matter. Bannerman saw the dark Rover draw up at the door and Allison get out; he returned to the table.

'So sorry to have kept you,' said Allison, 'I've been a bit snowed under this morning.' He beamed at the others and sat down.

Flowers said, 'Dr Bannerman thinks that we should mount a full scale investigation into the deaths at Stobmor and Achnagelloch; the time for low-profile sniffing around is past. I think I agree.'

Allison, urbane as ever, spread his palms in front of him in a gesture which appealed for calm. 'As I understand it,' he said smoothly, 'there has been another death.'

'Another three if we count the man's wife and employer,' said Milne, 'and pretty horrific deaths they were, too.'

'Yes, yes,' said Allison, his eyes betraying the slightest suggestion of irritation, 'but for the purposes of our interest, i.e. the brain disease problem, there has been only one. Am I right?'

'Yes,' agreed Flowers.

'And this man had nothing to do with sheep or cattle at all?'

'No,' said Flowers.

'So the connection . . .' Allison made the word 'connection' sound inappropriate, 'has been made entirely through his irrational behaviour?'

'His symptoms were identical by all accounts,' said Bannerman, 'and he was related to one of the men who died.'

'His symptoms, as I have been led to believe, amount to deranged behaviour. Is that right?'

'Well, yes,' agreed Milne.

'Nothing more specific than that?'

'No,' agreed Flowers. 'I suppose you could call it that.'

'The point I am making, gentlemen,' said Allison leaning forward to rest his elbows on the table and create the impression of being about to impart a confidence, 'is that this sort of thing happens all the time and all over the country. A man near the end of his tether grabs a rifle and shoots his way on to the front pages of the dailys. We've read about it all before! Her Majesty's Government is continually under pressure to review firearm regulations because of it!'

Bannerman had expected Allison to play things down; doing this was almost a government reflex, but he had to admit that Allison had a point. The man was good at his job; he had made a convincing argument and was now waiting to see the strength of the opposition. Bannerman steeled himself to keep his temper and said, 'My feeling is that this incident, happening as it did in Stobmor, is just too much of a coincidence. I firmly believe that this latest death is connected with the others and that there might be more if we do nothing. We have to pursue the source of this outbreak and identify it.'

Flowers and Milne sat on the sidelines, waiting for Allison's response. When he spoke there was a much colder, harder edge to his voice. He said to Flowers, 'Until yesterday you were prepared to give Her Majesty's Government a statement saying that there was no evidence of a direct link between brain disease in animals and similar conditions in man. Now, because of one man going off his head and running amok . . . are you saying that you won't?'

Flowers said calmly, 'I think we must wait a little longer before giving you the reassurance you seek.'

'How much longer?' asked Allison. He enunciated each word as if giving an elocution lesson.

'Until we are satisfied Mr Allison,' replied Flowers, earning Bannerman's admiration for his steadiness under strong pressure from the government's man.

Allison too seemed to sense that Flowers could not be bullied into committing the Council to something that he wasn't happy about. His manner relaxed a little and he said, 'Will you at least concede that this latest death *might* be due to the factors I've outlined. The man could have simply gone berserk after some domestic upheaval?'

Flowers, Milne and Bannerman all nodded.

'In that case,' said Allison, 'I have a proposal.'

Bannerman moved defensively in his chair but didn't speak.

'If we launch a major investigation right now,' said Allison, 'the press will have a field day – Killer Brain Disease Stalks Scottish Town – that sort of thing. The truth will be totally lost under banner headlines and the damage to the farming community will be inestimable.'

'What do you propose?' asked Milne.

I propose that we do nothing,' said Allison.

'Nothing?'

'Nothing, for an agreed period and if during that period there have been no further cases of people running amok and murdering their wives then we regard the *Scrapie* affair in Achnagelloch as an isolated incident which is now closed. You issue an interim report on brain disease in this country stating that, although there has been a rise, the statistics do not signify a connection with farm animals. If, on the other hand, there *is* another case, then you are free to go ahead and investigate in any way you choose.'

'What do you say gentlemen?' asked Flowers of Milne and Bannerman.

'How long?' said Bannerman.

'Three weeks,' said Allison.

'Four,' said Bannerman.

194

'Agreed,' said Allison, looking to Flowers and Milne. They both indicated their agreement.

Allison looked at his watch and said that he would have to rush. He left the room and Bannerman instantly felt more relaxed. He smiled and shook his head slightly. Men like Allison could steal your eye teeth and you wouldn't notice until dinner time.

'You don't really think that Bell's death could be coincidence do you?' asked Flowers.

'No I don't,' said Bannerman. 'Mind you, I hope with all my heart that it was.'

The days passed and Bannerman felt himself being drawn back into the routine lifestyle that he had known before going to Scotland. His friendship with Stella had changed however. They did not see each other as often as before and he no longer felt that he could do things like ring her up in the middle of the night to discuss some problem. He supposed that it was inevitable that the relationship should change and he felt sad in a way, but on the other hand his feelings for Shona were undiminished.

The highlight of each and every day was the phone call to Shona in the evening. For the first time in his life he wanted to tell someone everything. Matters that previously would have seemed too trivial to rate a mention had to be imparted to Shona in detail. He knew this made him vulnerable but it was a new and not unpleasant experience. He had been keeping people at arm's length all his life.

'Still no word from the north?' asked Shona.

'No,' said Bannerman. 'That's ten days now.'

'Do you still think there will be other cases?'

'Yes. I'm convinced Bell contracted the same disease as Buchan and the other two men. That means the outbreak did not end with the burial of the infected sheep on Inverladdie. If we can show there was some connection, then there is still a chance that the outbreak may be contained locally. If not, then there must be another source of the disease that we haven't even thought of. There's just so much about this whole affair that we don't understand.'

'Is there nothing you can do in the meantime?' asked Shona.

Bannerman said not. 'It's just a matter of waiting and hoping I'm wrong.'

'I'll hope with you,' said Shona.

'I think we all better do that,' said Bannerman.

'If there is another case, will you be involved in the investigation or will it be taken out of your hands?' asked Shona.

Bannerman hadn't considered the possibility of not being involved. He said, 'I'm going to see it through whatever they say.'

'I understand,' said Shona.

'Whatever happens, I'll come up for a long weekend at the end of the month, if that's all right with you? We've lots to talk about.'

'Of course,' said Shona gently. 'I'll count the days.'

'I'm sorry it can't be sooner,' said Bannerman.

'Come when you can,' said Shona.

After almost three weeks with no word from the MRC, Bannerman began to think that his worst fears might not after all be realized. One more week and the government would get the statement it wanted from the Council and that would be the end of the matter. The government would be happy, the farmers would be happy. Everyone would be happy . . . except Ian Bannerman. For him the fact would remain that seven people had died and a terrifying new disease had been created, even if it had disappeared for the moment. The outbreak would be conveniently forgotten by those in charge, those he saw as ostriches, happy ostriches with their heads safely back in the sand.

Newsnight had just finished on television and Bannerman was about to go to bed when the telephone rang. It was Angus MacLeod in Achnagelloch. Bannerman knew immediately why he must be calling and lost all trace of drowsiness.

'There's been another case?' he asked without preamble.

'Yes,' replied MacLeod.

Bannerman closed his eyes and swallowed. 'Tell me.'

'I was called out earlier this evening to see a young labourer.

His wife called me because she thought he was behaving oddly. I recognized in him the same symptoms displayed by Gordon Buchan.'

'But he's alive?'

'Yes,' agreed MacLeod. 'But for how much longer I don't know. I've sedated him and had him moved to the cottage hospital at Stobmor. What do you think about a transfer?'

'Where were you thinking of?' asked Bannerman.

'In view of what we both suspect, I thought we might try getting him admitted to the Department of Surgical Neurology at the Western General in Edinburgh but in another way I'm loath to do it.'

'What's the problem?' asked Bannerman.

'I think if we're honest we have to recognize that there's no chance of saving his life. We'd be moving him to get as much neurological information about the course of the disease as we can. DSN at the Western General has all the right equipment. But whether or not this would be fair on his wife is another matter.'

'I see,' said Bannerman, appreciating the moral dilemma. 'My own view is that the only conclusive data we'll get about the disease will come from post-mortem material. Reams of EEG print-out isn't going to tell us much.'

'In that case I think I should keep him here.'

'Agreed,' said Bannerman. 'I'm going to come up there. I'd like to see the man for myself.'

'Very good.'

'You said he was a labourer. A farm labourer?'

'No, he works at the stone quarry.'

'Any connection with the patients who have already died?'

'No family connection this time I'm afraid, but I did have one thought . . .'

'Yes?'

'The quarry lies to the west of Inverladdie Farm. It's not inconceivable that infected sheep could have wandered over there.'

'That's a thought,' agreed Bannerman, 'but he would still have had to come into close contact with the infected animals to pick up the virus through cuts or grazes.'

'Quarry workers invariably have plenty of these,' said Munro.

'I suppose so,' said Bannerman, still not convinced. 'I'd better have a note of some patient details.' He straightened up the pad by the telephone and flicked off the cap of his pen with his thumb.

MacLeod dictated, 'Male, twenty-eight years old, no medical history to speak of. Apart from headaches over the past week there was no real sign of illness until yesterday when his wife noticed lapses in concentration. She said he appeared at times to go into a trance. Today his behaviour became irrational and alarmed her so much that she called me in.'

'In what way irrational?'

'She found him eating the food in the dog's bowl, then he tried to go to work without any boots on. When she tried to talk to him, she says he looked at her as if he didn't know her, sometimes as if he hated her. They've always been such a loving couple; she's taking it very badly.'

'That's understandable,' said Bannerman.

'In view of what happened with Andrew Bell, I didn't think I could risk leaving Turnbull at home, even with sedation. That's why I had him moved to the cottage hospital.'

'Did you say "Turnbull"?' asked Bannerman.

'Colin Turnbull,' said MacLeod.

'Hell and damnation,' said Bannerman.

'You know him?'

'He was a regular in the bar of the hotel when I was up there, I liked him.'

'A bright chap,' said MacLeod. 'He was doing a degree part-time.'

'I remember,' said Bannerman.

'His wife, Julie, is the primary school teacher in Stobmor.'

Bannerman recalled the paintings in the windows of the school. He asked, 'Who knows about Turnbull's condition?'

'You can't keep secrets in a place this size,' replied MacLeod. 'Stories of another meningitis case will be all over town by now.'

'Damn,' said Bannerman.

'You can't keep this sort of thing under wraps for ever,' said MacLeod.

'That's isn't what was worrying me,' said Bannerman.

'Then what?'

'I think it would be an excellent idea if some kind of guard were placed on Colin Turnbull.'

'He's heavily sedated. I don't think he's a danger to anyone,' said MacLeod.

'It's the danger to him I was thinking about,' said Bannerman.

'I don't understand,' said MacLeod.

'Not everyone wants us to get to the bottom of this outbreak Doctor.'

'Are you serious?'

'Yes.'

'I'm going to spend the night at the hospital,' said MacLeod, and Julie Turnbull will be there as well, so he won't be alone.'

'I didn't realize you intended staying with him Doctor,' said Bannerman.

'I brought Colin Turnbull into the world twenty-eight years ago,' said MacLeod. 'I was a guest at his wedding to Julie and I was around when their child was stillborn three years ago. It seems that fate has decreed that Colin Turnbull will die soon, so I will be there to make him as comfortable as possible and to do what I can for Julie.'

'Of course,' said Bannerman, feeling alienated. Things weren't done that way at St Luke's. Somewhere along the line the personal touch had been superseded by bleeping monitors and chart recorders. If anyone else had said what MacLeod just had he would have found it corny, but because he knew and liked MacLeod he felt slightly ashamed.

'When can we expect you?' asked MacLeod.

'I intend getting the first British Airways shuttle to Aberdeen in the morning. I'll pick up a hire car at the airport and with a bit of luck I should make it by mid-afternoon.'

'Shall I book you into a hotel?' asked MacLeod.

'That would be kind.'

'Achnagelloch or Stobmor?'

'Stobmor. The hospital's there. Doctor . . . I hate to have to ask this but . . .'

'Yes?'

'Do you have the facilities for me to carry out a post-mortem?'

'There's a small operating theatre. You could use that.'

THIRTEEN

Bannerman watched the hours pass slowly by on the clock by his bedside. At two-thirty he knew that he was not going to be able to sleep, so he got up. He decided to go in to the hospital, changing his original plan about phoning staff later in the day. Going in personally would give him the chance to leave notes for those his absence would affect most, Olive, Charlie Simmons and Nigel Leeman. The hospital authorities would not be too enchanted with his sudden disappearance but going through official channels would take too much time, and he didn't have it; he suspected Colin Turnbull had even less.

He left word on Olive's desk that if the MRC were to phone she was to tell them he was already on his way to Scotland and would be in touch later in the day. His last act in the lab was to assemble a few post-mortem instruments. He didn't think he would have to take a full set with him, but concentrated on the type of instruments that the cottage hospital would not have. He left out the knives and scalpels that pathology and surgery had in common.

He knew that the ironware would present a problem at the airport when he went through the metal detector but he was carrying plenty of identification and was quite happy for the knives to travel in the hold of the aircraft. With a last look round, he turned out the fluorescent lights and locked the door. He was on his way.

Bannerman breakfasted lightly at Heathrow, more to break the monotony of waiting than through any feeling of hunger. Afterwards he telephoned Shona to say that he was travelling north. He apologized for phoning so early but she insisted that she was up and dressed and had already been for a walk on the beach.

'Then the weather's fine up there?' said Bannerman.

'At the moment,' said Shona, but there's a storm coming in from the west. It may stop the ferry sailing but if it doesn't I'll come across to the mainland and meet you in Stobmor.'

'I hoped you'd say that,' said Bannerman.

Shona's predicted storm swept across Scotland an hour later and was in full song when Bannerman's aircraft crossed the Perthshire hills; the captain apologized for 'turbulence' during the approach to Aberdeen airport. Bannerman lost contact with his stomach more than once during the descent, the worst moment being when the aircraft seemed to crab sideways on the final approach before steadying at the last moment to thump down on the tarmac. There were sighs of relief all round in the cabin and Bannerman even noticed a little smile pass between two of the stewardesses as they unbuckled their belts and stood up to prepare for disembarkation.

A 'mix-up' in the paperwork meant that his hire car was not waiting for him and he had to wait thirty minutes while uniformed girls made telephone calls and a car was eventually brought out from the city. He passed the time drinking luke warm coffee at a plastic table in the airport café, watching the rain pass horizontally across his field of view outside the window. If it was like this in the west, the ferries would certainly not be running.

The car arrived and Bannerman set off on the road north. The rain changed to sleet just north of Huntly, in distillery country, and became snow as he skirted Inverness, heading for the north west. The snow was lying on the minor roads and it took him over ninety minutes to negotiate the last twenty miles of the journey. It was six in the evening when he reached Stobmor. He dumped his things in his hotel bedroom and made straight for the cottage hospital.

* * *

Bannerman knew from the sound of sobbing as soon as he entered the hospital that he was too late. Through a half-glazed door, leading off the entrance hall, he could see Angus MacLeod comforting a woman he thought must be Colin Turnbull's wife. She had her back to him and MacLeod held up his hand to signify that he should stay outside for the moment. Bannerman nodded and moved along the hallway to the next room where he found a nurse making tea. He introduced himself.

'I'm Sister Drummond. Dr MacLeod expected you earlier,' said the nurse, putting the lid back on the tea pot.

'The weather,' said Bannerman.

'It is bad,' conceded the nurse.

'I take it Colin Turnbull's dead?' said Bannerman.

'Fifteen minutes ago.'

Bannerman could see, although the nurse was trying to give out signs of normality, that she was clearly upset. There was a definite quiver in her cheeks. 'Are you all right?' he asked gently.

The woman nodded but put a hand up to her face as if checking that there were no tears on her face. She swallowed as if preparing to speak. Bannerman waited.

'I have never . . .' she began, 'I have never seen anyone die that way . . .' The words seemed to act as a relief valve. She let out her breath and tears started to flow freely down her face. 'It was horrible . . . quite, quite horrible; he seemed possessed . . .'

The door opened and Angus MacLeod joined them. 'How's that tea coming along?' he asked.

'It's ready,' said the nurse.

'Perhaps you would sit with Mrs Turnbull for a bit Sister?'

'Of course Doctor.'

The nurse left the room and MacLeod said, 'Just too late I'm afraid.'

Bannerman nodded. He said, 'I hear it wasn't a very pretty end.'

'He was totally deranged. The sedation wasn't enough to keep him under. It wasn't easy to listen to. I only wish that Julie could have been spared that.'

'Where's the body?' asked Bannerman.

'Downstairs in the cellar, we're using it as a makeshift mortuary. Do you want to see him?'

'Yes,' said Bannerman.

'I'll just check that Julie's all right,' said MacLeod. He was gone for only a moment before returning and saying, 'It's this way.'

MacLeod led the way through a heavy wooden door that led to a flight of stone steps. Bannerman noticed an immediate change of temperature as they left the centrally heated hospital to descend into the unheated stone cellar.

MacLeod clicked on the cellar light, a single bulkhead lamp surrounded by a wire cage, drenched in cobwebs. It seemed to fill the room with shadows rather than light. Turnbull's body lay in the middle of the room on a slatted wooden bench; it was covered with a sheet which had been tucked in around the contours so that it was quite obvious what lay under it. The scene made Bannerman think of discoveries in the Valley of the Kings in Egypt, but Turnbull was no ancient pharaoh; he was currently the only clue to a terrible disease.

Bannerman walked over to the body, untucked the sheet from the head and pulled it back. He recoiled at the sight. Turnbull's eyes were open and his teeth were bared as if poised to leap up at him and grab his throat. But it was simply a death mask, the death mask of a man who had died in the throes of agony.

'I'm sorry, there wasn't time to do much about that,' murmured MacLeod. 'I had his wife to take care of. She was very upset.'

Bannerman tried to close Turnbull's eyes but found the skin stretched too tightly across his eyelids. 'Strange,' he said. 'Some kind of early rigor, maybe connected with the disease.' He found the same problem with the cheek muscles; they had contracted to tighten the skin at the sides of Turnbull's mouth. 'Will you ask Mrs Turnbull for PM permission?' he asked MacLeod.

MacLeod was obviously reluctant. 'She has just been through the most horrific experience,' he said. 'Could it wait until morning?'

Bannerman looked at the corpse, now re-covered with the sheet, and said, 'I'd rather you did it now, if you think it at all possible.'

MacLeod shrugged and said, 'I'll see what sort of state she's in when we go upstairs.'

'What on earth . . .' exclaimed MacLeod as he opened the door at the head of the cellar stairs and heard voices in the hallway. When Bannerman came out into the light he saw that there were three men talking to Sister Drummond inside the front door. He recognized one of them as the Dutchman, van Gelder; the other two were strangers, workmen by their appearance. The nurse stopped talking to the men and came over to MacLeod. She said, 'Doctor, Mr Turnbull's employer and two of his friends have come to see how he is.'

'You've told them?' asked MacLeod quietly.

'Yes Doctor. They'd like to see Mrs Turnbull.'

'Ask them to wait in the side room would you?' said MacLeod.

As the nurse turned away MacLeod said to Bannerman, 'I'll see if Julie will sign the permission form.' He left Bannerman standing in the hallway. Van Gelder saw him and smiled a greeting. He came over to shake hands saying, 'Good to see you again Doctor, I thought you had left the area.'

'I had,' agreed Bannerman.

'But no need to ask why you are back, eh? Another tragedy. What a terrible business. Turnbull was one of my most reliable workers. When are you chaps going to get to the bottom of it?'

'Soon I hope,' said Bannerman.

The other two men were looking across at them talking. The nurse was holding open the side room door, waiting to usher all three of them inside. Bannerman was aware that the look on the men's faces was distinctly hostile. He wondered why; he didn't know them.

'Are these men Colin's workmates?' he asked van Gelder quietly.

'I met them outside,' said van Gelder. 'They're old friends I understand,' replied the Dutchman, 'They're employed at the power station. One of them told me he was in Turnbull's class at school.'

'I see,' said Bannerman. He remembered how Turnbull had once warned him about the ill feeling he was generating among the nuclear power workers. This was how he had known. Some of his friends worked at the station.

'Is everything all right Doctor?' asked van Gelder.

'Yes,' replied Bannerman distantly.

Everyone in the hall was suddenly startled by the sound of a female voice raised in anger. It was Julie Turnbull. Embarrassed glances were exchanged as the sound of her voice grew louder and louder until she was screaming, 'No! No! On no account! Just leave my Colin alone!'

Julie Turnbull came bursting out of the room where she had been with MacLeod. She saw the two power workers and threw herself into the arms of one of them. 'They want to cut Colin's head off!' she sobbed. 'They want his brain!'

'Jesus,' said one of the men with open disgust.

'No one is going to touch Colin,' said the other man, holding Julie close to him.

Bannerman and MacLeod exchanged uneasy looks. MacLeod shrugged his apologies.

'Mrs Turnbull,' began Bannerman. 'Believe me, no one is going to cut . . .'

The man holding her interrupted him with a stream of abuse. 'Fucking doctors! What fucking use have you been, huh? Why don't you just piss off and leave us all alone!'

Bannerman backed off, sensing that the situation was beyond saving for the moment. Van Gelder stepped forward diplomatically and intervened. 'My dear Mrs Turnbull,' he said, 'perhaps you would allow me to drive you home? My car is just outside.

Or perhaps there is somewhere else you would rather go? A relative or friend?'

'Thank you,' replied Julie, recovering her composure. She turned to MacLeod and said, 'I'm sorry Doctor . . . but I meant what I said.'

MacLeod nodded and gave her a reassuring smile. Julie made a point of ignoring Bannerman completely and left the hospital, supported by van Gelder. The two power station workers followed behind. Both of them gave Bannerman looks that suggested he might be wise to steer clear of them on dark nights. One said, 'No one touches Colin's body. Understand?'

Bannerman did not dignify the threat with a reply. He just stared at the man balefuly until the man broke eye contact and left.

'I'm sorry,' said MacLeod. 'I made a complete mess of it.'

'It was my fault for rushing you into it,' said Bannerman. 'It would have been better to wait until the morning. The question now is, what the hell do we do?'

'You can enforce it legally,' said MacLeod.

'I know,' said Bannerman, 'but I'm not insensitive to what that would mean for you.' He knew that if MacLeod did not sign the death certificate Turnbull's death would be classed as 'sudden' and would therefore merit a post-mortem examination as required by Scottish law, whether his wife gave permission or not. The locals would construe this as treachery by their GP since he knew of Julie Turnbull's wishes.

'Thanks,' said MacLeod.

'What would you say to a compromise?' asked Bannerman.

MacLeod raised his eyebrows. 'A compromise?'

Despite the fact that he trusted MacLeod, Bannerman still felt a little wary of making his suggestion. He said cautiously, 'I could make do with a needle biopsy.'

MacLeod looked at him as if he hadn't heard properly.

'I could insert a wide gauge needle into Turnbull's brain and get the samples I need without doing the full PM head job. I could do it so that it wouldn't be noticeable to laymen.

That way no post-mortem will have been carried out and Mrs Turnbull's wishes will have been respected. You can sign the death certificate and your standing in the community will remain undiminished.'

'But surely the authorities and the MRC will insist on a full autopsy being performed?'

'The "authorities" will be only too happy to see this affair kept as low key as possible. They won't make waves if we don't.'

'I see,' said MacLeod thoughtfully. 'Well, if you're sure that you can get enough material I think you should go ahead. What do you need?'

Bannerman gave him a short list of his requirements.

'When will you do it?'

Bannerman walked over to the window. He could see the two power workers standing across the street watching the building. He said, 'Not now. I think I had better be seen to leave soon. If it's all right with you I'll come back later and do the biopsy, when the "guard" has been lifted.'

MacLeod joined him at the window and took his meaning. He said, 'I'll give you a key and show you where everything is. Could I be of any assistance later?'

Bannerman said not. 'It really shouldn't take long. I'm assuming these two aren't going to squat over there all night.'

MacLeod said, 'Why don't you go back to your hotel; I'll stay on for a bit and telephone you when they leave.'

Bannerman agreed. He went to his hotel and had a bath before getting something to eat. He had just finished his meal when MacLeod phoned. 'Sorry,' said MacLeod. 'They're still across the street and I'll have to leave now myself.'

Bannerman thanked him and said that he would wait for a couple of hours. He couldn't believe that the men would mount an all night vigil over the body. As he said it, the words, 'unless someone put them up to it,' came into his head.

Bannerman dismissed the thought for the moment and phoned Shona who, as he thought, was stuck on the island because of the ferry cancellations.

'The wind has dropped a good deal,' said Shona. 'There's a good chance I'll get to the mainland tomorrow.'

'That is the nicest thing I've heard all day,' said Bannerman.

'How's the patient?'

'He died shortly before I got here.'

'I'm sorry. That must alter your plans.'

Bannerman was wary about mentioning anything about a post-mortem examination of the body over the phone. He couldn't be sure that the hotel switchboard was 'safe'. 'I'll be going to Edinburgh next, to see the people at the Neurobiology Unit,' he said. He didn't say what he would be taking there. 'Come with me?'

'All right,' said Shona, without taking time to consider. 'That's the nicest thing I've heard all day.'

'Good,' said Bannerman. 'I'll see you tomorrow.'

Bannerman came downstairs to the hotel bar. He felt a chill come over him when he opened the door and saw Mitchell, the head of security at the power station, sitting there with another man. Mitchell looked up and smiled in a way that put Bannerman on edge. 'Well Doctor, still looking for nuclear skeletons in the cupboard?' he asked.

The smug look on Mitchell's face brought Bannerman's dislike for the man almost to boiling point, but he remained outwardly calm. 'The cupboard smells of detergent,' he replied.

Again the smug grin on Mitchell's face. 'Just a routine precaution Doctor. We do it every so often.'

'Of course,' said Bannerman, leaving Mitchell and going up to the bar where he ordered a tonic water. He stood with his back to Mitchell, indicating no further desire to continue their conversation. Mitchell returned to the conversation he had interrupted when Bannerman had come in. Bannerman watched them in the mirror behind the bar and deduced from the head movements in his direction that he was the current subject of their talk.

Was Mitchell's presence here a coincidence? he wondered, or was there something more sinister behind it? Could it be that *he*, as well as the hospital, was being watched to make sure that no one interfered with Turnbull's body?

Bannerman slid on to a bar stool and passed the time of day with the barman to create the impression of being a normal guest in the hotel. He was simply having a couple of drinks before going upstairs to his room for the night. There was no reason for Mitchell to know that he was only drinking tonic water, to keep his head clear. There was no reason for anyone to suspect that he was going to sneak out later, go to the cottage hospital under cover of darkness and perform an illegal autopsy on Colin Turnbull. But every time he glanced at Mitchell in the mirror he found that Mitchell was watching him.

Could the feeling possibly be prompted by paranoia? Bannerman wondered. It was true that Mitchell did seem to look a lot in his direction but that could be a legacy of their previous meeting. Having come to blows with someone in the past did tend to make one hyper-aware of their presence on subsequent occasions. He decided on a experiment. He would go to the lavatory down the hall to see if he would be followed. As he prepared to move he suddenly saw the door to the bar open and the two power workers who had been watching the hospital came inside. Mitchell nodded to them and one stopped to speak while the other came up to the bar to order drinks. He stood at Bannerman's elbow.

'Thought you'd be on your way by now,' said the man.

'Really?' said Bannerman drily.

'There's nothing here for you to do,' said the man.

'I'll be the judge of that,' said Bannerman.

'Julie will be the judge of that,' said the man. 'Don't you forget it or it'll be more than your car that gets hurt this time.' The man paid for his drinks and left the bar to join his companion and Mitchell.

So that's who they are, thought Bannerman. They were the two yobs who had vandalized his car on his last visit and Mitchell was pulling their strings.

Bannerman went to the lavatory. No one followed. As he washed his hands he began to think about how long he would have to wait before it was safe to return to the hospital. Pub closing time in the north was notoriously, or wonderfully, lax, depending on your point of view. He was beginning to think of the small hours of the morning. He dried his hands and opened the washroom door. His way was barred by one of the power workers.

This was the man who had stopped to speak to Mitchell while his companion had come to the bar counter. He was shorter than the other man but broad shouldered and stocky. His red hair was dry and frizzy and receded in the front although he could not have been older than mid-twenties.

'Excuse me,' said Bannerman, making to move past the man.

The man moved to bar his way and stood there staring at him.

'I said excuse me,' said Bannerman.

'Did you now,' said the man, his voice low with menace.

'Move!' said Bannerman firmly.

The man stood still. 'You are not wanted in this town,' he hissed.

'Believe me. I've got the message,' said Bannerman ruefully. 'But this isn't Tombstone Arizona and you're not Wyat Earp. I have a job to do and I'm doing it, so unless you really intend following a course of action which will end up with you inside Peterhead Prison, I suggest you move aside and let me past.'

The man considered for a moment before pursing his lips and reluctantly moving to one side to let Bannerman out through the door.

Bannerman went upstairs and locked his room door. He stood with his back against it for a moment, letting his breathing return to normal. His heart was thumping against his chest. He reflected for a moment that things might have been so much easier had he not got off on the wrong foot with Mitchell. After that first meeting there was just no point of contact between them. He steeled himself to keep vigil by his room window with the lights out.

* * *

Mitchell left an hour later and got into his car alone. It was another forty minutes before the two power workers came out into the street. The one Bannerman had left in the toilet was very drunk and was being supported by his companion. As they made their way down the street, the drunk struggled to turn round. He shouted back at the window of the hotel, 'I'll get you, you bastard . . . you see if I don't.'

'Not in that state you won't,' whispered Bannerman in the dark.

The hotel was too small to have a night porter or indeed any night staff that would warrant the front door being left open. Bannerman saw that it was locked when he came downstairs.

'Was there something?' asked the manager, who had just locked up and was preparing to turn in for the night.

'I thought I might go out for some fresh air,' said Bannerman.

'At this time?' exclaimed the man, looking at his watch but more by gesture than any real desire to see the time.

'Insomnia,' replied Bannerman. 'I'm a slave to it.'

The man gave Bannerman a key and requested that he lock up when he returned.

Bannerman said that he would.

The air was cold but mercifully still as he hurried along the deserted streets of Stobmor to the cottage hospital. Although it was after one-thirty in the morning and there were no lights on at all in the surrounding streets, Bannerman still felt as if a thousand eyes were watching him. He kept close to the shadows all the way and checked behind him before turning into the doorway of the hospital. He felt a surge of relief to be in the dark of the entrance porch. He got out the key MacLeod had given him and inserted it in the lock. It wouldn't turn.

Bannerman withdrew the key and re-inserted it, three times in all but it refused to turn. He cursed and tried one last time but to no avail. He was on the point of leaving when it suddenly occurred to him what the trouble was. He was trying to unlock a door that was already unlocked! He turned the handle and the door opened. MacLeod must have forgotten to lock it earlier!

*   *   *

Bannerman felt embarrassed that he had not thought of trying the door first. It confirmed his suspicion that he had no talent for cloak and dagger activities. What was required was a cool calculating mind. He was a bundle of nerves and his pulse rate was topping a hundred and twenty. He tiptoed into the room where MacLeod said that he would leave the equipment he would need for the brain biopsy on Turnbull. There was enough light coming in from the street lamps for him to find it without trouble. Surgical gloves, 50 ml capacity disposable syringes, wide-gauge needles, alcohol impregnated swabs and a range of specimen containers. Everything he needed to extract a sample of the dead man's brain.

Bannerman's pulse was still thumping as he collected the equipment together on a stainless steel tray and prepared to take it down into the cellar. As he lifted it he heard a sudden thumping sound from somewhere in the building. He nearly dropped the tray. Had MacLeod come back after all? The noise happened again and Bannerman was prompted to call out, 'Dr MacLeod? Is that you?'

There was no reply.

Bannerman felt unease grow inside him until it tightened his stomach muscles. For God's sake get a grip! he told himself. There are sounds in all buildings at night. Central heating noises, fridges switching on and off. You can hardly be afraid of the dead, you're a pathologist for God's sake! Get down into that cellar, get the needle biopsy over and done with and you can be on your way to Edinburgh in the morning.

Bannerman opened the door to the cellar and moved forward cautiously. He couldn't risk putting on a light until the door was safely closed behind him for fear that it would be seen from the street. Once more, he noticed the sudden change in temperature as he descended the stone steps. Another sound! A small shuffling sound. Surely it couldn't be rats at the body? He listened for the tell-tale scurry of paws. Silence.

*　　*　　*

213

Bannerman stood on the second last step and looked around the cellar. Nothing moved in the floor area lit by the single lamp but there were several dark corners. The sheet covered corpse lay undisturbed on its bench in the middle of the room. There was however, one loose fold of sheet on the right side of the head. Bannerman could have sworn that he had tucked the sheet round the head securely. He stared at it, his mind racked with unease.

He laid the instrument tray down by the side of the body and took off his coat. He rolled up his sleeves and put on a pair of surgical gloves, stretching his fingers and snapping the material back on his wrists to make sure the fit was perfect. He donned a second pair. There was no point in taking any risks with a disease as deadly as this. He fitted one of the wide-gauge needles aseptically on to a syringe and put the sterile plastic needle guard back on while he unwrapped the head of the corpse.

As he touched the sheet Bannerman experienced a moment of sheer terror; the corpse suddenly sat up straight. He could do nothing but stare wide eyed and open mouthed at the unfolding nightmare before him. The corpse's head, still covered with the sheet, turned slowly towards him and suddenly hit him full in the face with a vicious head-butt. Pain exploded inside Bannerman's head and consciousness was lost in a galaxy of stars.

FOURTEEN

Banneman came to with a blinding headache and the taste of grit in his mouth. He sat up slowly, spat the dirt out and gingerly touched his face to discover that his nose had been broken. He let out a grunt of pain as the bone moved under the skin. There was a good deal of congealed blood on his face but, as far as he could determine, there was no further serious damage. His ribs felt fine and his teeth were intact so it seemed that the assault had been confined to the single head butt that had laid him out. He looked about him and saw that he was now alone in the room. The 'corpse' had gone.

Painfully, he got to his feet and deduced from the stiffness in his limbs that he must have been lying in the same position for some considerable time. He had to pause half-way up the stairs and knelt for a moment when he felt consciousness start to slip away from him again. He tried putting his head between his knees to improve blood circulation but a protest from his aching head overruled the move. He compromised by resting for a moment before continuing upstairs to telephone Angus MacLeod.

'Who did you say did it?' said MacLeod, thinking that he hadn't heard right.

'The corpse, well, of course, it wasn't the corpse, it was someone pretending to be the corpse. Oh Christ, just get over here will you,' he snapped. He immediately regretted it but, for the moment, the pain in his head was dictating his behaviour. He found a bathroom and examined the damage to his face in the mirror. The blood made it look much worse than it actually

215

was and he recoiled from the sight that met him. He looked as if he had just been a spectacularly unsuccessful contender for the heavyweight championship of the world. 'Lucky punch Harry,' he murmured in true British heavyweight style. 'Lucky punch.'

MacLeod arrived and called out his name.

'In here,' croaked Bannerman.

MacLeod came into the bathroom and immediately took over. 'Let me do that,' he insisted. 'Come through here. It'll be more comfortable.' He led Bannerman to one of the treatment rooms where he set about cleaning up his face and resetting his broken nose. 'You're going to have two lovely black eyes in the morning,' he said. 'You can get dark glasses at MacPhail's in the High Street.'

'Thanks,' said Bannerman sourly. 'I found the front door unlocked when I arrived. Did you forget to lock it?'

'On the contrary, I distinctly remember locking it,' said Macleod.

Bannerman nodded. 'I should have thought of that,' he said. 'Whoever broke in tonight was inside when I arrive. It never even occurred to me to think that someone had picked the lock. I assumed you had left it open.'

'Should I call the police?' asked MacLeod.

'I don't think so,' replied Bannerman, thinking what the local constabulary would make of it all.

'But Turnbull's body. It's gone.'

'And I don't think we'll see it again,' said Bannerman. 'Whoever removed it obviously suspected that I'd try to get to the body for path specimens, permission or no permission, and they were right. They even saw me arrive to carry out what amounts to an illegal procedure. It could be argued that I am a bigger criminal than they are. They will maintain that they were only seeing that the grieving widow's wishes were respected.'

'Difficult,' said MacLeod. 'What do you want to do?'

'Sleep,' replied Bannerman, touching the bridge of his nose as if it were a butterfly's wing. 'I need some sleep.'

*　　*　　*

216

Bannerman woke early. The wind had disturbed him by attempting to rattle his bedroom window out of its frame as the latest gale swept in from the Atlantic to funnel through the streets of Stobmor.

'Bloody country,' he murmured as he lay listening to the sound which alternated between a moan and a howl according to wind velocity. After a few minutes he decided it would be better to get up. There was an electric kettle in the room in deference to the fashion for 'tea making facilities' in hotel bedrooms. He got up and switched it on. He checked the range of sachets beside the kettle while it boiled. Tea, coffee and hot chocolate. They all had one thing in common; they had obviously been lying in the room for a very long time. The packs were all brittle. Bannerman guessed that they had seen summer come and go in Stobmor. He tore open a sachet of instant coffee and braced himself for the taste. He was wise to do so. The 'coffee' tasted like salt water laced with floor sweepings and cigarette ash.

A couple of sips proved enough. He poured the contents of the cup down the wash-hand basin and caught sight of himself in the mirror. He drew his finger lightly round the dark purple circles under both eyes. 'Good Lord,' he murmured. 'If London Zoo are looking for a new panda, you're in with a chance.'

With a sigh of resignation, he crossed to the window where he drew open the curtains to look out on deserted, wind-swept streets. The sky was ominously dark and threatening. Rain wasn't far away. 'Bonnie Scotland,' he whispered, 'you're an absolute joy . . .'

Bannerman pondered on what he should do next. He felt frustrated and angry at having been beaten yet again by the factions determined to prevent investigation of the outbreak but he knew that he mustn't allow these feelings to dictate his actions. He must be practical. He felt sure that Turnbull's body would be kept hidden until a cremation took place. Alerting the police might force the handing over of the body but access would still be nigh impossible. He would still not be able to get the specimens he needed for lab investigation.

He still had the option of forcing the issue with court

involvement and Angus MacLeod's collusion but he'd ruled this out because of what it would do to relationships within the community. He decided on a conservative course of action. Despite the terms of the deal with Allison, which allowed him to call for a full-scale investigation if another case arose within the four week period, there was no point in doing so if there was nothing there to investigate! There were, however, a couple of other things he could do until he had decided what to tell the MRC. One was to talk to Gordon Buchan's widow.

The last time he had been in the area May Buchan had been recuperating on holiday. Presumably she was back now and perhaps she could throw some light on how her father had contracted the disease. First he would have to find out where she was staying.

He remembered that Sproat, the farmer at Inverladdie, had said she would be moving back in with her parents when she returned, but of course, they were now both dead and the family house in Stobmor had been burned to the ground. Would she still be staying in the tied cottage on the farm? he wondered. The girl who served him breakfast confirmed, between sidelong glances at the state of his face, that she was. When it seemed that she might have plucked up enough courage to ask what had happened, Bannerman said quickly, 'Don't ask.'

Wearing a pair of dark glasses which he purchased from MacPhail's in the High Street, as recommended by Angus MacLeod, Bannerman got into the car to drive up to Inverladdie Farm. There hadn't been a mirror in the dark, dusty general store so he looked at himself as best he could in the rear view mirror of the car. 'Very Jack Nicholson,' he murmured at the sight. He hoped he wouldn't alarm May Buchan.

The rain that had been threatening for the last two hours finally arrived as Bannerman nursed the car up the track to Inverladdie Farm. One moment he was driving up a clearly defined farm road, the next he was moving slowly up the bed of a fast flowing river.

When he eventually reached the cottage he was pleased to see that someone was at home. There was a light on in the kitchen.

He made a run for the shelter of the porch and knocked on the door. It was answered by a very tanned woman in her thirties; her hair had been bleached almost blonde by recent exposure to the sun. She was wearing tight-fitting jeans and a white sweater with a small gold crucifix dangling over it. Her feet were bare.

'Mrs Buchan? I'm Ian Bannerman. I wonder if I could ask you a few questions?'

May Buchan looked as if she might have argued the point had the weather been kinder but rain and wind were funnelling in through the open door. She said, 'You'd better come in.'

Bannerman explained who he was and expressed his sympathy at the death of her husband and parents.

May Buchan thanked him automatically and stared at his glasses. 'It's not exactly sunny,' she said.

Bannerman touched the glasses self-consciously and said, 'I have a slight eye problem.' He thought it rather rude of May Buchan to have made the comment, but at least it told him what kind of person she was. On the other hand, maybe the loss of three close relations in quick succession had simply stripped the veneer of social nicety from her?

'I see,' she said, still staring.

Bannerman tried to establish some kind of rapport with her. 'You have a wonderful tan,' he said. 'You didn't get that in Bonnie Scotland.'

'Nassau,' said May Buchan.

'The Bahamas?' exclaimed Bannerman.

'The Sproats have been very kind. They paid for the trip. They thought it would help me get over Gordon's death.'

'That was very nice of them,' said Bannerman, thinking that he had misjudged John Sproat.

'It was a surprise,' said May Buchan. 'Unfortunately while I was away my father . . . well, you know.'

'Yes, I'm sorry,' said Bannerman. 'I'll come straight to the point. I'm trying to establish a connection between your husband's death and your father's and I'd like you to help me find it.'

May Buchan looked uncertain. 'But Gordon died of meningitis. Dad wasn't ill. Something just snapped inside him and he

219

went on the rampage. What sort of connection could there be?' she asked.

'I think they were both suffering from the same illness,' said Bannerman. 'Your husband was working with the infected sheep on the farm before he fell ill wasn't he?'

'Yes, he and the others were burying them in the lime pit.'

'Was your father involved in this at all?' asked Bannerman.

'My father?' exclaimed May Buchan as if it was the most ridiculous thing she had ever heard. 'No, of course not. He never came near the farm at the best of times. Apart from that he and Gordon didn't exactly see eye to eye.'

'So they didn't see each other socially?'

May Buchan shook her head. 'Once a year at most.'

'But you saw your mother and father?'

'I visited them in the town, usually once a week.'

'Can you think of any way your father could have come into contact with the infected sheep on Inverladdie Farm?'

'No,' said May Buchan shaking her head in annoyance. 'What's all this about sheep? Why do you keep going on about sheep? Gordon died of meningitis.'

'The truth is that we're not quite sure what your husband and the others died of. It is just possible that infected sheep were involved,' said Bannerman.

May Buchan looked as if she had been struck. Despite her tan, Bannerman saw her pale visibly. 'What the hell do you mean, "involved"?' she rasped. 'The sheep died of *Scrapie*; the vet said so.'

Bannerman proceeded carefully. He said, 'It is possible that it wasn't an ordinary strain of *Scrapie* but something that could be transmitted to man.'

'Oh my God,' said May Buchan.

The air was electric. Bannerman knew he was on the verge of finding out something important. He mustn't push May Buchan too hard. He let the silence put pressure on her.

'Oh Christ!' said May Buchan, burying her head in her hands.

Bannerman remained silent.

'I can give you your connection,' said May Buchan between

sobs. 'Gordon and the two others . . . and my father . . . ate meat from one of the sheep.'

'They ate it?' exclaimed Bannerman.

May Buchan nodded. 'In the past when there's been a *Scrapie* outbreak old man Sproat has got the beasts off to market as quickly as possible.'

'But surely that's illegal?' said Bannerman.

'Everyone knows that *Scrapie* doesn't affect human beings so where's the harm? If the farmers declare the disease, government compensation isn't anything like market value so what can you expect?'

'But Sproat didn't send them to market this time,' said Bannerman.

'It all happened too quickly for him,' said May Buchan. 'The sheep were dropping like flies. He called in the vet and after a lot of discussion old man Sproat and the vet told Gordon and the others it was *Scrapie*. They were to bury the carcasses in a lime pit.' May Buchan had to pause for a moment to compose herself before going on. 'Gordon thought this was a bit of a waste so he and the others kept one of the sheep and brought it here. They butchered it and I put it in the freezer.'

'And they all ate it?'

'Gordon asked the two other sheep workers to Sunday dinner to thank them for their help.'

'But you?'

'I'm vegetarian,' replied May Buchan. 'And so is my mother.'

'But the connection with your father?' asked Bannerman.

May Buchan dabbed at her eyes with a paper tissue. 'Just before I went off on holiday I went to see my mother. I took some mutton chops from the freezer. I thought they would do for Dad's dinner.'

'I see,' said Bannerman. His mind was reeling from the information. Here surely was the proof that sheep *Scrapie* had been implicated in the men's deaths. 'Mrs Buchan did you know a man called Colin Turnbull?' he asked.

May Buchan looked at him blankly. 'Never heard of him,' she replied.

'Are you sure?' Bannerman pressed. This was the one remaining link he had to forge.

'I'm certain,' said May Buchan. 'Who is he?'

'He was a quarry worker. His wife is the primary school teacher in Stobmor.'

'Sorry. Don't know them.'

'Is there any chance that your husband might have known Colin Turnbull?'

'I suppose so,' said May Buchan, 'But I think not. If Gordon had known him, so would I; it's as simple as that in a place like this.'

Bannerman nodded, disappointed that he had failed at the final hurdle. Then suddenly he had a thought which wiped out all thoughts of disappointment. 'Mrs Buchan,' he said, trying to disguise the excitement he felt welling up inside him, 'Do you have any of the sheep left in the freezer?'

'Well . . . yes,' replied May Buchan.

Bannerman closed his eyes momentarily and gave silent thanks. 'I need some for testing,' he said.

May Buchan got up and went through to the kitchen. Bannerman followed her and watched as she raised the lid of a chest freezer. She lifted out a couple of white plastic bags and handed them to Bannerman. 'Will this be enough?' she asked.

'Perfect,' said Bannerman. 'What happened to the remains of the carcass?'

'Gordon buried it out the back.'

'In lime?'

'No.'

'Can you show me where?'

May Buchan opened the kitchen door and pointed to the dry-stone dyke at the foot of the garden. She said, 'Just there,' pointing to a far corner.

'I'll need a shovel.'

'In the shed round the corner.'

Bannerman fastened up his collar against the weather and asked if May had any plastic bags. She opened a drawer and handed him a couple of bin liners. 'Anything else?' she asked.

'Kitchen knives, sharp ones.'

May Buchan pointed to a wooden block next to the draining board. It held half a dozen knives. He selected two.

Bannerman was wet through in no time but it didn't matter. His excitement at having found a source of pathological evidence took precedence over all other considerations. He even took comfort from the fact that the rain had made the ground soft and easy to turn over with the spade. The remains of the sheep were not deep. At the first sign of them he stopped using the spade and knelt down to remove earth with his hands, like an archaeologist uncovering precious artefacts of a long-departed civilization.

He found the head and lifted it clear of the mud. A worm crawled out of an eye socket but apart from that it seemed to be in reasonably good condition. He carried it over to the tool shed to gain some protection from the elements while he got to work with the knives.

As he worked, he reassured himself with thoughts that the *Scrapie* agent was one of the toughest infective agents known to man. It could survive treatment which would sterilize any other known virus or bacterium in the world. A relatively short time lying in the soil would have no adverse effect at all. He managed to recover at least fifty grams of brain material and knew that that would be quite sufficient for analysis. With all his samples safely into plastic bags, Bannerman secured the necks and left them in the shed while he re-buried the remains of the sheep.

'Did you get what you wanted?' asked May Buchan when he returned to the house.

Bannerman nodded.

'When will you know for sure?'

'Probably within three to six weeks,' replied Bannerman. He saw the look of self-recrimination in the woman's eyes and said, 'You really mustn't blame yourself you know.'

'I served it up to them. I killed them.'

'There was no way you could have possibly known. As you say, *Scrapie* has always been considered harmless to human beings.'

'Why should it be any different this time?'

Bannerman shook his head and said, 'I don't know, but with a bit of luck, and these,' he held up the bags, 'I'm going to find out.'

Bannerman turned as he got to the door and said, 'Mrs Buchan I would be very grateful if you would say nothing about this to anyone. Nothing has been proved as yet.'

'I promise,' said May Buchan.

'One more thing. You must destroy the entire contents of your freezer. Burn everything.'

'There's not much in it anyway,' said May Buchan. 'I'm going to have to move out of here very soon. The Sproats will be wanting the cottage. They've been very good about letting me stay on here so long. Oh my God . . .'

'What is it?'

May Buchan stood for a moment with her hands up to her mouth. She said, 'I've just realized . . .'

'Realized what?'

'I would probably have given the meat away to friends before I left here.'

'Thank God I came,' said Bannerman.

Bannerman's euphoria at having made progress at last was tempered on the way back to Stobmor by the fact that he still had to make one of the pieces fit, and that piece was Colin Turnbull. Could Turnbull have eaten infected meat too? And if so, where had it come from? What was probably more important, was there any more still around? He had been assuming that the original infected sheep presented no problem because they had been buried in lime but maybe more than one had found its way into the freezers of Achnagelloch? He would have a word with MacLeod about it. The people respected their GP. A word about the possible dangers of eating sheep meat which had 'fallen off the back of a lorry' would be heeded. As for Turnbull, it seemed unlikely that he would have dined alone on illicit meat and it would be stretching coincidence a bit far if Turnbull's wife should turn out to be vegetarian too.

Thinking of Turnbull's wife made Bannerman realize that he

would have to speak to her and judging by her behaviour yesterday, he wasn't exactly her favourite person.

As he entered the main square at Stobmor he was still thinking about how best to approach her. He got out of the car and saw a bus pull up across the street. Shona got down from it.

Bannerman suddenly felt good, as if the sun had come out. He smiled broadly and called out 'Hello there!'

Shona crossed the street, smiling and Bannerman wrapped his arms around her. 'It's so good to see you,' he said.

Shona laughed at his obvious pleasure and asked, 'Have you suddenly become a film star or haven't you noticed that it's raining?'

Bannerman lifted the dark glasses and Shona gasped. 'What on earth have you been doing?'

'It's quite a story. Come on inside.'

They went into the hotel and Shona registered.

'Will the adjoining room be all right?' asked the clerk.

'Fine,' said Bannerman, choosing to ignore the smirk on the man's face.

'Will there be anything else?'

'I'd like some ice,' said Bannerman.

'Ice?'

'Yes, lots of ice. Have it sent up to my room will you?'

'Yes sir, if you say so.'

Bannerman turned to Shona and said, 'That's given him something to think about.'

'Me too,' replied Shona, with a quizzical look, as they headed for the stairs.

Bannerman filled Shona in on everything that had happened.

'But will the specimens be all right packed in ice?' she asked.

'I can't ask the hotel to put them in their freezer,' replied Bannerman.

'But if it was well wrapped?'

'I can't risk it,' replied Bannerman. 'We can't put infected material like this anywhere near foodstuffs. I'll just have to keep changing the ice until we leave for Edinburgh in the morning. A polystyrene box would help with insulation. Any ideas?'

'Lots of things are packed in polystyrene these days. Why not ask the desk clerk? He might be able to come up with something.'

Bannerman phoned down to the desk.

'A polystyrene box?'

'Yes, and more ice.'

'I'll see what I can do.'

A few minutes later the clerk appeared at the door with an armful of polystyrene and a full ice bucket. 'This was the packing from a new microwave oven,' said the man. 'Will this do.'

'Nice and thick,' said Bannerman. 'This will do perfectly.'

Bannerman closed the door and saw that Shona was smiling broadly. 'What's up?' he asked.

'That poor man was obviously wondering what we were up to,' said Shona.

'Really?' said Bannerman. He turned and looked at the closed door, wondering if the clerk was outside listening. 'Use the polystyrene!' he said suddenly in a loud voice suffused with mock passion.

Shona had to cover her mouth.

'Now the ice! Oh God yes, the ice!' 'More polystyrene! My God that's wonderful.' Bannerman moved around the room feigning the sounds of sexual ecstasy while Shona collapsed on the bed in fits of laughter. 'You're crazy!'

'Not usually,' said Bannerman, suddenly serious. 'I think it comes with being happy.'

Shona got up and came over to him. 'Then long may you be crazy,' she said softly. She reached up to kiss him.

'Mind my nose,' said Bannerman.

Bannerman fashioned the polystyrene packing into a container for the sheep samples and packed ice around it before sealing the package with adhesive tape. 'Perfect,' he said, admiring his handiwork. 'That just leaves Mrs Turnbull to deal with, then we can have a nice quiet dinner, a good night's sleep and we're off to Edinburgh.'

'From what you've said, she's not going to be very pleased to see you,' said Shona.

Bannerman nodded and said, 'I think I'll try getting Angus MacLeod to approach her first. She was very upset yesterday but I'm sure she'll be calmer today.' He called MacLeod and asked for his help.

'Are you going to try to persuade her that her husband's body should be handed over for post-mortem?' asked MacLeod.

'No I'm not,' replied Bannerman. 'Apart from anything else, that would be accusing her of complicity in its removal. I just want to ask her a few questions. I promise I won't upset her and there will be no mention of post-mortems.'

'Then I'll do my best,' said MacLeod.

'There's one more thing Angus,' said Bannerman.

'What?'

Bannerman told him about the infected sheep which had escaped destruction in the lime pit. 'Do you think you could make discreet enquiries to see if any more sheep "escaped" from Inverladdie and quietly warn people off?'

MacLeod said that he would.

Ten minutes later MacLeod called back. He said, 'Julie Turnbull has agreed to talk to you. I will hold you to your promise not to upset her.'

'Don't worry,' said Bannerman. 'When can I see her?'

'Seven-thirty this evening.'

'Her address?'

MacLeod read it out and Bannernman copied it down. 'I'm grateful to you,' he said.

'Just don't upset her,' said MacLeod.

Bannerman left the hotel, assuring Shona that he shouldn't be any longer than half an hour. He had dressed casually, hoping that this might help dispel Julie Turnbull's initial impression of him as a ghoul, hell-bent on stealing her husband's brain. Shona had suggested that a suit and tie might be deemed more respectful but Bannerman decided that Julie would have seen enough black ties in the last twenty-four hours. He wore a sweater, slacks and a leather jerkin.

Bannerman followed MacLeod's directions and found the house in a quiet street three blocks north of the primary school where Julie worked. The blinds were half drawn. There was an air of neatness and order about the place, an air which extended to others in the row with one exception. The house which stood three doors away from the Turnbull's cottage had two wrecked cars in its drive. It's garden was unkempt and a motor cycle with its back wheel missing was propped up against the front wall. 'There's always one,' thought Bannerman.

Julie Turnbull was wearing black. Her face was pale and her eyes were ringed with redness. She took a pace back to indicate that Bannerman should come in but didn't say anything until they were in the living-room. 'I really didn't want to see you Dr Bannerman but Dr MacLeod persuaded me that I should.'

'I'm grateful to you, Mrs Turnbull,' replied Bannerman. 'Please believe me when I say that you have my deepest sympathy. I met your husband on several occasions when I was last here and I liked him a lot.'

'What is it you want to know?' asked Julie Turnbull.

'I want to know if Colin knew any of the other men who died recently in Achnagelloch and Stobmor.'

'He knew the man who worked at the garage. Colin had his car serviced there.'

'Were they close friends?'

'No.'

'How about the men from Inverladdie Farm?'

'He didn't know them at all.'

'Are you sure?'

'He may have known them to nod to in the street, but no better than that,' said Julie. 'He steered clear of sheep farmers whenever he could.'

'Why was that?'

'Colin was a clever man, Dr Bannerman. He worked as a labourer but he had a good brain. He was bored by constant talk of sheep. He resented the fact that so much of the life of the town revolved around sheep and sheep farming. I think that's what made him decide to do a part-time degree. It exercised his mind. It gave him the stimulation he needed.'

Bannerman nodded. He asked, 'Did you and Colin ever eat apart?'

Julie Turnbull's face registered surprise at the question. She half shrugged her shoulders in bewilderment and said, 'No, not that I can think of, except for lunch of course.'

'Lunch?'

'Colin took sandwiches to the quarry.'

'Who made them?'

'Me. What are you suggesting Doctor? That Colin was killed by something he ate?'

Bannerman was reluctant to commit himself to a straight answer. He said, 'Mrs Turnbull it's important that I establish certain details about Colin's diet over the past two weeks or so. Please bear with me.'

'What details?' asked Julie Turnbull.

'Sheep products in particular. Mutton, lamb.'

'That's easy, none.'

'None?'

'Colin disliked sheep meat. He never ate it at all.'

'Never?' repeated Bannerman, feeling failure descend on him like a lead yoke.

'Never.'

'Does this mean that Colin was vegetarian?'

'No. He liked nothing better than a good steak. He simply didn't like mutton or lamb.'

Bannerman tried desperately to think of another way that Turnbull could have contracted the disease. He knew he would probably not have another chance to question Julie Turnbull. He asked a broad general question, 'Did anything change about Colin's lifestyle in the past two to three weeks? Did he do anything out of the ordinary or different?'

Julie shook her head slowly as she considered. 'No, I don't think so, except for the geological survey of course.'

'Tell me about that,' said Bannerman.

'He's been doing geology for his degree. He thought he would impress Mr van Gelder if he carried out a survey of the land in the surrounding area.'

'I remember him saying something about that the last time I saw him,' said Bannerman. 'He was hoping for a better job with the company.'

'That's right,' replied Julie. She paused as she considered that this would not now ever happen.

'When did he do this Mrs Turnbull?'

'At the weekends.'

'Was he out last weekend?'

Julie Turnbull nodded.

'Do you know where?'

Julie shook her head but she got up and went over to a writing desk to open the drawer. She pulled out a series of charts and said, 'These are Colin's notes on his work.'

'May I borrow them?'

Julie handed them over without saying anything.

Bannerman got up to go. He thanked Julie, offered his sympathy again and said, 'I'll see that these are returned to you.'

'How did it go?' asked Shona when Bannerman got back to the hotel.

'Not good,' replied Bannerman. 'Turnbull never ate mutton or lamb. He didn't like it.'

'What rotten luck,' said Shona. 'Just as it all seemed to fit together.'

Bannerman smiled wryly and said, 'That's the way it goes.'

'Perhaps he ate it without knowing?'

'How?'

'In a stew or a curry or something.'

Bannerman hadn't considered that possibility but he dismissed it after a little thought. 'Turnbull ate nothing but what his wife cooked except for lunch-times when he ate sandwiches prepared by her. She wouldn't have given him something he didn't like.'

'I suppose not,' agreed Shona. 'Maybe a restaurant meal she forgot about?'

'If infected meat had been served in a restaurant there would have been lots of cases,' said Bannerman.

'So how did he get it?' asked Shona.

'I wish to hell I knew.'

FIFTEEN

Bannerman and Shona were sitting in the hotel bar just after ten o'clock when the barman came over to say that Bannerman's car had been bumped in the car-park by a leaving customer. He didn't think the damage was great but would he mind taking a look? The driver concerned was waiting for him in the car-park.

'I don't believe it,' said Bannerman. 'The hire company will have me black-listed if this goes on.'

'Don't lose your temper,' cautioned Shona with a smile.

'Won't be long,' said Bannerman.

He walked round to the hotel car-park and over to his car. The car-park wasn't well lit – a single lamp was mounted on the back wall of the hotel – but he should have been able to see anyone waiting there. There was no sign. He took a look round the car for signs of damage and failed to see anything. After a second inspection he thought he detected a small scrape on the rear bumper but when he bent down to touch it he found that it disappeared when he rubbed it; it was dirt. He stood up and took another look around the car-park; it remained silent and empty.

Bannerman shrugged his shoulders and decided that the man must have left when he saw that there were no real signs of damage after all. Modern plastic bumpers could take much more in the way of impact than the old metal ones without showing signs of damage. He started to walk back up the lane leading to the front of the hotel when, suddenly, he was gripped from

231

behind and pushed hard up against the wall of the building. His broken nose came into contact with the rough stone and he let out a yelp of pain. Tears welled up in his eyes.

'Where is Colin Turnbull's body?' rasped a voice behind him.

'I've no idea,' gasped Bannerman, as he fought against having his arms twisted up his back.

'You were told that Julie Turnbull didn't want the body interfered with, weren't you?' said the voice. The statement was punctuated with another painful jerk on his arms. 'But that wasn't good enough for you was it?'

Bannerman let out a gasp of pain and tried to lean forward to take some of the pressure off his shoulder sockets. As he did so a knee came up and caught him between the legs. He cried out and the grip on him was relaxed, allowing him to fall to the ground.

'Where is the body?' repeated the voice.

Bannerman thought he recognized it despite the fact that the man was angry and rasping rather than speaking. He turned over and saw his attackers. There were two of them. Mitchell, the security chief, and one of the two power workers who had been plaguing his life. 'You should bloody know!' he replied through his pain.

'What does that mean?' demanded Mitchell, drawing back his foot as if to kick Bannerman on the ground.

Bannerman curled up defensively. When the kick wasn't delivered he said, 'What's this pantomime all about Mitchell? Your lot took it away last night. How do you think I got a face like this?'

Mitchell took a closer look at Bannerman's face and saw the black eyes and damage to his nose. He seemed lost for words for a moment. 'Are you trying to tell me that you didn't have Turnbull's body removed for pathology?' he said.

'Of course I didn't,' gasped Bannerman. 'And you were the only ones interested in preventing me doing that. You have interfered with my work here through every step of the way because you imagine I'm trying to close you down, so what is all this crap about me taking the body?'

'We haven't got it,' said Mitchell.

'Jesus,' gasped Bannerman, overloaded with pain and frustration. 'I don't believe this place . . .'

'Who else would want it?' said Mitchell.

'You,' accused Bannerman.

'Why do you keep saying that?' demanded Mitchell. 'Julie Turnbull didn't want you quacks getting your hands on Colin. We're just seeing that her wishes are respected.'

'Like hell you are,' rasped Bannerman.

The power worker, the man Bannerman had the run in with in the hotel washroom on the previous evening, moved as if to strike him but Mitchell put out a restraining hand.

Bannerman looked up at the man and said, 'All the sheep aren't on the hills are they Mitchell?'

The insult proved too much for the power worker who lashed out with his foot and caught Bannerman in the solar plexus.

Bannerman brought up the contents of his stomach and curled up in agony. Through his pain he heard Mitchell berate the man then turn his attention back to him. 'If it's any comfort Doctor,' he said, 'I believe you. Perhaps you will believe me when I say that . . . we haven't got it either.' The men left, leaving Bannerman lying on the cobbles.

Bannerman got to his knees and paused for a moment with one hand against the wall of the hotel. He could hear the engine of an approaching car. It slowed and turned into the lane leading from the main street to the hotel car-park. As its headlights swung round they caught him in their glare and the car came to a halt. Bannerman shielded his eyes and heard a car door being slammed as the driver got out.

'My dear Doctor. What on earth happened?' asked a friendly voice. It was Joop van Gelder.

'I was mugged,' replied Bannerman.

'This is awful,' exclaimed van Gelder. 'Are you hurt badly? Can you stand? Let's get you inside and then I'll call the police.'

'No, no police,' said Bannerman.

'But . . .'

233

'Really, no police. It's personal. Just leave it.'

'Personal?' exclaimed van Gelder. 'You mean you know who did this to you?'

'Just give me a hand up will you.'

Van Gelder helped Bannerman to his feet and supported him on one side, up the lane leading to the front of the hotel. As they passed the Dutchman's car, Bannerman saw that there was a man sitting in the front passenger seat. For some reason he couldn't fathom, alarm bells started ringing in his head. He felt sure that he knew the man but in his present state he couldn't think clearly enough to put a name to him.

Shona came rushing over as soon as he was through the front door. 'I was just coming to find you. Just look at you! What happened?'

'Let's say there was a misunderstanding over the fate of Colin Turnbull's body,' said Bannerman.

'Come upstairs. Can you manage?' Shona took over from van Gelder and helped Bannerman upstairs. Van Gelder called after them, 'I still think you should let me call the police.'

'No,' said Bannerman. 'Thanks for your assistance.'

Shona closed the room door and said, 'Tell me. What happened out there?'

'It was Mitchell from the power station and one of his pet monkeys. They thought I had stolen Turnbull's body to carry out an autopsy.'

'They thought *you* had taken the body?' exclaimed Shona. 'But you were sure that *they* had taken it!'

'That's about the size of it,' agreed Bannerman, holding his stomach.

'What hurts most?' asked Shona.

'I'd rather not say,' said Bannerman.

Shona smiled sympathetically. She said, 'You don't believe in taking the easy way do you Ian?'

'Character-building stuff,' said Bannerman through gritted teeth.

'So who did take the body, and why?' asked Shona.

'An embarrassing question,' said Bannerman.

'Embarrassing?'
'Because I haven't a clue.'

Bannerman changed out of his soiled clothes and cleaned himself up. Shona helped by applying cotton wool soaked in antiseptic to some new superficial cuts and grazes.
'Will you be fit enough to travel in the morning?' asked Shona.
'Yes . . . if you'll drive?'
'Don't I always?' said Shona.
Bannerman smiled. It turned out to be more of a grimace.
'Can I get you a drink?'
'Brandy.'
'Large?'
'Enormous . . . and Shona?'
'Yes?'
'If you get the chance, try to find out who van Gelder was with this evening, will you?'
'Still playing detective?' smiled Shona.
'Not for much longer,' said Bannerman. 'But I feel sure I know the man who was sitting in his car. I just can't place him and it's bothering me.'
'I'll see what I can do,' said Shona.

Shona left the room and Bannerman got to his feet to walk slowly round the room. His aches and pains were beginning to subside and the question of who had taken the body was now uppermost in his mind. Julie Turnbull could not have known about it or she would have raised hell at their meeting, unless, of course, she had arranged it! That seemed to be the most likely explanation. Julie Turnbull had arranged for her husband's body to be removed from the hospital for safety. Perhaps he should let sleeping dogs lie. His first priority was to get the infected sheep brain to Munro in Edinburgh. Searching for Turnbull's body would only delay matters. He and Shona would set off for Edinburgh first thing in the morning. Events in Stobmor could take their natural course.

Shona returned with the brandy and the information that the man with van Gelder was his son, Peter.

'His son?' exclaimed Bannerman.

'I asked the barman,' said Shona.

'Then I must have been mistaken,' said Bannerman. 'I've never met his son.'

'Good looking chap. How are you feeling?'

'Much better.'

'You'd better get some sleep.'

Bannerman nodded.

'You look all in,' said Shona, coming over to him. She kissed him lightly on the cheek. 'See you in the morning.'

For once the weather was kind to them. The sun shone down on Stobmor from a blue sky and fluffy white clouds raced each other in a stiff breeze. There was a strong smell of the sea in the air as Bannerman loaded the polystyrene box containing the samples into the boot of the car and checked that it wasn't leaking. He had opened it earlier to replace the ice.

Shona and Bannerman made good time on the journey down to Edinburgh, stopping only twice on the way. Once to have lunch and fill the tank with petrol and the second time to have coffee and stretch their legs in mid-afternoon. Bannerman phoned the Medical Research Council to keep them appraised of his whereabouts.

Once in Edinburgh, they booked in to a small hotel on the south side of the city and Bannerman called Hector Munro at the Neurobiology Unit.

'Can I bring the samples over?' he asked.

'We're all waiting,' replied Munro. He gave Bannerman directions on how to find the unit which was situated in the university's science complex at Kings Buildings in West Mains Road. Before he left, he thought it polite to call Morag Napier at the university medical school and tell her that he had succeeded in getting some infected brain samples.

'That's good news,' said Morag. 'How did you manage it?'

Bannerman told her about the sheep carcass that had escaped the lime pit.

'What a piece of luck,' said Morag. 'Will you set up the tests yourself?'

Bannerman said that he was giving them to Munro at the Neurobiology Unit but if she would like some to complete the mouse experiments that her department had started then he would see to it that some tissue was sent to her.

'Thank you Doctor,' replied Morag. 'Perhaps you could tell me what tests you are asking Dr Munro to do so that we don't duplicate our efforts?'

Bannerman said that a stained brain section was a first priority. Subsequent tests would depend very much on that.

'Call me when you know,' said Morag.

Bannerman said that he would.

Bannerman spoke into the grille at the side of the entrance door and said who he was. The electric security latch was energized, and he was allowed to enter. At the top of the stairs he met Hector Munro, who was waiting to greet him.

'Whatever happened to you?' exclaimed Munro, when he saw Bannerman's face.

'A long story,' said Bannerman, 'and it would do me no good to relate it. This is what you've been waiting for.' He handed over the polystyrene package containing the sheep samples.

'This is exciting,' said Munro. 'Will you wait for the brain section report?'

'Wouldn't miss it for the world,' smiled Bannerman.

The samples were taken away by two technicians who had been briefed on what was to be done to them.

'Coffee?' asked Munro.

'Please.'

As the two men sipped their coffee in Munro's office, Bannerman broached the subject of the MRC report on brain disease. He told Munro what Milne had said about classifying the Achnagelloch agent as a new virus. Munro smiled and said, 'I suppose he's right in a way. We can hardly classify this thing as a *slow* virus if it has an incubation time of two to three weeks.'

'But the point is that it is a form of *Scrapie!*' insisted Bannerman.

'We've yet to prove that,' said Munro.

'Agreed,' conceded Bannerman. 'But if your tests show that

to be the case, can I count on your support in making the point forcibly to the government?'

Munro looked at him thoughtfully over the rim of his coffee cup. 'Take on the government?' he said. 'And the farmers? You're not asking much are you.'

'All I'm asking is that we tell the truth,' said Bannerman.

'Ah yes, the truth,' said Munro slowly. 'Wouldst it were so simple.'

'Isn't it?' asked Bannerman.

'I don't think it is. We have to consider what is right in this case as well as what the truth of the matter is. We are talking about half-a-dozen deaths here, probably as a result of some freak, biological accident. Against that, we have the whole future of the meat trade in this country.'

'But if it has happened once it could happen again.'

'Maybe,' said Munro, looking down at his desk.

'Then I can't count on your support?'

'Look around you, Doctor; this unit exists on government grants . . .'

Bannerman smiled ruefully.

'Let's wait and see what the tests tell us,' said Munro.

Bannerman nodded with an air of resignation.

The buzzer on Munro's internal phone sounded. He answered it and held a brief conversation before saying to Bannerman, 'Excuse me, there's a problem.'

Munro returned ten minutes later and stood in the doorway of his office. He said, 'I don't quite know how to tell you this.'

Bannerman turned to face him.

'My people have done a couple of brain sections . . .'

'And?' asked Bannerman.

'They're quite normal. No sign of *Scrapie* damage at all.'

'But that's impossible!' protested Bannerman.

'Come and see for yourself.'

Munro led the way through to a laboratory where one of the sections was set up under the microscope. Bannerman sat down and examined the preparation for himself. It seemed perfectly healthy. 'I just don't believe it,' he murmured.

'We've also carried out an antibody test for *Scrapie* associated fibrils. It was negative.'

'Shit,' said Bannerman, feeling utterly deflated.

'Sorry,' said Munro, removing the slide from the microscope. 'Back to the drawing-board.'

'I don't believe it!' stormed Bannerman.

'I think you have to,' soothed Shona. 'Unless you are going to suggest that Dr Munro is part of the conspiracy to cover this thing up.'

Bannerman looked at her and Shona regretted having said it when she saw Bannerman was seriously considering the possibility. 'The other samples!' he said.

'What other samples?' asked Shona.

'I kept some back to give to Morag Napier at the medical school for ethical reasons. 'I could do some preps myself!'

'Aren't you being a little paranoid about this?' ventured Shona.

Bannerman thought for a moment before saying, 'I just cannot believe that three men died after eating this sheep and the sheep had nothing to do with it.'

Shona conceded that he had a point. 'Do what you have to do,' she said.

It was just after eight in the evening when Bannerman drove into the quadrangle at the medical school. He was counting on the fact that most of the staff would have left by now and probably only the duty technicians and perhaps a night security man would be around. He did not want to explain why he was repeating tests that Munro's people had already carried out.

Having been a recent visitor, the technician who answered the bell recognized him and let him in without question. 'Working late, Doctor?' the girl asked. She hadn't realized that he had been away.

'A couple of hours,' smiled Bannerman.

Bannerman turned the corner at the end of the ground floor corridor and found himself face to face with Morag Napier.

'Dr Bannerman?' she exclaimed. 'This is a surprise.'

239

'I was hoping I might catch you,' said Bannerman, recovering well from his shock.

Morag had on her coat and was obviously just about to leave. 'What can I do for you, Doctor?' she asked.

Bannerman came clean about the tests. 'Munro's people found no sign of *Scrapie* infection at all,' he said. 'I just wanted to be absolutely sure.'

I'll help you,' said Morag, taking off her coat.

'There's really no need,' insisted Bannerman. 'I can manage if you don't mind me using your lab?' Bannerman felt uncomfortable, knowing that Morag must have worked out that that was what he had intended doing anyway.

'It's no trouble,' said Morag. 'It'll be quicker if I help, and I wasn't doing anything this evening anyway. My fiancé is away at the moment.'

'That's very kind of you,' said Bannerman. 'I appreciate it.' He removed the brain sample vial from his pocket and handed it to her. They walked back to her lab and she laid the sample down on the bench while she donned her lab coat and put on surgical gloves. Bannerman felt a tingle of anticipation grow inside him as he watched Morag prepare the section. 'I just find it so hard to believe that there was no sign of infection,' he said.

'Are you sure this came from one of the infected sheep?' asked Morag.

'Yes,' replied Bannerman.

'Then we'll see,' said Morag.

Bannerman grew nervous as they waited for the final staining procedure to complete. After a few minutes the electric timer sounded and Morag rinsed away the stain with fresh distilled water. He was pleased to see her hasten the drying procedure by placing the slide under the bulb of an anglepoise lamp for a couple of minutes instead of allowing it to dry naturally in the air like all the books said.

'Now then,' Morag murmured, as she set up the slide under the microscope and adjusted the focus. 'Let's see what we have here . . .'

It took less than thirty seconds for the feelings of excitement to die inside Bannerman. He read the expression on Morag's face as she got up to let him take a look for himself. Each new field he turned to confirmed what Munro had said. He was looking at normal, healthy brain tissue.

Bannerman had been angry and confused when Munro's people had come to this conclusion, but now he was just thoroughly fed up. He jettisoned the slide into a contaminated-waste container and let his head slump forward on his chest for a moment while he thought.

'Most peculiar,' said Morag.

'I just don't understand,' said Bannerman.

'If you have another sample with you I could set up animal tests,' said Morag. 'Maybe this animal was at a very early stage of infection. Perhaps it's just not showing up on section analysis.'

'I don't have another one with me,' said Bannerman. 'I'll bring one in tomorrow if that's all right?'

'Of course. Did Dr Munro set up animal tests?' asked Morag.

Bannerman shook his head. 'I was so disappointed at the section result I forgot to leave him a sample,' he confessed.

'Never mind,' said Morag sympathetically. 'I'll send up a full range.'

Bannerman thanked Morag for her help and wished her goodnight. It started to rain as he crossed the quadrangle to get into his car.

Bannerman was on his second gin and tonic in the hotel bar before he realized how badly he was behaving towards Shona. He had hardly said a word to her since his return. 'I'm sorry,' he said. 'It was just such a disappointment. I can't stop thinking about it.'

'I understand,' said Shona, giving his arm a squeeze. 'Why don't you get plastered. You deserve it.'

Despite promising not to, Bannerman periodically returned to the subject of the sheep brain, expressing disbelief that fate could be so cruel.

'You'll just have to accept it,' said Shona. 'This particular sheep didn't poison the men.'

241

Bannerman stared at the glass on the table and said slowly, 'What did you say?'

'I said, you'd just have to accept it,' said Shona.

'No, the rest,' insisted Bannerman.

'I said the sheep didn't poison the men, why?'

'You used the word "poison". I'd forgotten all about the possibility of chemical mutagenesis of the virus!' said Bannerman. He got up from his chair, left the bar and ran upstairs. He came back down with his coat on and his hands searching through his pockets for his car keys. Shona watched him in the hall with wide eyes. 'I won't be long, I'll explain later,' he said.

Bannerman disappeared through the front door leaving Shona wondering what on earth was going on. Within seconds, he had reappeared in the doorway and was looking embarrassed. 'I've had rather a lot to drink,' he said. 'Will you drive?'

'Don't I always?' said Shona, holding out her hand for the keys.

'Where are we going?' she asked as she started the car.

'The Royal Infirmary.'

Shona stopped the car outside a shop that was still open. She got out without saying anything and returned a few minutes later with some chewing gum and a packet of peppermint sweets. 'Eat,' she said, handing them over. 'If you go into the infirmary smelling like a distillery they'll call the police. Now say after me, the quick brown fox jumped over the lazy dog . . .'

'That's for typists,' protested Bannerman.

'It'll do, clever dick!'

'The . . . quick . . . brown fox . . . jumped over the lashey dog.'

'Close,' sighed Shona. 'Again!'

Bannerman continued with his elecution practice until they reached the hospital. 'Remember,' said Shona. 'Speak slowly and don't get excited. Do you have your ID?'

Bannerman checked his inside pocket and said that he had. 'I won't be long,' he said and disappeared inside the building. He returned fifteen minutes later.

'Did they agree to do what you wanted?' asked Shona.

'Yes,' said Bannerman. 'They agreed. I'll know tomorrow. Thanks Shona.' He leaned over and kissed her gently on the lips.

'Peppermint,' she said. 'Are you going to tell me what all this is about?'

'I used to be a great fan of old war films,' said Bannerman.

'So what?' said Shona.

'There used to come a point in just about all of them when someone would say, "It's a long shot but it might just work." Well, this is my moment.'

'I see,' said Shona with an inflection in her voice that made it clear that she didn't.

Next morning, as they walked through Holyrood Park after breakfast, Shona asked Bannerman when he would call the hospital.

'After lunch,' he replied.

'What exactly did you ask them to do?'

'The Royal Infirmary has a poisons reference laboratory. When you used the word "poison" last night it made me realize that chemical involvement was something I hadn't really considered. The presence of the power station had blinkered me to everything except radiation as a cause of mutation. I had a look around the barn at the farm but that's about all.'

'So you think that the *Scrapie* virus was altered by some chemical agent?' said Shona, without much enthusiasm.

'It's possible,' said Bannerman. 'But, unlike radiation damage, traces of the chemical might be present in the tissue samples.'

'But there was no sign of *Scrapie* in the brain samples yesterday,' said Shona.

'It occurred to me that the mutant virus acts so quickly that there wouldn't be time for the brain pathology to develop the signs that we normally associate with *Scrapie*. That's why the slides appeared normal yesterday!' But if the samples are injected into mice I bet they'll be dead within days.'

'But the slides that were sent to London showed typical *Scrapie* brain damage,' protested Shona.

243

'Quite so,' said Bannerman, thoughtfully. 'The slides that Gill sent us. I think I just might be able to explain that too.'

Their walk took them down past Holyrood Palace where the Royal Family would stay when in the Scottish capital. At the moment only a handful of workmen were in evidence in the courtyard which, in the summer months, would be thronged with tourists anxious to be led through the rooms where Mary Queen of Scots had once collected her tears in a small glass bottle. They came back on to the high road which climbed up the side of Arthur's Seat, the hill – an extinct volcano – which lay like a recumbent lion in the park. Several joggers from the nearby university halls of residence complex passed them by as they stopped to admire the view across the Firth of Forth to Fife, and the Kinross Hills beyond.

'You haven't explained how the first slides were different,' said Shona.

'I think there was something wrong with them,' said Bannerman. 'I think that's why Gill tried to send the brains to the MRC when he was on the run.'

They stopped on the south side of the hill to look down at Duddingston Loch, a nature reserve which was clad in the grey hues of winter. A few ducks paddled their way through the reed beds like busy tug boats while two swans sailed serenely past in open water, too elegant to notice.

'What was wrong with them?'

'I don't want to say just yet. I need to think.'

'We haven't talked about us,' said Shona.

'I know,' said Bannerman.

'Why not?'

'I don't know where to begin,' confessed Bannerman. 'I don't know where we go from here. Do you?'

Shona smiled and Bannerman asked her why. 'Like I said,' she replied, 'the easy way is never for you.'

'What is the easy way, Shona?'

'Follow your heart,' said Shona.

Bannerman opened his mouth to reply but Shona put her index finger on his lips. 'Ssh!' she said softly. 'You are about to tell me that it isn't that easy. Don't.'

Shona made to walk on but Bannerman called after her. She turned round and Bannerman said, 'I do love you, you know, very much.'

'I know,' said Shona.

They turned to the hotel to be met in the lobby by two men in dark suits. Bannerman had noticed the desk clerk nod to them as he came through the door.

'Dr Bannerman?'

Bannerman nodded.

One of the men flicked open an ID wallet and Bannerman saw the photograph and read the name.

'I'm Inspector Morris. This is Sergeant West. We're from Special Branch.'

'What can I do for you?' asked Bannerman, quite bemused.

'We'd like you to come with us, sir,' said Morris.

'Am I being arrested?' exclaimed Bannerman.

'No, sir,' replied Morris evenly. 'We'd just like to ask you a few questions.'

'About what?'

'Later, sir.'

Bannerman shrugged his apologies to Shona. 'When will I be back?' he asked Morris.

'Can't say, sir.'

'Don't worry,' said Shona . . . 'I'll wait for you.'

Bannerman was shown out to an unmarked, dark green Austin Montego and ushered into the back. Morris got in beside him. West sat in the front passenger seat and said something to the driver – also in plain clothes – which Bannerman couldn't quite catch. He felt that there would be no point in asking where they were going and assumed that it would be the police headquarters. He was surprised therefore when the car turned in through the west gate of the Royal Infirmary. Bang went his theory about it having something to do with the disappearance of Colin Turnbull's body. The car drew to a halt and he was invited to get out.

SIXTEEN

Their footsteps echoed along the corridor that took them to Seminar Room eight. There was no mistaking that they were in a hospital. Even if he had been blindfold, Bannerman would have recognized the distinctive smells of anaesthetic and disinfectant that pervaded hospitals the world over.

'In here, sir,' said West as he opened the door and stood back to allow Bannerman to enter.

There were three men inside. They were seated at a plain wooden table but got up when Bannerman entered.

'Good of you to come Doctor. Please sit down.'

Bannerman remained standing. He said, 'You know who I am but I'm afraid you have the advantage of me.'

The two men in suits looked at each other and then said, 'I'm Jackman.'

'And I'm Mildrew.'

Mildrew indicated to the white coated man on his left, 'This is Dr Mellon of the poisons bureau.'

'Are you Special Branch too?' asked Bannerman.

'No we're not,' replied Jackman.

'Then who are you?' asked Bannerman.

'I can vouch for these gentlemen, sir,' said Morris, attempting to defuse the tension.

'I want to know who they are,' said Bannerman, evenly.

'We are from the Ministry of Defence,' said Jackman with an air of reluctance.

'Special Branch and the Ministry of Defence,' said Bannerman slowly. 'Then presumably this is not in connection with a parking offence?'

Mildrew ignored the comment and said, 'You are Ian Bannerman, consultant pathologist at St Luke's Hospital in London?'

'Correct.'

'Last night you brought in a sample of sheep brain to the Poisons Reference Bureau and requested toxic analysis on it?'

'Yes.'

'Where did you get it?'

'Why do you want to know?'

'Surely it's a reasonable question, Doctor,' said Jackman.

'So is mine,' said Bannerman.

'Frankly, Doctor, I think I should warn you that if you continue to be obstructive you could be in very serious trouble,' said Mildrew.

'What did they find in the sheep brain?' asked Bannerman. 'They did find something, didn't they? That's what this is all about.'

'Where did you get it?'

The impasse continued in silence for a few moments before Bannerman said, 'I'd like to make a telephone call.'

'Do you think you need a lawyer, Doctor?' asked Jackman.

'I'm not calling one,' said Bannerman. 'I would like to speak to Mr Cecil Allison of the Prime Minister's office.'

'The Prime Minister's office?' repeated Jackman. 'What do you have to do with the Prime Minister's office?'

'I've been carrying out an investigation on behalf of the Medical Research Council in conjunction with the PM's office,' replied Bannerman.

Mildrew and Jackman looked at each other and then at Morris who shrugged his shoulders. 'We were unaware of this,' said Jackman. 'There seems to have been a breakdown in communications somewhere.' His look to Morris indicated where he thought it lay. 'Perhaps Inspector Morris will place the call for you.'

Morris moved to an adjoining room and returned a few moments later to say to Bannerman, 'Mr Allison is on the line, sir.'

Bannerman closed the door behind him and picked up the receiver.

'I understand you are in a spot of bother, Doctor,' said Allison.

Bannerman never thought he would be pleased to hear the sound of Allison's voice, but he was. He told him about the sheep brain and about his having requested a chemical toxin analysis on it.

'But what did they find?' asked Allison. 'What's all the fuss about?'

'They won't tell me and I won't tell them where I found it, so we're sitting here, looking at each other.'

'Perhaps I should speak to them,' suggested Allison.

'I'd be grateful.'

Mildrew spoke to Allison in private, then returned to the room and indicated to Bannerman that Allison wanted to speak to him again.

'Bannerman, I suggest that you cooperate fully with Mr Mildrew and his colleagues,' said Allison.

'Without question?' said Bannerman.

'Yes.'

'No way,' said Bannerman, flatly. 'I've not come this far to be fobbed off like this. I want to know what was in the sample.'

'I thought you'd say that,' said Allison. 'I warned Mildrew you might. Mr Mildrew is prepared to tell you more but first you will have to sign the Official Secrets Act.'

'Ye gods! What next,' exclaimed Bannerman.

'If you lab boffins had got this right in the first instance, none of this would have been necessary,' said Allison and put down the phone abruptly.

'Well thanks a lot,' said Bannerman to the dialling tone.

'Sign where I've marked it,' said Jackman, handing Bannerman a copy of the Official Secrets Act.

Bannerman signed without comment and pushed the form to one side.

'The brain sample you presented last night contained traces of a chemical called NYLIT,' said Mildrew.

'Nylit,' repeated Bannerman. 'Never heard of it.'

'We would have been surprised if you had.'

'Where does it come from?'

'This is the cause of our interest, Doctor,' said Mildrew. 'NYLIT is not a by-product of any chemical process, as so many toxins are. It was a specific component of a biological weapon developed in 19 . . . some time ago.'

'A weapon?' exclaimed Bannerman.

'It was one of a chain of compounds developed by our defence establishment.'

'And it's a powerful mutagen?'

'Among other things, yes.'

'So how the hell did it get into a sheep in the north of Scotland?'

'That's what we intend finding out, Doctor, with your help of course.'

'I'll give you all the information I have,' said Bannerman.

It was after ten in the evening before Bannerman got back to the hotel. He was exhausted, having told Mildrew and Jackson every single detail he could remember about the investigation in Achnagelloch and Stobmor.

'I've been so worried,' said Shona. 'What did they want?'

'The sheep were exposed to a powerful mutagen,' said Bannerman.

'Where did it come from?'

'We don't know, but the best guess at the moment is that some canister was washed up on the beach at Inverladdie and through time it leaked and contaminated the ground. Grazing sheep which were incubating the *Scrapie* virus at the time were affected by it, and the rest you know.'

'That still doesn't explain how Colin Turnbull came to be affected,' said Shona.

'No it doesn't,' agreed Bannerman but there was a more pressing question on his mind. He was again considering why the brain sections taken from the dead men at Inverladdie had shown such perfect signs of classical Creutzfeld Jakob Disease when the sections from the poisoned sheep showed no brain degeneration at all? He feared that the answer to that must lie with the people responsible for the pathology on the dead men, Lawrence Gill who was dead and Morag Napier . . . who was not.

It was late and Bannerman did not want to voice his suspicions to Shona. Despite the fact that it was he who had finally worked out the puzzle he was smarting over his earlier certainty about the involvement of the Invermaddoch nuclear power station. He seemed to have been so wrong so often in this affair that he decided he would keep his thoughts to himself for the moment. He would go into the medical school in the morning and try out a little test of his own. He still had the samples of sheep brain. He would let Morag go ahead with the animal tests she had promised to do.

Bannerman had just left for the medical school when the phone rang and Shona answered.

'May I speak to Dr Bannerman please?' asked a female voice.

'I'm afraid he's just gone out. Can I give him a message?'

'This is Morag Napier at the medical school. I wanted to remind him about the sample he said he would bring in for animal inoculation.'

'I think he's on his way to see you now, Dr Napier, with the news.'

'What news?'

'Apparently the sheep were affected by some poison on the land, but Ian will tell you all about it himself when he gets there.'

'That sounds interesting, thank you,' said Morag Napier.

'Hello again,' said Bannerman when he entered Morag Napier's lab.

'Good morning,' smiled Morag. 'You've brought the sample?'

Bannerman took out a small bottle containing sheep brain. 'Here you are. Can I watch you do the innoculations?'

'If you like,' said Morag. She took the bottles over to a fume hood and switched on the extractor fan. It accelerated slowly into life and settled down to a steady hum.

Morag, now gloved and gowned, transferred the contents of the first bottle into the heavy glass reservoir of an emulsifier. She added sterile saline solution and fitted the cap which housed a sharp metal blade mounted on a long shaft that reached to the foot of the bottle. She clamped the reservoir to its platform and made the motor connection to the upper end of the shaft. She then switched on the power and the blade started whirling inside the glass, emulsifying the brain into a smooth, injectable solution.

Morag inspected it by eye and then gave it another couple of minutes. She then loaded the contents of the reservoir into two sterile plastic syringes. She fitted needles to both and said, 'Shall we go down to the animal lab?'

There was still a vague smell of burning about the animal laboratory despite the fact that it had been completely reconstructed since the fire. It mingled with animal smells and that of fresh paint in an unpleasant cocktail which made Bannerman wrinkle up his nose as they went in. He noticed that Morag used her own key. There was no one inside.

'I thought I would do six mice,' said Morag.

'Good,' said Bannerman watching her every move.

'I wonder, would you get me the experiment register from the office?' asked Morag.

Bannerman went to the office but as soon as he turned the corner he turned back to look at what Morag was doing. He saw her take out two filled syringes from a drawer below the bench and replace them with the two she had brought down from upstairs.

'Is that how you did it last time?' asked Bannerman from behind her.

Morag jumped, but regained control quickly. 'I don't know what you mean,' she said.

'It had to be you. You faked the brain sections and the animal tests to make it look as if the men in Achnagelloch had died from sheep *Scrapie*. Lawrence Gill must have found out what you'd done and tried to send true samples of the men's brains to the MRC for proper analysis but he was murdered before he could say anything about it.'

'He wasn't murdered!' insisted Morag with flashing eyes. 'He fell from the cliff. It was an accident! The whole thing was an accident! If the farm workers hadn't been so greedy the sheep would have been safely buried and none of this would ever have happened!'

'How about Colin Turnbull, Morag? What did he do wrong?'

'Perhaps I can answer that Doctor,' said a foreign voice.

Bannerman turned round to see a man emerge from the animal food store. He was holding a gun.

Bannerman felt himself go cold when he looked into the man's eyes. He had seen them before. They had been above a ski mask up on Tarmachan Ridge. He'd only seen them for a second but now it all came back to him. There had also been two other occasions when he had seen this tall, fair, good-looking man. The first had been when he had been partially obscured behind Morag Napier when they had both come into the restaurant where he was eating in the Royal Mile and the second time had been in van Gelder's car up in Stobmor on the night he had been assaulted in the car-park.

'You're van Gelder's son,' he said.

'My fiancé, Peter,' said Morag. 'We met and fell in love when I first went up to Scotland with Lawrence.'

Bannerman reckoned that Peter van Gelder had to be at least ten years younger than Morag and he was very handsome. 'Really,' he said.

'We didn't want any of this to happen,' said Morag, who was now sobbing. 'It was a simple accident. There was a leak of a chemical they use for treating the quarry stone and it killed a few sheep. It all stemmed from that, a tragic accident. That's all it was. The company would have been forced to close down if the accident had been made public. There was so much resentment to their success among the locals. Peter's father would have been ruined and we couldn't have got married as we planned.'

Bannerman looked at Morag and shook his head. 'Stupid, stupid, stupid,' he said.

'What do you mean?' snapped Morag.

'Will you tell her van Gelder, or shall I?' asked Bannerman.

'I don't know what you're talking about,' said van Gelder.

Bannerman turned back to Morag and said, 'You've been used. The story about a chemical to treat stone is rubbish. They're using the quarry as a dump for dangerous, illegal chemicals. The one that killed the sheep workers and Colin Turnbull was a powerful mutagen developed for biological warfare.'

'Tell him it isn't true!' demanded Morag.

'He also murdered Lawrence Gill,' continued Bannerman, as he saw all the pieces start to fit. 'He was the fair-haired man who pretended to be Gill at Cairnish post office. He even tried to push me off the Tarmachan Ridge and the only person who knew I was going there was you; I told you on the phone the morning before I left. You must have passed on that information to him.'

Bannerman could see by Morag's expression that he was right. 'You were the one who told him where Lawrence Gill was going because you overheard the conversation on the phone with Shona MacLean.'

'But Peter just wanted to reason with Lawrence!' protested Morag. 'He just wanted a chance to explain why I had switched the slides.'

'The slides came from Creutzfeld Jakob patients?' asked Bannerman.

Morag nodded.

'Why?'

'I knew that Lawrence would make the connection with the official report of *Scrapie* in the sheep. All the affected sheep had been destroyed so I thought everyone would be keen to write it off as a freak accident and that would be the end of it. Unfortunately Lawrence found out about the switch.'

'How?'

'He overheard me talking to Peter on the phone.'

Bannerman stared at Morag in silence. 'And now Peter is going to kill us,' he added.

253

Morag looked bemused. She turned to van Gelder. 'Tell him this is nonsense,' she pleaded.

'I'm afraid the man has a lot more brains than you, you stupid bitch,' said van Gelder, matter-of-factly.

Morag looked stunned, as if she couldn't believe her ears. 'But we love each other . . .' she said distantly.

'Love?' mocked van Gelder. 'What do you think I could possibly see in you, you dried up old bitch. You were useful and now you are not. It's as simple as that.'

'Toxic waste is big business Morag,' said Bannerman. 'Governments pay through the nose to get rid of it. It's an embarrassment and a political liability.'

Morag did not register having heard what Bannerman had said. She was staring wide-eyed and unblinking at van Gelder, the man who had just shattered all her dreams with one viciously unkind outburst. Van Gelder held her stare with an amused smirk on his lips. Bannerman used the opportunity to move his hands slowly along the bench behind him until he felt his fingers wrap round the thin, wire bars of a rat cage. He heard the rat scuttle about inside it and hoped it wouldn't go for his fingers.

'And now the end is near, as Mr Sinatra would say,' smiled van Gelder.

'I did everything for you,' said Morag in a low whisper. 'I lied and cheated. I let you . . .'

'That was a treat,' sneered van Gelder.

'You bastard!'

Van Gelder raised the pistol higher when he thought that Morag was going to rush at him, and she stopped. 'Relax,' he said. 'But then you always did have trouble relaxing . . .'

Bannerman sensed Morag tense beside him. 'And how do you plan to dispose of our bodies?' he asked van Gelder.

'I'm going to drive you both back up to Achnagelloch. You'll be buried under a thousand tons of rock on the next blasting day, along with Turnbull.'

'Why did Turnbull die?' asked Bannerman.

'He was doing some stupid little geological survey to impress us. Unfortunately he stumbled on to a cave where that greedy

254

old bastard Sproat had hidden a pile of dead sheep because he was too mean to bury them properly. It was Turnbull's own fault for ignoring the warning signs to keep out of the area. He must have contaminated himself when he examined the sheep.

Morag snatched a scalpel up from the bench and started to move towards van Gelder. The look in her eyes said that she was not to be reasoned with.

'Put it down!' commanded van Gelder.

Morag kept moving towards him.

'Drop it, you stupid bitch!'

The latest insult made Morag raise the scalpel above her head and lunge at van Gelder. The Dutchman fired and Morag was jerked backwards by the impact of the bullet. She collapsed like a discarded rag doll, a red stain spreading over the front of her white lab coat and an expression of surprise etched on her face.

'And now you, Doctor,' said van Gelder.

Bannerman swung the rat cage round and threw it hard at the Dutchman. It caught him on the face and knocked him over backwards, where he hit his head off the wall and slid to the floor. The cage burst open when it struck him and the rat was now perching on his face, sniffing around his mouth and nostrils.

Bannerman saw that van Gelder still had hold of the gun; he was not totally unconscious. He was groaning and lifted his left hand up lazily to brush the rat off his face as if it were a playful kitten disturbing his sleep on a sunny afternoon. Bannerman gambled on making a bid to get the gun, and failed. He was still a metre away when van Gelder opened his eyes and levelled the gun at him. 'You'll pay for that,' he grunted, his eyes red with anger. I'll blow your bloody knees off first.'

There were four rat cages on the bench above where van Gelder lay. Bannerman reached up and shoved the one nearest to him so that it pushed the others off the end and down on to van Gelder. The Dutchman cursed and struggled to free his gun arm from the tangle while Bannerman made a lunge for the door. It was locked. He turned to see van Gelder getting to his feet. A rat was attacking his ankles. He kicked it across the room.

There were half a dozen animal watering bottles on the table next to the door. Bannerman started throwing them at van Gelder but the Dutchman avoided them with ease and they smashed harmlessly off the far wall. Van Gelder raised the gun and Bannerman closed his eyes. He opened them again when he heard van Gelder let out a scream.

Morag Napier was on her feet behind him and she had just plunged a full syringe of emulsified sheep brain into van Gelder's back. Bannerman had never seen such hatred in anyone's eyes. It was clear that hate was the only thing that was keeping Morag Napier alive. Even as van Gelder hit the floor she kept pushing the plunger of the syringe into his back.

When the entire contents had been injected into the prone Dutchman she looked up briefly at Bannerman and smiled enigmatically. It only lasted a split second before her eyes glazed over and she fell backwards to the floor.

Bannerman approached van Gelder's body cautiously. He wasn't quite sure whether he was dead or not. It was possible that Morag had managed to hit something vital with the needle and kill him or it may just have been shock that had caused the Dutchman to pass out. The gun was lying about half a metre from van Gelder's right hand. He reached down slowly to pick it up.

His fingers had almost touched the butt when van Gelder's hand shot out and clamped Bannerman's wrist in a grip of iron. One look at van Gelder told Bannerman that he was totally deranged. He deduced that the contents of the syringe must have been injected directly into his spinal canal, giving the agent immediate access to his brain. Van Gelder's eyes had a quality that filled him with fear. People in this state could sometimes command superhuman strength. Bannerman swung his foot round and thumped it into van Gelder's chest to provide a firm base to pull his arm free. He did so with difficulty and staggered backwards as he broke away.

Van Gelder's body jerked in muscle spasm as he tried to get to his feet. He writhed and scratched himself as if plagued by an itch. Bannerman was pleased to see that he no longer had an interest in the gun, but he backed away as van Gelder's gaze settled on him. He was appalled at the sight of the Dutchman. What had been a handsome man a few minutes before was now a feral monster.

Bannerman's plan was to circle round the bench keeping van Gelder coming after him. If he kept moving in a clockwise direction, as he was doing, he would come back to the spot where the gun lay on the floor. He reckoned he could pick it up and fire before the Dutchman reached him.

Van Gelder, or whoever the deranged creature in van Gelder's body was, grew tired of edging forwards and made a lunge at Bannerman. Bannerman moved easily out of range but stumbled over one of the animal cages behind him on the floor. He fell over backwards and lay spreadeagled and helpless. Above him, van Gelder loomed into view. He threw himself at Bannerman.

Bannerman felt his hand touch something metal on the floor. He brought it round between van Gelder and himself. It was the scalpel that Morag Napier had tried to attack van Gelder with earlier. The Dutchman impaled himself on it.

Bannerman had to struggle to free himself from the dead weight lying on top of him. The first thing he did when he had finally got to his feet was to rush to the sink and be sick. He sluiced cold water up into his face again and again until the horrors of the last few minutes stopped threatening his sanity. When he could breathe evenly again he picked up the telephone and called for help.

Bannerman enjoyed three days of rest and relaxation with Shona in Edinburgh before Special Branch, in the shape of Inspector Morris, called on him again.

'The scale of the operation took our breath away,' admitted Morris. 'They were bringing the stuff in by sea to the terminal at Inchmad. Ostensibly they were loading road stone on to the ships but in reality they were unloading toxic waste from the ships and bringing it by rail up to the quarry in containers disguised as fuel trucks. God knows what we're going to do with it all. We're not even sure if we've found all the underground dumps.'

'I think I can help you there,' said Bannerman. He brought out Colin Turnbull's survey charts from his bag and said, 'A young man named Colin Turnbull prepared these geological charts of the area. I think they'll help.'

'I'm sure they will,' said Morris. 'I'll pass them on.'

'When you've finished with them, see that they are returned to Julie Turnbull; she's the primary school teacher in Stobmor. I think she'd appreciate knowing what a help they'd been.'

'I'll see to it,' said Morris.

'What about Sproat and the vet, Finlay,' asked Bannerman.

'It's pretty much as you suspected,' said Morris. 'They both knew about the chemical leak from the quarry which happened about a year ago. Van Gelder came clean at the time and bought their silence. He had to, because the chemical killed the sheep nearest to the leak outright. When the others developed a form of *Scrapie* a year or so later and started dropping like ninepins they suspected that the chemical had been involved. Van Gelder bought them off again. The new cars were a dead give-away.'

'Bastards,' said Bannerman. 'That's why the Sproats sent May Buchan away on holiday. Conscience money.'

'Take a look at life again soon,' said Morris.

'Can I go now?' asked Bannerman.

'Not exactly,' said Morris.

'What does that mean?' asked Bannerman.

'I have a message for you from Mr Allison. He says that he would like to see you in London as soon as possible.'

'I see,' said Bannerman.

'And one more thing, sir, he says to remind you that you signed the Official Secrets Act and that everything to do with this affair is covered by it.'

'Why?' snapped Bannerman angrily. 'A bloody Dutchman starts using Scotland as a dump for all the world's shit. A sheep virus starts killing people and Whitehall wants to keep it an official secret!'

'Best discuss that with Mr Allison, sir,' said Morris.

*   *   *

258

'Something wrong?' asked Shona, when Bannerman emerged from his conversation with Morris.

'I have to go to London,' said Bannerman.

'Have to?' asked Shona.

'I'm not running away,' said Bannerman softly. 'The establishment wants a word with me.'

'And then what?' asked Shona quietly.

Bannerman looked at Shona and said, 'I feel as if I'm walking a tight-rope and I'm going to fall at any moment.'

'But the important question is, on which side?'

'Come with me?' said Bannerman, taking her into his arms and resting his cheek against her hair.

Shona remained silent in his arms for a few moments and then drew back again to smile and shake her head. 'No,' she said softly. 'I'm beginning to miss my island. I'm going home.'

Bannerman nodded and said softly, 'I'll call you.'

Shona just smiled as she turned away. 'Take care,' she whispered.

The taxi carrying Bannerman across London ground to a halt in heavy traffic for the umpteenth time.

'A bit busy today,' smiled the driver.

Bannerman smiled at the blind optimism that prevented the driver from seeing that it was like this *every* day.

'Park Crescent you said?'

'The Medical Research Council.'

'Doctor, are you then?'

'A pathologist.'

'Like that, do you?'

Bannerman found himself lost for words. It was a simple question but there seemed to be no simple answer. 'It's a living,' he smiled.

'Just like me mate,' said the driver. 'Life begins when you clock off.'

Bannerman tipped the driver well and returned his wave as he drove off. He sighed as he looked at the official Rover parked near the entrance to the MRC. It was Allison's car.

* * *

'My dear Doctor Bannerman, how nice to see you,' exclaimed Allison when Bannerman was shown in. He rose to shake Bannerman's hand warmly. John Flowers and Hugh Milne got up to do the same.

'I can't tell you how grateful we are to you for clearing up this awful business,' said Allison.

Flowers and Milne sat quietly while Allison conducted the proceedings. Bannerman watched the government man's eyes. The rest of him was animated and exuding *bonhomie* but his eyes remained cold and calculating.

'I know it sounds strange in view of the terrible circumstances up north but Her Majesty's Government is profoundly relieved.'

'Relieved?' exclaimed Bannerman in surprise.

'That the deaths had nothing to do with *natural Scrapie*.

'*Natural Scrapie?*' repeated Bannerman.

'You know what I mean,' said Allison, waving his hands. 'These poor men died from this mutant monster thing that the chemical created.'

'But nevertheless it was created, Mr Allison. There is now a form of *Scrapie* which will infect people.'

'But the government has seen to it that every sheep on Inverladdie Farm has been slaughtered and disposed of by incineration. There is no further source of the agent.'

Bannerman was lost for words for a moment. He couldn't believe the aura of complacency about the man. 'But it's what happened before we found out the truth that matters!' he exclaimed.

'What do you mean?'

'I mean that sheep carcasses were lying around all over the place because Sproat was too mean to dispose of them, and for God knows how long!'

'I think that's a bit of an exaggeration,' said Allison condescendingly.

'One bird feeding off one infected carcass a few weeks ago will by now have spread the virus to another part of the countryside. Sooner or later a new flock will become infected and just maybe a few infected lambs will make it

260

to market before the regulations step in. Then what happens?'

'I feel we are moving in to the realms of fantasy here doctor,' said Allison. 'You can't seriously be suggesting that we quarrantine every sheep in the land?'

'I'm suggesting that you tighten up the regulations immediately. You make *Scrapie* a notifiable disease and you offer compensation to farmers for infected sheep at a level above market value so there will be no "slipping through the net" before notification.'

'If we do that then it will appear that something is wrong,' said Allison.

'Something *is* wrong!' insisted Bannerman.

Allison thumped his hands angrily on to the table. 'No,' he exclaimed. 'This is over the top! You'll be suggesting next that we ban people from crossing the road so that road accident figures will drop!'

Bannerman recognized Allison's attempt at blustering to gain the initiative. He remained calm and said. 'That is not the same thing and you know it.'

Allison changed tack. He suddenly became reasonable. 'Look doctor, we both know that very little is known about the spread of *slow* virus infection. A lot more research needs to be done. Her Majesty's Government has agreed to fund an extensive programme of research. The programme will be administered by the Medical Research Council who will set up a new board specifically for that purpose. We would all be delighted if you would chair that board.'

Bannerman felt as if he was being swept along by a freak wave. He shook his head and looked down at the table in silence.

'At least think about it,' said Allison, getting to his feet.

Bannerman held up his hands and said, 'Not so fast.'

The silence that ensued could have been cut with a knife. 'You have not said one word about the business at the quarry,' said Bannerman.

'What's there to say?' asked Allison. 'Thanks to you we've been able to put a complete stop to it.'

'What about charges, Mr Allison? A foreign company has been using our country as a dump for some of the most dangerous substances on earth and there has not been one mention of it in the papers or on the radio or on television. Why not?'

For the first time Allison displayed real vulnerability. He sat down again slowly and Bannerman noticed a small smile flicker across the lips of Flowers, who had remained silent throughout.

'Frankly Doctor, the government believes that it would be in the best interests of the people of this country if the full extent of this outrage was not made public. Don't you agree?'

'No, I do not!' said Bannerman forcefully.

'Doctor, you force me to remind you that . . .'

'I signed the Official Secrets Act. Yes, I get the picture and "D" notices will fly like confetti while you and your cronies conduct yet another cover-up of what really goes on in this country!'

'We have to do what we think best,' said Allison.

'Why Allison? Tell me that. There's got to be more to it than "the best interests of the people". Just tell me why?'

Allison laced the fingers of his hands together in front of him and took a deep breath. Even then, there was one false start before the words started to come out. 'The waste . . . the toxic chemicals . . .'

'Yes?'

'They were British.'

'British?' exclaimed Bannerman in disbelief. He saw that Milne and Flowers had already been told this.

'The government awarded a disposal contract to a Dutch company we believed to be reputable. As it turns out they were not.'

Bannerman's mouth fell open as he realized what had been happening. 'You mean that you were loading it on to ships at one end of the country and they were unloading it at the other? God, what a farce! So to save your blushes, you hush it all up?'

'There's more,' said Allison, avoiding Bannerman's eyes. 'The chemicals were manufactured in this country at a time which puts us in contravention of an international agreement banning such work. The Dutch company knows this.'

'My God,' said Bannerman, shaking his head.

'The Russians broke the agreement, the Americans too, everyone knows they did' said Allison.

'Though it was never proved,' said Bannerman. 'But if you pursue the Dutch they'll crucify you on the world stage?'

'More or less.'

'I need some fresh air,' said Bannerman, getting to his feet. Flowers and Milne shrugged their embarrassment at him.

'You will think about that offer I mentioned earlier,' said Allison. 'You are the man for the job.'

Bannerman left without replying. He returned to St Luke's and called Shona from his office. She answered after the third ring.

'I've fallen off the tight-rope,' he said.

'On which side?'

'Can I come up?'

'I'll be waiting,' laughed Shona.

'Do you think the island could use a GP?'

'I'm sure,' said Shona. 'But we'll talk about that later. When are you leaving?'

'Now,' said Bannerman.

'I love you,' said Shona.

'I'm so glad that you do,' said Bannerman softly.

'Get a move on.'

Bannerman put down the phone and cleared out his desk. Without looking back he left the building and was nearly at the front gate when he heard his name being called. It was the hospital psychiatrist, David Drysdale. 'I've been trying to get hold of you for ages,' said Drysdale.

'Really?' asked Bannerman.

'It's about that problem you had, you know, with the night-mares and the feelings of uncertainty and lack of confidence.'

'What about it?'

'We all thought it was down to mid-life crisis at the time but it wasn't. I've finally worked it out. You may find it hard to believe but . . . you don't like being a pathologist. You never did. It's just unfortunate that you're so good at it. It never occurred to you to change.'

Bannerman broke into a broad smile. 'Tell me about it,' he said as he walked away and out through the gates.

As the train slid out of the station for the long journey north Bannerman took out his newspaper and started to read. The lead story concerned a man in a Norfolk village who had slaughtered his entire family with an axe before taking his own life. There were family snaps of his wife and three small children at the beach. 'In happier times,' said the caption. 'He was a quiet man,' said one of the neighbours. 'He kept himself to himself,' said another. Everyone in the village was stunned by what had happened, said the story.

'Tragic,' said the man across from Bannerman who had been reading the same story. 'Seems to happen a lot these days.'

Bannerman nodded and put away his paper to look out of the window. You ain't seen nothing yet, he thought to himself.